The Body in the Gravel

Books by Judi Lynn

Mill Pond Romances
Cooking Up Trouble
Opposites Distract
Love on Tap
Spicing Things Up
First Kiss, on the House
Special Delivery

Jazzi Sanders Mysteries

The Body in the Attic
The Body in the Wetlands
The Body in the Gravel

Published by Kensington Publishing Corporation

The Body in the Gravel

Judi Lynn

LYRICAL UNDERGROUND
Kensington Publishing Corp.
www.kensingtonbooks.com

LYRICAL UNDERGROUND BOOKS are published by

Kensington Publishing Corp.
119 West 40th Street
New York, NY 10018

All Kensington titles, imprints, and distributed lines are available at special quantity discounts for bulk purchases for sales promotion, premiums, fund-raising, educational, or institutional use.

Special book excerpts or customized printings can also be created to fit specific needs. For details, write or phone the office of the Kensington Sales Manager: Kensington Publishing Corp., 119 West 40th Street, New York, NY 10018. Attn. Sales Department. Phone: 1-800-221-2647.

Lyrical Underground and Lyrical Underground logo Reg. US Pat. & TM Off.

First Electronic Edition: September 2019
ISBN-13: 978-1-5161-0838-1 (ebook)
ISBN-10: 1-5161-0838-8 (ebook)

First Print Edition: September 2019
ISBN-13: 978-1-5161-0841-1
ISBN-10: 1-5161-0841-8

Printed in the United States of America

Acknowledgments

I'd like to thank John Scognamiglio, my editor at Kensington, and Lauren Abramo, my agent, for everything they've done for me. And I'd like to thank everyone at Kensington—the publicity people who work with me, the designer of my book covers—I think they're awesome—and every copy editor who catches my many mistakes. Many thanks.

Chapter 1

A spider scurried up the left sleeve of Jazzi's flannel shirt. She was about to put down her hammer to squash it when a big, tanned hand reached over to smoosh it for her. Ansel flicked the small corpse off her sleeve and grinned at her.

"I know you hate eight-legged creatures."

That, she did. Snakes? No big deal. There weren't many poisonous ones in northeast Indiana. Worms? She liked. When she dug them up in her flower beds, she carefully relocated them. A teeny, weenie spider? It must die. "Thanks for killing it."

His grin grew wider. "When I gave you the engagement ring, that's what I signed on for. To honor and protect."

Jerod, driving the last nail into the frame they were building, snorted. Her cousin had spent most of their childhood tormenting her, and Jazzi had happily repaid him in kind. "My Franny hates spiders, too. Must be a girl thing." He sat back on his heels to survey their work. A flower bed had rimmed this side of the house at one time, but only a few sagging mums and sedums remained. After they'd dug a trench to expose the crumbling foundation at this corner, they'd built a frame to hold new cement. Jazzi's back wasn't used to so much bending. Jerod pressed a hand to the small of his back, too. "I'd say we're ready to call Darby to pour the concrete."

They'd worked with Darby ever since they'd started their fixer-upper business. He was a cantankerous old coot, but he charged decent prices and was dependable. He'd given them a fair estimate for the concrete to rebuild this section of the foundation. They'd had to jack up the corner of the house to repair it. The driveway's cement was in even worse shape and needed to be completely replaced. Darby had given them a lower bid than they'd expected for that job, too.

Jazzi started toward the two-car garage at the back of the yard. She'd left her toolbox there. Some of the houses in this older neighborhood had only small, one-car garages that faced an alley, but the house they'd bought had been a standout when it was built—three stories of yellow brick, with its own drive. When they finished renovating it, it would be a standout again. "Let's ask if Darby can come in an hour. I'm ready for lunch."

They'd known it would be a bear to fix the sagging corner, and the job had taken even longer than they'd estimated. It had taken all morning to finish the framing, and Jazzi needed a break. She'd brought a cooler full of chips and buns, and sloppy joe mix in an insulated container. When the weather was hot, she'd brought a cooler filled with cans of beer, too, but once the temperature dropped, she lugged two large thermoses of coffee instead.

Jerod punched Darby's number on his cell phone and set up a time for him to deliver the cement. When he finished, he nodded to Jazzi. "He'll be here at about one-thirty."

Perfect. They trundled inside the empty house and gathered at the card table and four chairs they'd brought. Ansel's pug, George, opened an eye to greet them, then returned to his nap. Ansel took the dog with him everywhere possible. He swore George got depressed when he was left alone. Jazzi wasn't sure about that, but Ansel's doggie devotion never wavered, so she didn't argue the point. If Ansel loved her half as much as he did his pug, they'd be together forever.

Ansel glanced around the room and shook his head. "I'm glad this is early October. We should be able to get all of the outside work done before we start in here. We might *never* get everything finished inside."

Jazzi looked at the list of projects, arranged in the order they should tackle them, tacked to the kitchen wall. They'd never bought a fixer-upper that needed so much work. "This house should keep us out of trouble for a long, long time."

Jerod went for a second sloppy joe. "This is going to make working on my basement on Saturdays look like a piece of cake."

After working on her sister, Olivia's, house, Jazzi had sworn she'd never work on Saturdays again, but how could she say no to Jerod? His Franny was carrying their third child. She and Jerod would have three kids under five running underfoot. Gunther was four now and Lizzie one-and-a-half. She understood why Jerod wanted to make the dry, deep basement of his big, square farmhouse into a playroom. Jerod had sweetened the deal by promising that he'd never expect them to show up to work before ten in the morning. He knew how Jazzi liked to sleep in on the weekends.

Ansel scanned the list again. "Your project's going to be a breeze compared to this. If we're lucky, we can have yours done in a month."

Jerod gave a wicked grin. "Let's hope so. You two tie the knot on November tenth. You'll be feeling frisky for a while after that. Won't be interested in installing ceiling tiles or indoor-outdoor carpet."

Jazzi rolled her eyes. Jerod was always giving her free advice and opinions. "We already live together. We're not going on a honeymoon until late February when we're sick of winter and can fly somewhere with sunshine. Nothing's going to change that much."

"Yeah, yeah, I thought the same thing when I said *I do* to Franny, but believe me, when you make it official, it feels different."

"It means there's no going back." Ansel looked absolutely delighted with that. "Jazzi will be stuck with me till I conk off."

She'd be living every girl's dream. Women looked at Ansel and melted. She gave a dramatic sigh. "Poor me."

Jerod laughed, ready to tease them, when they heard a vehicle pull into the driveway. They tossed their paper plates in the trash as they went to see who was there. Had Darby come early? But her sister Olivia's live-in boyfriend, Thane, was walking to the house when they spilled out of it. He saw them and gave a quick wave. "I had a minute, so thought I'd come over and look at the furnace you're worried about. My crew and I are installing a new high-efficiency one not far from here."

Jerod motioned to Thane's van. "You'd better park it on the curb. We're having cement delivered in fifteen minutes."

Thane knew about work sites. He moved his van, then followed Jerod into the basement. Jazzi was glad she'd opened its windows to get rid of some of the musty smell down there. When a house was closed up for a while, smells bloomed and lingered. Jerod was saying, "The furnace still kicks on when we turn up the thermostat, but the thing looks ancient."

He and Thane disappeared inside, and Ansel went to the front porch to grab the trowels they'd need to smooth the cement. He handed her one when Darby backed into the cracked driveway. He parked so the chute from his truck could reach the back corner of the house. They had to yell to be heard over the noise from the tank mixing the concrete. Man, what a racket! But it was quick work to fill the wooden frame they'd built; then Darby turned off the truck's engine. Hopping down to inspect his job, he gave a satisfied nod. "Looks good to me."

"Me, too," Ansel agreed.

Darby had always been a bit rough around the edges, but Jazzi had never seen him so unkempt. He was in his mid-fifties, and his longish gray hair flew around his head. His huge mustache and bushy eyebrows reminded her of Yosemite Sam on the old cartoons, and his sideburns could double as fuzzy slippers. Even his clothes looked like they could use a wash.

Jerod came out to inspect the job, too. "This'll do it. When the cement sets, we can lower the jacks and bolt the house to the foundation."

Ansel pinched his lips together and turned to Jerod. "I'm almost afraid to ask, but what about the furnace?"

"It's shot. We have to replace it. Probably some of the ductwork, too."

Of course. Why wouldn't the big metal arms sprawling off the furnace need work?

Darby stepped back to get a better view of their new investment. "This is one of your fixer-uppers?"

Ansel nodded. "This'll be our biggest project yet."

Darby studied it. "Mind if I ask what you paid for it?"

Jerod answered. "Fifty-six thousand."

"Will you make money on it?"

"We're hoping to make forty-five grand if we can keep our budget under control," Jerod said. "We're going to be at it awhile. Our time is worth something."

"How do you split the profits?"

Jerod frowned at him. "You're getting a little personal."

Darby squirmed. "Just curious. I've been saving money for a while. Have a hundred and fifty thousand. Was kind of thinking of buying a fixer-upper for me and the guys to work on during our slow season."

"Not a bad idea," Ansel said. "Don't start with something this major, though. Start small. We split the profits three ways. The costs, too."

Jerod frowned. He scratched his chin, thinking it over. "Do you know anything about construction or contractor work? You don't pour much cement through January and February, do you? If you got a house that didn't need a lot of work, you could finish it in a couple of months *if* you knew what you were doing."

Darby tugged on his beard. "Don't know a thing, but the timing's right. It's something to think about. Mind if I take a look around your place and see what needs work?"

"Go for it," Jerod told him, "but we have to get busy on the cement before it sets. Look at anything you want to."

"If you look at everything, you'll be a while," Ansel warned.

"Thanks. 'Preciate it." And Darby ducked inside the house.

They were smoothing the cement at the top of the frame when raised voices caught their attention. Darby and Thane must be near the furnace, not that far from the open basement window.

Darby barked a laugh. "It's none of your business what happened, boy! What? You're still sad Walker didn't move in with you? Wasn't natural how much you liked him, if you ask me."

Thane's voice was harsh. "You always did have a dirty mind. I'm not surprised you went there, but Walker would still be here if it wasn't for you. Funny that he and Rose both left during the night and no one's heard from them. Where are they, Darby? Buried near some tree at the back of your property?"

"Take that back!" The sound of a fist hitting flesh made them all jump to their feet. Was Darby nuts? Thane was as tall and big as Jerod and Ansel. Of course, Ansel was all muscle, whereas Thane and Jerod were heftier, with more bulk. Darby must only be five-eight and scrawny. He drank more than he ate, from what Jazzi heard.

Ansel pounded down the basement stairs first. Thane had both arms forward, holding Darby away from him. Ansel grabbed Darby's sleeve and yanked him behind him. "Enough!"

"He started it!" Darby yelled.

"Like hell." Thane glared, and Darby turned away from him to stomp up the stairs. "Don't call me if *he's* here," he snarled at Jerod. "If I see him, I'll turn my truck around and leave."

They heard the front door slam. Soon, Darby's cement truck rumbled out of the driveway and disappeared.

Jerod blinked at Thane. "Darn, bud, I've never seen you lose it before."

Jazzi studied his face. Thane looked more than angry. He looked upset. "You okay?"

Thane started for the steps, too. "I'm fine. Darby's old history." He glanced back at the furnace. "I filled out an estimate. If you decide on a new model, here." He handed the sheet of paper to Ansel and left.

The three of them looked at each other. What the heck had just happened?

Chapter 2

"I didn't even know Thane had a temper," Jerod said. "I saw him in protective mode when that idiot gutter and siding guy harassed Jazzi in Thane's driveway once, so I know he can be intimidating when he wants to be. He looked like he'd stuff the guy in his van and kick the van to the next subdivision."

Ansel wrapped an arm around Jazzi's waist. "I'd forgotten about that. God help anyone who gives Olivia a hard time when he's there. Thane's usually so low-key, I don't see that side of him much."

Jazzi tilted her head, thinking. "I wonder what Darby did to get on his bad side. It would take a lot."

Ansel handed Thane's estimate to Jerod. He looked at it and winced. "I'm betting we'll never know. Didn't look like Thane wanted to talk about it."

That's the impression Jazzi had gotten. They started upstairs and got back to their trowels. Cement didn't wait. Even with her heavy work gloves on, Jazzi could feel her hands drying out. Concrete did that—stole the moisture from your skin. She was glad when they finished with it and returned to the kitchen and the list that they'd pinned on the wall.

Jerod let out a long breath when he took a close look at its length. "Okay, we can cross off fixing the foundation. Next, we have breaking up the driveway, building frames for it, and pouring a new one."

Ansel said, "The way the driveway slants, it wouldn't hurt to pour a gravel base."

"Not a bad idea." Jerod scribbled that on the list, too. "We'll call Darby for a load of gravel, lay the wire on top of that, then pour the concrete."

"That'll keep us busy for a while. Every job we start here needs extra work." At the rate they were going, Jazzi would be surprised if they finished the house before she and Ansel left for their honeymoon.

Jerod waved that away. "We're a great team. We'll have the driveway done by the end of the week."

Ansel raised a blond eyebrow. "Ya think?"

"Not really, but did it make you feel better to hear that?"

Her Viking nodded; she'd chosen the nickname for him since he was tall, fair, and Norse. His voice dripped sarcasm. "Yeah, I like fairy tales."

Jerod nodded in her direction. "You haven't seen Jazzi man a wheelbarrow."

If he expected her to sprint with a full load of broken cement, he'd lost his grip on reality. It wasn't going to happen.

Jerod took his cell phone out of his pocket to glance at the time. "Three-thirty. What if we call it quits today and drive to my place to look at the basement?"

Ansel nodded agreement. "No need to lean on the jackhammer and start breaking up the driveway now. It can wait till tomorrow."

Ansel picked up George to carry the pug to his work van. Jazzi locked up the house behind them; she slid onto the passenger seat, and they followed Jerod south to his place. When they passed a house on Fairfield, Jazzi noticed Thane's work van parked in its driveway. They'd make sure that Darby had finished making deliveries at their place before they called Thane to put in a furnace. He and Darby must have more history than he wanted them to know.

They turned off Fairfield onto Airport Express. George, as usual, curled on the back seat and slept. Jerod's old farmhouse lay fifteen minutes past the south side of River Bluffs on two acres of property. A sturdy picket fence surrounded the pond Jerod had dug at the back of the long yard—a safety measure to ensure the kids never tried to swim unchaperoned. The white two-story had green shutters and a green tin roof. Franny opened the door for them when they climbed the steps to the front porch, and Jazzi squeezed past her stomach. Franny wasn't due until the middle of February, but she looked ready to pop now. Gunther and Lizzie ran to hang on Ansel's legs when they saw him, and he stomped around the entry while they laughed and giggled.

Jerod looked disgusted. "I see how I rate. I only feed you and keep a roof over your heads, and you ignore me for Norseman."

"Norseman!" Gunther cried. Ansel's other nickname. Jazzi's fiancée was mostly Norwegian with white-blond hair and blue eyes. When he knelt on the floor for the two kids to climb on his back for a horsey ride, Jazzi watched his luscious fanny as he crawled away from her.

He must have felt her gaze on him, because he glanced at her over his shoulder with a grin.

Franny was drooling, too, until she winced and put a hand to her stomach. At Jazzi's questioning look, she said, "The baby kicked. He does that a lot."

"He?" Jerod stared at his wife.

She pushed loose strands of carrot-colored hair away from her face and smiled. "I visited the doctor today, remember? He sent me for an ultrasound."

Jerod raised his arms in a victory symbol. "A boy!"

Franny frowned. "Would you have been disappointed if it was a girl?"

"Not if she has orange hair and freckles like you."

He had chosen the right answer. Franny practically glowed.

Ansel circled the dining room table and crawled back to them, nodding for the kids to get off him. They went to pet George. The pug took them in his stride. When Ansel stood, he clapped Jerod on the shoulder. "Congrats! Got a name picked out?"

Jerod raised his eyebrows at Franny. "We're still haggling. She read a romance where the guy's name was Zane, and she's voting for that. It doesn't do it for me."

"I kinda like it." Jazzi looked at Ansel.

He gave a noncommittal shrug. "It's okay, I guess."

Franny's gray eyes lit up. "Oh, Jazzi, you have to read it! Zane's a prince who can turn into a dragon, and he's so *hot*! *Dragon Among Them* by Kyra Jacobs. You can download it to your Kindle."

When was the last time she'd read a book that got her hot and bothered? She'd have to look it up.

Jerod looked horrified. "We're not naming our kid Zane. You'll have hot flashes every time you think of that prince."

Franny laughed. "You're just jealous. We have plenty of time to worry about a name. Right now, I need to go check on supper, and you need to show Jazzi and Ansel the basement."

Franny started toward their big country kitchen with its huge island, and Jerod led Jazzi and Ansel down the basement steps. He'd rebuilt them so they were sturdy and had railings on both sides. "I don't want Franny or a kid to fall."

The basement had plenty of room. Ansel's attention went to the cement blocks that formed the foundation. "Good and solid," he said. "All we have to do is put up a moisture barrier, then build frames for drywall."

Jazzi checked out the cement floors. "The cement's chipped in places and crumbling on top. Nothing deep. We can pour a thin layer and smooth it out."

Jerod poked at a small patch of chipped cement with the toe of his work boot. "I don't want to spend a fortune on this. I thought I'd buy cheap indoor-outdoor carpet to cover the floor once we smooth out the cement. Then the kids can jump rope and skateboard down here if they want to. I want to hang a flat-screen TV, too, so they can watch movies or play video games, and Franny wants me to build a craft table for the far side."

Ansel looked impressed. "Sounds like kid heaven to me."

Jerod grinned. "I sure hope so. I'd rather they brought their friends to our house instead of disappearing on us."

When they climbed the steps again, Franny yelled from the kitchen. "You're welcome to stay for supper if you want to. I made plenty."

An acrid smell drifted toward them. Ansel said, "Thanks anyway, but Jazzi has fish thawed at home. It's been out all day, so we'd better cook it."

Jazzi gave him a look. She didn't know her Norseman was so good at fibbing. But he sniffed again and shook his head at her. Jerod had told them over and over again that his wife wasn't the best cook in America, and Ansel loved good food. He wasn't willing to risk this.

Jerod raised an eyebrow, but his lips curved in a grin. "I've held you up long enough. Go make your supper, and thanks for coming."

They grabbed George and made their getaway before Franny dished up. On the drive home, Ansel said, "It's late, and fish does sound good. Let's stop at Big-Eyed Fish to grab some on our way home."

He'd get no arguments from her. She loved the fried pollock, wild rice, and coleslaw. George loved fish, too. And she wouldn't have to cook. Win/win. Besides, her muscles protested more than usual after a job. They'd had to crouch and bend to build the frame for the foundation. When she took a shower tonight, she was going to stand under the hot water for a long time.

Chapter 3

When Jazzi opened the kitchen door, pushed off her work boots, and carried the bag of takeout inside, she was attacked by two naughty, furry troublemakers. Inky and Marmalade wove around her ankles, meowing for their supper. While George made a habit of begging for people food, the cats ran to their food bowls, waiting for their cans of Fancy Feast.

"Have you been good today?" Jazzi filled both bowls and stroked the cats' smooth fur. She stood to survey the room for damage, and sure enough, another pitcher of flowers was knocked over and the glass pitcher broken. Jazzi had given up using her good vases for the flowers she bought at the grocery store. Now she used rinsed-out pickle jars, bottles, and chipped mugs. Fussing, she went to clean up the mess and find something new to put the bouquet in.

Ansel carried George inside after parking the van in the garage. Instead of walking to his food dish, the pug came to the kitchen island and stared at the plastic sack the food was in. Ansel bent to pat his head. "George always gets hungry when he smells food all the way home."

Jazzi rolled her eyes. "George is always hungry, no matter what."

Ansel grinned. "It's genetic. He's my dog."

"I'm not sure it works that way." Jazzi put out paper plates and went to get them each a beer. They sat side by side on the kitchen stools to eat their meal.

"I wonder what Thane and Olivia are eating tonight. Pizza?" Ansel couldn't get over the fact that Jazzi's mom and sister didn't like to cook.

"There's a big variety of takeout where they live—Mexican, Chinese, lots of big chains."

He wrinkled his nose. "That's great for once in a while."

"Thane doesn't mind. He knew Olivia didn't cook when he moved in with her."

Ansel was quiet a minute, frowning. "Do you think the thing between Thane and Darby goes long-term, or do you think it's been since Thane met your sister?"

"Beats me. I didn't know they had a thing until today." She lowered her fork for a second and let her gaze wander around their kitchen.

Ansel shook his head, alarmed. "No, no, no. We're knocking down walls at the Southwood Park house. The kitchen and dining room will have plenty of space for people to get together, and we can do a deep sink and an island, too, but we have to stay in budget. Butcher-block countertops instead of granite. Ceramic tiles instead of real wood."

She grimaced. "I was thinking about the backsplash."

"Subway tile does the trick, babe, and it looks good."

"But glass is so pretty, and it comes in so many colors."

"And it costs five times more." He turned to argue with her, saw her cocky grin, and glared. "You're just giving me a hard time."

She wasn't repentant. "It's your own fault. You started it. You didn't even know what I was thinking about when you went into *no* mode."

"Okay, I have to give you that, but you had that look…the one that usually costs money." He quirked an eyebrow. "So, what *were* you thinking about?"

"How much I love our house, how perfect it is for us." When Jazzi and Jerod had bought the stone cottage, they'd meant to fix it up and flip it, but the longer Jazzi worked on it, the more she wanted to keep it. So she'd bought out Jerod's half, and once she and Ansel grew more serious, they'd planned its renovations together.

Ansel glanced at their surroundings with a satisfied smile. "We were lucky. We got the right house at the right time, and we ended up in it together. Olivia and Thane got lucky, too. Their house suits them."

Jazzi pinched her lips together at the mention of Thane. He wasn't what she'd call good-natured, but he was usually easygoing and tended to be on the quiet side. "I can't imagine what Darby said or did that could make Thane that angry."

"Darby was talking about someone whom Thane liked a lot, someone he'd invited to move in with him. And Thane accused Darby of driving that person away or worse."

Jazzi blinked, remembering. "Thane asked if Darby had buried him."

"And a Rose. Two people disappeared and were never heard of again." Ansel finished his supper, gave George one last bite of fish, and started to clean the island.

Jazzi stood to help him, still deep in thought. "You don't think Darby *did* kill two people, do you? He has an attitude if you aggravate him."

"If two people disappeared, I'm sure the cops looked into it."

"What if they did, but they just didn't find enough evidence?" Inky leapt onto the sink counter to bat at the flowers again, and Jazzi lifted him off. Of the two cats, Inky was usually the instigator. Since she was at the sink, she grabbed the dishcloth and went to wipe off the island.

The kitchen clean, they headed upstairs for quick showers and changed into their pajamas. The hot water had soothed Jazzi's aching muscles. They'd ache more tomorrow after she rolled a wheelbarrow around all day. But for now, it was time to relax. Ansel started for the living room and his favorite couch. Jazzi and George followed behind, and Ansel lifted George so that he could stretch near his feet. On the couch across from him, Inky and Marmalade took up their favorite spots beside Jazzi.

Ansel turned to her before turning on the TV. "Do you think we could ask Thane about Darby, or would we get another short answer?"

"I don't know. It'll probably depend on his mood, but he's been harboring his grudge against Darby for a while. I'd sure love to know what happened between them."

"So would I. If I find the right opening, I'm going to ask."

He was braver than she was. She meant to avoid the subject if she could. Sure, she was curious, but she didn't want Thane to get aggravated with her.

Ansel turned to her again. "Do you think Olivia knows?"

"I'm betting she does. That was my game plan. I thought I'd bring it up when we go out on Thursday." Jazzi and her sister met at a restaurant for dinner every Thursday night, their "girls' night out." Jazzi had her family over every Sunday for a family meal, so they could all catch up with each other, but there were so many people that there was no guarantee she and Olivia would get a chance to talk.

Ansel leaned back on his couch cushion, looking satisfied. "That sounds like a better plan than me pestering Thane about it."

They let the conversation drop and enjoyed some TV until Ansel stretched and yawned. "I'm ready to call it a day. You?"

Jazzi jostled the cats to stand up. "I'm tired, too."

They turned off lights and started up the stairs. Ansel bent to scoop up George, and Jazzi relaxed. When Ansel carried George upstairs with them, there'd be no hanky-panky, just sleep. Her muscles still ached enough that she was fine with that. The cats raced up the stairs after her, and soon George snored in his dog bed, and Inky and Marmalade snuggled against her legs. Ansel's hand slid under the sheets to rest on her hip, and she drifted off to sleep.

Chapter 4

Ansel worked the jackhammer. Jazzi and Jerod manned the wheelbarrows. The Southwood Park house's driveway wasn't incredibly long, but it would take them most of the day to break it up, clear it, and build the frame for a new one. Even though George didn't like the constant rat-a-tat-tat of the hammer, he stayed on the small back porch to watch them with a pained expression on his doggy face.

The morning had started out cool, but the temperature rose until they could toss off their flannel shirts. For Jazzi, this was distracting, since Ansel wore only a white T-shirt under his. Watching his muscles strain as he worked proved the only happy moments of today's job. Lifting chunks of concrete into her wheelbarrow and rolling them to the dumpster they'd rented strained Jazzi's arms and back. Nothing a hot bath and two Advil couldn't fix, but she was feeling the ache the longer they worked.

The leaves on a tree a block away had changed to brilliant orange before any fellow maples flamed with color. It would be another week or two before yellows and reds joined this tree's vivid glory.

They'd started early today and took a quick lunch break, so that by two, Jerod could use their backhoe to dig out a new drive. Jazzi and Ansel hammered the wooden forms as soon as Jerod had a section ready, and by three-thirty, they were ready for Darby to arrive with the gravel, as planned. Only three-thirty came and went, and Darby didn't show up.

Ansel swiped sweat. "You don't think he crossed us off his deliveries list because he got mad at Thane, do you? I was hoping we could level out the gravel and tamp it before we left tonight."

Jerod was walking toward the backhoe but called over his shoulder, "If we finish the base tonight, we could pour concrete tomorrow."

That meant working overtime, but Jazzi was okay with that. She'd like to get the gravel done, too.

"Only one way to find out." She dug for her cell phone and called Darby's office.

Someone picked up, but it wasn't Darby. "Earl here. How can I help you?" She explained that they were waiting for a delivery that hadn't come.

"Darby never came in today," Earl told her. "He has the gravel loaded, though. I'm finished for the day and can drive it over for you, if that's okay."

"Better than okay. We'd appreciate it," Jazzi said. "See you soon."

Ansel asked. "What's up?"

"Darby didn't show today. One of his drivers is going to deliver the gravel."

Jerod's frown matched Ansel's. "Darby's never left us in the lurch before. It's not like him."

"Maybe he's sick." But Ansel shook his head, dismissing that idea almost before he'd finished talking. "You'd think he'd call in. I mean, he owns the business."

"Maybe he drank too much last night and has a killer hangover." Jerod sounded like that might be a possibility. "I can't remember him missing a day of work, though."

"But he's never punched anyone on a job site either," Jazzi reminded him. "At least, not one of ours."

They went to sit on the back-porch steps to stretch their legs until the truck arrived. George scooted closer to Ansel, and Ansel stroked his smooth fur. Jazzi rolled her shoulders. They ached. Her back hurt. Her legs felt stiff. Hauling concrete was heavy work. When Earl backed the truck into their drive, she cringed when she stood up.

Ansel grinned at her. "I give great massages if you need some attention when we get home."

"I think every part of me is sore."

His grin widened. "Even better."

Jerod shook his head in disgust. "I'd tell you to get a room, but you might like that idea."

Laughing, they walked to greet Earl.

"This where you want it?" the man called. At Jerod's nod, Earl partially tipped the bed of the truck to let gravel fall in a thick layer as he drove forward. He'd made it a third of the way down the drive when a tangle of legs and arms tumbled out of the truck and landed, facedown, on the gravel. Jerod threw up his hands to stop work.

"Hold it!" Ansel shouted.

Earl stepped on the truck's brake and turned off the engine. Ansel ran to stoop over the body. They all gathered around when he reached to turn it over, but he hesitated. "Can I touch it?" he asked. "Or will that ruin the crime scene?"

"You're wearing work gloves. Besides, what's Gaff going to find?" Jerod asked. "Someone tossed this guy in the truck and covered him with gravel."

Gravel dust coated his hair and clothes. Earl bent to get a better look and shook his head. "He has longish hair like Darby. Looks like it might be auburn, too. Do you think...?"

"Flip him over!" Jerod said.

Ansel gripped the man's shoulder and turned him onto his back.

"No, no, no." Earl rubbed his eyes. "Is there a pulse?"

Jerod gave him a surprised stare. Gray dust stuck in the dead man's bushy eyebrows and sideburns and was embedded in his skin, but Jerod bent to press his fingers over Darby's wrist. "Dead," he announced.

A big dent cratered Darby's forehead, shaped a lot like the blade of a shovel.

Chapter 5

Jazzi couldn't believe she had to do this again, but she pulled her cell phone out of her jeans pocket and called Detective Gaff.

He answered with, "Don't tell me there's another one."

"It's not like I planned it, you know."

There was a pause. She understood his hesitation. How many times could this happen to a person? Finally, he said, "Give me the details."

She explained about finding Darby in the gravel.

"No one leave, and don't touch anything. I'll be there in twenty minutes."

She grimaced as she turned to the others. "We can't leave, and we can't touch anything."

Jerod gave an exasperated sigh. "You know what this means, don't you? The crime scene guys will drape yellow tape around the driveway, and we won't be able to do anything until they give us permission. It's not fair! How many projects have we had to wait on because they became a crime scene?"

Earl stared. "You mean this isn't your first dead body?"

The poor man looked pale despite his tan, and his hands shook. Jazzi guessed him to be in his early forties, going bald in the back with a fringe of brown hair circling his head. He was half a foot taller than her five six. He had beautiful blue eyes rimmed by long, dark lashes.

"Do you want to sit down?" she asked him.

His balance was unsteady as he walked to the porch steps. "Darby was all fired up when he came back to the company yesterday. I've never seen him so bent out of shape. He swore he was going to get even, that no one had the right to talk to him the way Thane had."

"Do you know Thane?" Jazzi asked.

Earl nodded. "I've worked for Darby for twelve years. Thane used to hang out with his kid, Walker. Darby never liked Thane, complained he was a bad influence on Walker. But when Walker and his mom took off two years ago, Darby didn't blame him. That made me wonder."

Jazzi's curiosity got the better of her. "No one knew what happened to Walker and his mom?"

"Darby might have, but he never said." Earl put his hands on his knees, trying to steady their trembling. "When he didn't show up this morning, I thought he'd gone to have it out with Thane."

"Thane. I should call him."

Ansel nodded. "He'll want to know that Darby's dead."

"Is that smart?" Jerod asked. "When Gaff hears that they argued yesterday, Thane's going to move to the top of his suspect list."

Jazzi shrugged that off. "That'll happen anyway. It'll be better if Thane's here to answer Gaff's questions and clear his name."

Ansel reached to pet George. He did that when he was upset. Comforting the dog helped soothe him. "At least warn him that Gaff's on his way."

"Gotcha. Will do." Jazzi walked a little away from the others to make the call and heard Ansel ask Earl, "Can we get you something? We have a leftover sandwich from lunch. It might steady you."

Earl shook his head. "I've only seen dead bodies at funerals before. And to have one fall out of the dump truck..." He stammered to a stop.

When Jazzi returned, Ansel raised his eyebrows at her in a question. Jerod was never that subtle. "Did you get Thane?"

"He's leaving his job site now. He'll be here soon."

She didn't add that he'd said, "The bastard probably deserved it" before he hung up.

Instead, she turned to Earl. "Do you know when Darby filled the dump truck with gravel?"

Earl took a minute to ponder that. "He must have done it after we left the job site yesterday. He slammed into his office when he got back from his concrete run and didn't come out until quitting time. I'd guess he was drinking."

"Did he do that on the job?" It sounded dangerous to drink and drive a concrete truck.

"Only once in a while, when he wasn't going anywhere the rest of the day and he wasn't happy about something. Believe me. He wasn't happy yesterday. Got in a ruckus with us before we left."

"A ruckus?" Ansel was about to follow up on that when Gaff's car pulled to the curb. The detective got out and walked toward them. As usual, his suit jacket was rumpled, and the top button of his dress shirt was undone. He nodded at the four of them and then went to look at the body. They joined him. Gravel was stuck in Darby's hair and beard. Scratches and cuts covered his face and neck. Someone had shut his eyes before tossing him in the truck bed and burying him under the small, jagged stones.

Gaff looked at Earl. "Are you the truck driver?"

"Earl Lahr." Earl started to hold out his hand to shake with Gaff, thought better of it, and dropped it to his side.

Gaff asked, "Any idea how your boss ended up in the gravel?"

Earl let out a long sigh and shook his head. "Darby was alive when we left to go home yesterday."

Gaff reached for the notepad and pen in his shirt pocket. "We? How many of you worked for Darby?"

Earl blinked. "Worked? What does that mean? Will we still have jobs?"

Gaff paused the pen over his paper. "Too soon to tell. Right now, I'm just looking for his killer."

Earl's tan faded again. He jammed his hands into his jeans pockets. "Three of us drove for him, but we all walked to our cars at five and pulled out of the lot at the same time like we usually do."

Jazzi started to ask about the ruckus Earl had mentioned, but just then, Thane's work van pulled to the curb behind Gaff's car, and Thane walked toward them. His lips pinched when he saw Darby's body, and he looked unhappy. "He would go and get himself killed. Now I'll never know what happened to Walker and Rose."

Gaff gave him a closer look. "You had a beef with Darby?"

"Couldn't stand him. Really hated him once Walker and his mom disappeared."

Gaff's gray brows rose in surprise. "Are you just trying to make yourself our top suspect?"

"Figured I would be anyway since I argued with him yesterday."

Another van pulled behind Thane's, and the crime-scene techs started toward them. Alex and Ben saw Jazzi and gave her a quick wave. Earl noticed, frowning. Gaff went to talk to them a while. The medical examiner arrived next. He and Gaff exchanged a few words, then Gaff motioned for Jazzi, Jerod, Ansel, Thane, and Earl to follow him into the house.

Jerod and Ansel dragged two beat-up lawn chairs from the back porch into the kitchen and arranged them close to the card table. The square table sat only four comfortably, but they crowded around it anyway. The kitchen was small and cramped. They wouldn't start work on the interior of the house until they'd finished everything outside. Jazzi grimaced at the wall they wanted to knock down. This room needed to be expanded. It felt claustrophobic now.

Gaff pointed his pen toward Thane. "Let's start with you. You say you argued with Darby yesterday? I want to hear all about it."

Jazzi leaned forward in her chair. She was curious about what Darby had done to make Thane despise him forever.

Chapter 6

Thane's jaw locked, and he gripped the edge of the card table. He didn't kill Darby, Jazzi was sure of that. Thane was too nice, too thoughtful. Sure, he had lost his temper with the old man, but that in itself was a novelty for him.

Gaff put his notepad on the table and got comfortable. "Okay, what happened between you two? What's the background story?"

Thane scraped a hand through his longish auburn hair and swallowed nervously. "Darby was my best friend's dad. Walker and I hung out together since second grade. We were close, shared everything. He came to our place whenever he could to get away from his old man. Darby was always giving Walker grief, wouldn't leave him alone, but he sure put him to work. Walker had chores at the cement company—heavy chores—as long as I knew him. When we were little, I used to ride my bike there on weekends to pitch in, because then Walker could finish faster and we could play. But Darby just started adding more jobs to the list, and together it took us just as long as it once took Walker alone. My dad finally went over and talked to him, and I wasn't allowed to work there anymore."

"But Walker could still come to your house?" Gaff asked.

"Only because his mom stuck up for him and told Darby there was a law about child labor and if he didn't knock it off, she'd report him."

Gaff rested his pen on the notepad, thinking. "How did Darby and his wife get along? Did he listen to her?"

"He belittled her all the time, but he could push Rose only so far, and he knew it. And he hated it when she got really mad at him. If she stopped talking to him, gave him the silent treatment, he went crazy—bought her flowers and candy, followed her around, begging her to forgive him."

Jazzi frowned, trying to add things up. "But then he'd do the same thing again?"

"He couldn't quit being Darby. He didn't have it in him."

She wondered when things had reached the breaking point.

Gaff must have wondered the same thing. He asked, "What finally happened?"

"The older Walker got, the more things he was responsible for. By the time we graduated from high school, he almost ran the company. The more Walker did, the more money they made. He was a natural at business. And the better things ran, the worse Darby treated him."

The word popped out of Jazzi's mouth before she realized it. "Why?"

"Darby always resented Walker. He was all the things Darby couldn't be. That, and Darby always needed to have a whipping boy, someone to be his scapegoat."

Earl's eyes went wide. "*That's* why he started picking on Andy. Walker left, and he needed someone new to be mean to."

Thane clenched and unclenched his hands. "*If* he left."

Gaff's pen poised over his notepad again. "You don't think he did?"

Thane leaned forward, his expression intent. "When I started the internship with my company, I got paid while I trained and worked. I got an apartment and asked Walker if he'd like to be my roommate. That way, he wouldn't have to spend any more time with Darby than he chose to. Walker turned me down, told me he loved the cement business and his mom, that he'd never leave her alone to deal with the old man. He meant to take Darby in his stride. But things got worse and worse between them. Then two years ago, he came to my place, and we played cards for most of an evening. He left, and I got a call from him late that night. He said his mom and him had to leave, that he couldn't be around Darby anymore, that he needed a fresh start. I never saw him or Rose again. I called him over and over again, but he never answered. He and Rose just vanished."

Jazzi stared. "That's why you accused Darby of burying them somewhere on his property."

"What would you think?" Thane curled his hands into fists. "If Darby thought Rose was walking out on him, he'd go berserk, especially if she was leaving with Walker. I drove to Darby's place and demanded to know what happened, but he cussed me out and told me to get lost. I finally called the cops, told them my story, and they let me walk every inch of the grounds with them. They brought a dog trained to find corpses."

"And?" Jerod demanded.

Thane shook his head. "We didn't find anything, and somehow Darby convinced them that Rose got tired of him, ran off, and took Walker with her."

Earl rubbed his forehead, a worried scowl on his face. "Darby poured a cement slab a month after Walker left. Odd, because it's stuck in a strange spot, doesn't serve any purpose."

Thane flinched and pinched his lips together in a tight line. "When I accused Darby of killing them yesterday, that's when he punched me."

Gaff's expression had grown more and more thoughtful the longer he listened to Thane. "It must have stirred up lots of old memories when you saw Darby yesterday."

"It ruined my mood, that's for sure."

Gaff straightened his shoulders. "I hate to say it, boy, but you sound like a top candidate for someone who'd like to see Darby dead."

Thane scanned the rest of them at the table. "I can't deny that, but I didn't kill him."

Gaff asked, "Could you tell me where you were last night from five p.m. to this morning?"

"That's easy. I left my job site and drove straight home. Olivia doesn't work at the salon on Mondays, so she was there when I got back."

"Was she with you all night?"

Thane leaned forward, put his elbows on the table, and rested his chin in his hands. "No, she went to a meeting for small business owners that started at eight. Was gone about two hours."

Gaff raised an eyebrow. "Plenty of time for you to drive to Darby's place, smash in his head, and drive back."

Ansel sat up straighter in his chair. "Is that when Darby died?"

"It's too soon to know for sure." Gaff used his professional voice when he looked at Thane. "You're a suspect, so don't leave town. I'll probably have to ask you more questions later."

Thane gave a curt nod. "It's not like I had plans anyway."

Earl squirmed in his chair.

Gaff turned to him. "Since you're here, let's get your questions done before I meet the two other drivers."

Earl gripped his hands together and swallowed hard. "I can tell you right now, I live alone. Once I left my parents' place last night, I was by myself."

"Why were you at your parents'?"

"Mom called and asked me over for supper—a big pot of vegetable soup and her homemade bread."

"When did you arrive and leave there?"

"I went there after work, probably left around eight. Dad's retired, but Mom and I still have to get up for work in the morning."

"No neighbors saw you drive into your garage? No one can vouch for your timing?"

"I have a small house a few miles out of town. No one can see my place. I like it that way."

Jazzi thought about their house. One of the reasons she and Ansel loved it was because of the privacy. Where they lived, homes were set so far apart, with bushes or fields between them, that you didn't pay much attention to your neighbors. Besides, even if people lived close, how many could vouch for you anyway? She didn't sit looking out her window to keep track of her neighbors' comings and goings. And what if Darby died at one or two in the morning? Who could swear you'd never left your house then?

Gaff flipped his notepad to a fresh page and nodded at Earl. "I'll take your full statement anyway. We'll see what we come up with."

Earl nodded but looked worried.

Chapter 7

Jazzi went to the cooler she'd packed with lunch things and carried two open bags of chips to the table. Taking out a handful for herself, she passed the bags to Ansel. He dumped a small pile from each on a napkin and handed them to Jerod. When they reached Earl, he took the last of them. Jazzi stood to throw away the empty bags and brought back a cold can of Pepsi for each person.

Gaff ate a handful of chips and took a few sips of cola before turning his attention back to the interview. "Okay, Earl, let's start at the beginning. How many years did you work for Darby?"

"Twelve."

"Your name?"

"Earl Lahr. Two other guys and I drove for Darby. He paid us good wages. We had steady work except for the down season. Every cement driver has that. The business did better when Walker ran it. Since Darby's been in charge the last two years, things have been slipping."

Gaff frowned. "Why's that? He ran it until Walker got old enough, didn't he?"

Earl rubbed his chin. He glanced over at Thane. "Darby hasn't been the same since Rose left. I don't think he'd ever harm her, so I don't think he killed her. He might not have been nice to live with, but she was his rock, his foundation. He's been off-kilter without her. He drank more, forgot to write down deliveries if he was in one of his moods, and just didn't seem to care as much as he once did. We were beginning to wonder how much longer we'd have jobs."

"How did you and the other two drivers get along with him?"

Earl rubbed his palms on his jeans. "No one got along with Darby. He could get under anyone's skin. From one breath to the next, he could flip from laughing and joking with you to saying the meanest thing you've ever heard. We used to joke that he was bipolar, but then we decided he was just mean. Once he found your soft spot, he wouldn't leave it alone."

"Did he find yours?"

"The best he could do was call me a momma's boy. He'd say I'd rather hang on to Mom's apron strings than find a woman of my own."

"Did that bother you?"

"Not much. I was married once. Met my wife when we were both studying to be dental hygienists."

Jerod stared. "You worked in a dentist's office?"

Jazzi rolled her eyes at him. Her cousin had no tact. Whatever thought flew through his mind had a chance of popping out of his mouth.

Earl glanced down at his flannel shirt and work jeans. "Hard to believe, isn't it? I cleaned and X-rayed teeth for three years. Hated it. My wife loved it, but I didn't like being stuck indoors. I wouldn't have been happy doing any office work. When I quit to drive a truck, she filed for divorce. I made more money, but she thought it was a low-class job. I steered away from women for a long time after that."

Gaff finished scribbling notes and asked, "Did Darby pick on his other two employees?"

"Anyone was fair game," Earl said, "but he especially heckled Andy. He's the youngest of us, and I got the idea that made Darby think he was more vulnerable. That, and Andy has a kid with autism."

Jazzi couldn't believe anyone would use autism to badger a parent. What kind of sadistic person would make fun of a father trying to cope with a child who had a disability?

Gaff's expression hardened, too. The detective was close to his two grown boys, Jazzi knew, and crazy about his three grandkids. He wouldn't appreciate jokes about kids with problems. "Is Andy working today?"

"We're all on the schedule, but it's getting close to quitting time. If you want to talk to them, you'd better call them and ask them to stay."

Gaff made the call and gave a curt nod. "We'd better go. They're going to stay long enough to clean their trucks and promised to hang on a few more minutes, but Andy has to get home so that his wife can meet friends tonight. He's watching their son so she can have a break."

Earl rose to leave, too, and Gaff glanced at Thane. "Want to come with us? We can check out the new cement slab."

"If Jazzi comes, too." Thane gave her a pleading look.

"Why me?" She'd be happy to go home to hear the results.

Thane turned to Ansel for backup. "She knows the right things to say, right? She makes things easier."

Ansel grinned. "She's the best, all right."

"I have to agree." Gaff motioned for her to come, too.

No fair. She was about to argue when Thane added, "I'm still a suspect. I could use some help clearing my name. Olivia would want you to help me."

Olivia would have a fit if Jazzi didn't go with him. With a sigh, she went to join them.

"What if I drive and we follow you there?" Thane asked Gaff. "I have to come south again when we're done, and I can drop Jazzi here on my way home."

Jerod looked at the kitchen clock. "Ansel and I will start ripping off the back porch while you're gone, Jazz." He gave Gaff a sour look. "We can't finish the driveway with police tape roping it off."

Everyone, including Jazzi, grumbled as they left the kitchen. A murder did that, put people on edge. Would it have been asking too much for Olivia to have been home all night last night? For Thane to have a rock-solid alibi? For Darby to have fallen out of the gravel in someone else's driveway?

Chapter 8

As Thane drove west toward Darby's place, Jazzi spotted a few trees that were beginning to change color. Not many yet. But a few reds and yellows were scattered here and there in the woods they passed.

She cracked her window an inch. The air was cool but had no bite. They took the same route she used to drive to Jerod's house, except that they turned off before they reached the highway. Darby's house and business were close to a series of gravel pits on the southwest side of town. At one time, a warm shallow sea covered the entire area. Geology students got special permission once to take a field trip to the bottom before the pit grew so huge and deep. They found prehistoric fossils poking from the sand. She'd been fascinated with the trilobites on exhibit at the local college. Had the sea existed before the Ice Age? Or had the glacier that moved across northeast Indiana dumped all of the sand and gravel here? She tried to remember. The sea came first, she decided.

Thane interrupted her thoughts. "I'm sort of dreading digging up the cement slab. Part of me has always suspected that Darby killed Walker and Rose, but I sure hope we don't find skeletons under the slab Earl told us about."

"Me, too. Finding Aunt Lynda in the trunk at our house was enough." When she and Jerod had bought the cottage she and Ansel now lived in, they never expected to find the skeleton of her mother's sister folded in a trunk in the attic. Everyone had thought Lynda had gone to New York, but she'd never left River Bluffs.

Thane wrinkled his nose. "It was hard enough seeing Darby's body when he was still fresh. Walker and Rose disappeared two years ago.

Would they be skeletons by now? Or would they look like the bodies you found near the wetlands?"

Jazzi pushed those images away. Thane hadn't gone with Ansel, Jerod, and her when they led Gaff to two shallow graves near his and Olivia's subdivision. She grimaced. "I don't know how long it takes for bodies to decompose. I just know it's not a pretty sight."

Thane slowed to turn into a long drive that led to a tri-level house. They passed it and wound around to three metal outbuildings at the back of the property. One of them had an office sign hanging next to the front door. Gaff's car was already parked close by. When she and Thane walked into the office, Gaff, Earl, and two more men sat in stiff-backed chairs, waiting for them.

"Good, we can get started." Gaff reached for his notepad and pen. "Earl, you can introduce your friends to Jazzi and Thane."

"I know them," Thane said. "I used to come here to pick up Walker. He always had work to finish, so I ended up hanging around for a while."

Earl motioned toward Jazzi. "This is Jazzi. Thane lives with her sister. She and her friends are fixing the house I delivered gravel to. Darby's body landed in their driveway. Jazzi, this is Andy." He motioned to a guy who looked to be close to her and Thane's age. "And this is Colin." Colin looked older, like he might be in his late thirties.

"Let's start with you." Gaff turned to Andy. "How long did you work for Darby?"

"Six years. I'm the newest driver. I started a year after my son was born."

"How did you get along with Darby?"

"We did all right until Walker left. Then things got rocky. When Darby was in a mood, he could be really mean."

"Can you elaborate?"

Andy looked uncomfortable. "My son is autistic. When he wanted to needle me, he'd ask where the screwed-up gene came from, me or my wife?"

Jazzi gaped. Who'd say something like that?

Colin snorted. "You were an easy target. You always took his crap, never stuck up for yourself."

"Didn't matter," Earl said, sticking up for Andy. "Darby wouldn't quit, no matter what you did. Look at how he treated Walker and Rose, and they let him know he was pushing it."

"If he treated me like that, I'd walk," Colin said.

Gaff turned his attention to him. "Darby didn't give you any grief?"

"Oh, sure he did, but nothing personal, nothing downright mean. Darby couldn't leave anyone alone. He had to heckle, but he paid good wages. What did I care what he said? He was a paycheck. I didn't have to like him."

"Did he ever push hard enough that one of you would snap and smash his head in with a shovel?"

Andy's jaw dropped. "Is that what happened to him?"

Gaff nodded. "Looks like a crime of impulse, like Darby said the wrong thing, and somebody hit him to shut him up."

Jazzi was surprised that Gaff was telling them this, but then she remembered that Earl had seen Darby's body. He knew how Darby had died.

Colin leaned back in his chair and stretched his legs out. "Sounds like the old coot finally went too far. When did he die?"

"I don't have the coroner's report yet," Gaff told them. "Did any of you see or hear from him after you left work yesterday?"

Andy shook his head. "We all left at the same time. That's the last I saw him."

"You?" Gaff glanced at Colin.

"He doesn't pay me enough to put up with him on my off hours."

Andy fidgeted. "Will we have jobs now? Should I start looking for something else? We don't have much in savings, mostly live paycheck to paycheck."

Gaff spread his hands in a helpless gesture. "I don't know. We're going to try to find Walker and Rose, but I don't know what will happen to the company. We're going to look for a will, too."

"I doubt he has one," Earl said. "I don't think he liked anyone enough to give them anything."

Gaff turned to Jazzi and raised his eyebrows. She took her cue and asked, "Did Darby have *any* friends, anyone he was close to?"

Earl looked thoughtful. "He had a drinking buddy he met a few times a week, but I don't remember his name. Do you guys?"

Andy and Colin shook their heads.

Earl frowned, then brightened. "Whiskers! That's what he called him, but I never heard his real name."

With no name, how would they find him? Jazzi decided Gaff would find a way.

Gaff wrote it down, then said, "I need to know where Andy and Colin were last night after you left work. I already asked Earl."

Andy answered quickly. "I went home. My wife and I stayed in and had a quiet night."

"You?" Gaff asked Colin.

"I met a friend at the bar for a burger, then I went to the store to restock the fridge. I ended up drinking a couple beers at the Black Dog Pub before I went back to the apartment."

"Can anyone vouch for you?"

"Off and on. I don't like to stay in one place very long."

"The restless type?" Gaff asked.

"That's why I like this job. I can come and go, making deliveries, not be stuck in one room all day."

Gaff got the friend's name whom Colin had met and made a note to check his alibi at the Black Dog Pub and grocery store. "I'm pretty sure there'll be big enough gaps, though, that you could have snuck out here to kill Darby."

"If I'd wanted to," Colin agreed. "But I didn't."

When he finished with his questions, Gaff handed them each one of his cards. "If you think of anything else, give me a call. And don't leave town. I might need to ask you more questions." Then he turned to Earl. "Can you show us the slab of cement you told us about?"

Colin's eyes lit up. "Funny about that slab. Darby poured it where no one would ever use it." He followed them when Earl led them to it, but Andy mumbled a quick good-bye.

"I have to babysit our son so my wife can leave."

Gaff nodded. "Earl explained about that. And remember, don't leave town."

"Like I could. My wife can't raise our son alone." Andy hurried to his car.

They left the outbuildings and crossed a stretch of grass that led to Darby's fenced-in backyard. Most of it was taken up by a huge cement patio. A gas grill and a smoker sat on one side of it. Two umbrella tables, circled by chairs, sat on the other side.

"Did Darby like to entertain?" Jazzi asked. Ansel was thinking about buying a big smoker. They had her family over every Sunday, and he had visions of smoked ribs, briskets, and chickens, but they'd have to expand their patio to make room for it.

Earl scoffed at her question. "Darby left on Sundays a couple times a month to go fishing with Whiskers. They drank beer on his pontoon and usually came home empty-handed. Rose invited us over whenever he was gone. Walker manned the grill and smoker." Earl let out a deep breath. "There wasn't a nicer person on this earth than Rose."

"She didn't have any family around here?" Jazzi asked.

Earl looked sad. "She told me that when she married Darby, they all drifted away from her. She was pretty much on her own."

Jazzi motioned toward long, raised garden beds tucked between the patio and fence. "Rose liked to garden?"

He smiled. "That woman canned enough green beans and tomatoes to last an entire year. Dried herbs, too."

They were approaching the slab, and Jazzi scanned the area. There was nothing but grass. Nothing.

When they reached the square of cement, they circled it, staring at the four-by-four slab. It wasn't big enough to cover two bodies. Had Darby used it as a grave marker?

Colin gestured at the lack of anything close by. "The old man dug up a big chunk of sod and stuck this here. What sense does that make?"

None, as far as she could tell. The slab was completely out of place.

"I'll call for a jackhammer," Gaff said. "We'll see what's under it."

Jazzi was glad she wouldn't be here when they dug for bodies, but Thane grinned.

"Jerod let me borrow theirs. It's in the back of my van."

She'd have to thank Jerod for that. Not.

Thane went to get the jackhammer. He was grunting by the time he dragged it back to them. Colin and Earl walked to one of the buildings and came back with shovels. Jazzi thought about walking to the picnic table near the office and grabbing a cup of coffee from the machine inside. She'd be far enough away, she wouldn't see anything, but she was too nosy. She wanted to know if Walker and Rose had never left River Bluffs, just like her Aunt Lynda.

Thane pressed on the jackhammer, and soon its loud racket drowned out all other noise. Rat-tat-tat-tat. Rat-a-tat-tat. Dust and dirt flew in the air. Jazzi coughed and stepped back. Thane made short work of the slab, and she helped the men move chunks of cement out of the way, then Colin and Earl began to dig. About a foot down, their shovels hit metal.

"Darby didn't stick them in a metal drainage pipe, did he?" Colin asked.

"Wouldn't put it past him," Earl said.

When they dug enough to clean off what he'd buried, they stared in surprise at a heavy metal safe.

"What the heck?" Earl scratched his head.

It took some serious lifting, but they finally managed to free the safe from its hole and set it on the grass. A heavy sheet of plastic was duct-taped to its top, protecting an envelope stuffed into a plastic sheath. They scraped dirt off it and read the message: FOR WALKER.

Thane shook his head in disbelief. "Well, I'll be. If Darby buried this for Walker, then my friend must still be alive. Somewhere."

Earl turned to Colin. "Isn't that the safe that used to be in Darby's office? I wondered why he'd gotten rid of it."

"You don't think it's booby-trapped, do you?" Colin bent closer to it. "I don't see any wires. The old man was royally fuming for weeks after Walker disappeared."

"Would he do that?" Jazzi asked.

Earl barked a laugh. "You didn't know Darby."

She stepped farther away from the safe.

"Does anyone know the combination?" Gaff asked.

Earl answered. "Only Walker and Darby. The boss guarded everything to do with that safe. You'd think it was Fort Knox."

Gaff considered it for a while. "You guys are all strong. Let's put it in the trunk of my car, and I can take it to the station. Maybe we can figure out how to open it there. And I'll start searching for Walker and Rose."

The safe was heavy, but nothing Thane, Earl, and Colin couldn't handle. They put it in Gaff's trunk, and then everyone got ready to leave.

"Remember. Don't leave town," Gaff warned them.

"Do we show up for work tomorrow?" Colin asked.

Gaff gave that a moment of thought. "Might as well until we know what will happen to the company."

"Will we get paid on Friday?" Colin's question was legitimate. Did Darby have anyone as backup in case he got sick or hurt?

Gaff shrugged his heavy shoulders. The detective wasn't tall, but he was stocky. "That I don't know."

Earl sighed. "I hope you find Walker soon. He might know what to do now."

They climbed into their vehicles to part. On the drive back to the fixer-upper, Thane brooded for a while before blurting out, "Walker could have called me. He could have let me know he was alive. If Gaff finds him, I don't want anything to do with him."

"Maybe he had a good reason."

"Not good enough. We were like brothers. He knew I'd worry. Even if he's alive, he's dead to me."

Jazzi didn't argue. She understood why Thane was hurt. He'd deserved better treatment from his friend.

Chapter 9

When Jazzi got back to Southwood Park, Jerod and Ansel had yanked the entire back porch off the house and were throwing the last of the debris into the dumpster.

"*Now* she gets here!" Jerod teased. "After all the work's done."

She waved off Thane and gave her cousin a sweet smile. "You can go with Gaff next time, and I'll stay to work with Ansel."

"No way. You win. I don't want any part of murder investigations." Jerod took off his work gloves and stuffed them in his back pocket. "Did you find any bodies?"

"No, but we found a safe buried under Darby's cement slab." She brought them up to date on things.

The guys listened with interest, then Jerod dusted off his flannel shirt and swatted rubble off his baseball cap before returning it to his head. "It's been a big enough day for me. I'm ready to head home. Gunther has to collect a dozen different kinds of leaves to take to nursery school tomorrow. They're going to have a lesson on trees and then do an art project."

A dozen seemed like a lot to Jazzi for a four-year-old. Were preschools offering college degrees these days? "Do you have that many different trees on your property?"

"No, but Foster Park does. I'm going to drive him there."

Ansel looked tired, so she motioned toward their vehicle, too. He grabbed George and headed to his white work van. They followed Jerod's pickup to Fairfield, then he turned south and they turned north. On the drive home, Ansel said, "Maybe we should plant more trees on our property and get ready ahead of time. Then when our kids have to collect a dozen leaves, we'll be ready."

She liked the idea. "I'd love to have more flowering trees around our house—maybe some crab apples, magnolia trees, and flowering pears."

Ansel turned onto Main Street. Traffic was heavy this time of night. "In the spring, we can plant as many trees as you want. Anything else?"

"I like azalea bushes."

"Those, too, then." He pressed a hand to his stomach. "I'm starving. What's for supper tonight?"

"I started a pork loin in the slow cooker."

"Did I see you add coconut milk and dried apricots?"

"And I rubbed it with a spice blend, too."

He smiled. "You got that recipe off the Food Network, didn't you?"

"You owe Sunny Anderson a special thank-you."

"I'll remember that."

"If we're up for it, I thought I'd make vegetable soup for tomorrow and take a round of crusty bread out of the freezer." She happened to know that Ansel had a soft spot for the stuff. Once it was sweater weather, they craved more soups, stews, and one-dish meals.

"I'm never leaving you. You know that, right? I'm like George. We can be swayed by food." He glanced at the pug on the back seat. Sometimes, his ears perked up when he heard his name, but tonight he never blinked.

Once Ansel got out of city traffic and turned onto Coliseum Boulevard, he asked, "How was Thane? Okay?"

"He's pretty upset." Jazzi explained.

"I'd be upset, too," Ansel said. "Thane thought Walker and his mom were dead the last two years. Not knowing what happened to them would eat at you."

Jazzi thought of her mom, wondering what had happened to Lynda. It had been a relief when Jazzi and Jerod found her skeleton. At least, she *knew* Lynda had died and hadn't deserted and ignored them.

Ansel turned onto the road that led to their house. As always, once their stone cottage came into view, Jazzi's spirits lifted. The house was larger inside than it looked, with a massive kitchen and living room downstairs, and three good-sized bedrooms and two baths up. It sat on a large piece of property with a pond Ansel had dug in the back.

As always, Ansel stopped to drop Jazzi off at the kitchen door before he drove to the garage. She was filling the cats' bowls when he carried George inside. Inky and Marmalade purred loudly as they ate. Jazzi loved that sound. George went to his bowl, too, and Ansel fed him. The pug liked dry dog food, as long as it was augmented with table scraps at meals.

Ansel inhaled a deep breath. "The kitchen smells wonderful."

The magic of a slow cooker. The aroma of the pork roast made Jazzi's mouth water.

Before they worried about sides for supper, Jazzi and Ansel climbed the steps to their bedroom and took quick showers. They planned on staying inside the rest of the night, so changed into their pajamas early.

Ansel looked especially appealing in his drawstring, striped PJ bottoms and roomy T-shirt. Darn, her guy was sexy. The way he was looking at her let her know he appreciated her in pajamas, too. Then his stomach rumbled, and Jazzi laughed.

"Let's finish making supper." Half an hour later, she put butter and parsley in the pot of drained potatoes, and Ansel tossed their salad. They settled at the kitchen island to eat, and George hunkered by Ansel's feet to beg.

The coconut milk she'd added to the pork had thickened into a gravy, and she poured some over her potatoes. Ansel wasn't so subtle. He drowned his plate in it before tossing a piece of the roast to George. When he'd finished his first helping and dished up a second, he slowed down a little. He turned toward her, finally ready for their usual dinner conversation. "You never left River Bluffs, did you? Do you have any friends that go back to second grade like Thane and Walker?"

"You've met Leesa and Suze when our group meets at restaurants some Fridays. We've been friends a long time."

"You've known them since grade school?"

She shook her head. "Nope, since high school. The kids I hung out with in grade school ended up in different middle schools and high schools. I lost track of them. What about you? Do you have any longtime friends?"

"Ethan and I did a lot of stuff together once we met in middle school, but then he got married right out of high school, and I left Wisconsin and moved here."

Jazzi finished her supper and stood to carry her dirty dishes to the sink. "Right now, it's harder for Leesa, Suze, and me to get together. They have babies and young kids."

"Kids change everything." Ansel carried his dirty dishes over to join her. "I think it's great that they still make time to see you." With a grin, he added, "Especially since they let their husbands and me tag along."

"So do I." She finished rinsing dishes for him to load in the dishwasher and began wiping down the sink area. "I'm going to take a break and watch some TV before I start the soup for tomorrow."

"When you're ready, I'll help you." Ansel walked behind her and put his arms around her waist. He leaned closer to say, "But I can think of something better to do than watch TV."

"You can, can you?" She swiveled out of his embrace, took his hand, and started to the stairs. George raised his head, saw where they going, and lowered it again. The cats didn't take the hint and ran ahead of them, only to have Ansel scoot them out of the room and shut the door.

An hour later, freshly showered again, she and Ansel returned to the kitchen. She tossed stew meat in the food processor and pulsed it into smaller pieces before adding it to the hot oil in the Dutch oven. She seared it, then added the beef broth and seasonings while Ansel chopped and added vegetables. They let the soup simmer while they watched TV.

By the time they called it a night, tomorrow's supper waited in the fridge, and crusty bread thawed on the countertop. Once in bed, she and Ansel turned on their sides, butts touching, to drift into slumber. Marmalade jumped on the bed and pressed against Ansel's leg. Inky snuggled into the curve of Jazzi's thighs and stomach. In a sleepy voice, Ansel asked, "Do you think Gaff will find Walker and his mom?"

"If they're not dead, sure. I doubt they changed their identities and went into hiding."

"What do you think Thane will do if Walker comes back to River Bluffs?"

"Probably cuss him out and warn him to stay far away from him."

"That's what I'd do." Ansel's hand slid under the blankets to touch her fanny. Her Norseman liked having her within reach.

Jazzi wondered if Walker would even bother to return here when he learned Darby was dead, or if he did, if he'd return with a wife and maybe a kid. What kind of explanation could he give Thane for making him worry all this time? Maybe Walker wasn't as good a friend to Thane as Thane had been to him. Maybe Thane was lucky Walker was no longer a part of his life.

Chapter 10

Jazzi sliced the leftover pork roast to make sandwiches for their lunch today. She topped it with plenty of pickles because the guys loved them. She added two bags of chips to the cooler, and Ansel grabbed it and one of the coffee thermoses to carry to his waiting van.

"Come on, George!" he called. "You have to walk this morning."

The pug rose to follow him while Jazzi reached for the second thermos. Inky gave her a dirty look. George got to go with them. The cats didn't. He leapt onto the countertop and went straight to the glass jar holding her new bouquet of flowers, put his paw on the side, and knocked it over. As usual, the glass broke, and water ran everywhere.

"You brat!" Jazzi grabbed for him, but he took off before she could reach him. She put down her thermos and cleaned up the mess. This time, she went to the pantry and returned with a heavy ceramic jar her grandma used for making sauerkraut. She jammed the flowers in that. Not ideal. The brim was too wide, and the flowers sprawled, but let Inky try to knock it over! Then she headed to the van.

There was more traffic than usual this early on a Wednesday morning. Jazzi had tugged on a sweatshirt and her insulated flannel since the temperatures had dropped during the night. The inside of the van felt cold, and Ansel flipped on the heater to take off the chill. He wore his long-sleeved thermal shirt beneath a worn sweater. She loved it when he looked like a rugged outdoorsman.

On the drive south, Ansel saw flashing lights a few blocks ahead, so he turned onto Anthony. They passed strip malls before they reached a section of well-tended older houses. Tudors jostled alongside American Foursquares and two-stories with deep front porches. Jazzi could remember when this street was lined with majestic American elm trees, but elm disease had ravaged all of them. Now crab apple trees took their place. In the spring, white flowers formed a corridor for traffic.

Ansel stayed on Anthony until they reached Rudisill, then drove to Southwood Park. The trip took longer with this route, but there was less traffic. Jerod's pickup slid in behind them when they pulled to the curb.

"'Morning, guys!" He strapped on his work belt before he started toward them. "Time to build the new back porch. You ready?"

They buckled on their work belts, too. Ansel handed Jerod the cooler to lug inside, then he carried George to the backyard. After Jazzi put the two thermoses on the kitchen countertop, she tugged on her work gloves and went to join Ansel. They'd decided to build a deck across the entire back of the house, with a roofed area over the kitchen door. It would be large enough for grilling and entertaining.

They had the frame and floor done when Thane called. Jazzi winced when she heard his gruff, angry voice. "Detective Gaff found Walker and Rose. They moved to Dayton, Ohio, not that far from here. He asked them to come to River Bluffs so he can talk to them. Rose can't make it. She has to work, but Walker's on his way. Gaff wanted to bring him to my work site, but there's no privacy here. Besides, I don't want to see him. No such luck. Gaff insisted, so I told him to bring Walker to your fixer-upper."

"Are you going to be okay?"

"I have to be, don't I? It's not like I have a choice."

"I'm sorry, Thane. We'll be here for you."

"Thanks. I'll see you in an hour."

When she put her phone back in her pocket, Jerod shook his head. "We heard. Thane's not a happy camper. His voice carried."

"Everyone should be here in an hour," Jazzi said.

Jerod nodded, walking toward a pile of railing posts. "That's long enough to finish the deck so no one falls off it."

They didn't waste time talking. They got busy. By the time Gaff strolled up the walkway to the house, the railing was finished. A tall man with crisp, chestnut-colored hair walked behind him. He was good-looking, but not drop dead gorgeous like Ansel. Jazzi hurried to greet them and hustle them inside before Thane got there.

Gaff introduced them. "Walker, this is Ansel, Jazzi, and Jerod. And this is Darby's son, Walker."

Ansel had already crowded six chairs around their card table. They were settling in place when Thane gave a quick knock and walked through the door. He glanced at Walker, and his expression turned hard.

Walker pinched his lips together. "I'm sorry, bud. I promised my mom I wouldn't talk to you."

"Doesn't matter." Thane sat between Jerod and Ansel. "Ancient history."

"But Darby's dead now. I can explain."

Thane crossed his arms over his chest. "No need to. We've both moved on."

Gaff opened his notepad and focused on Walker. "Well, *I'd* like to know what happened and why you disappeared two years ago."

Walker tried to make eye contact with Thane, but he turned his head. Walker let out a ragged breath. "My dad and I got into a fight like we always did. When Mom tried to smooth things over, it ticked Dad off. He said he'd never been sure if I was really his son, that he was pretty sure Mom had been having a little fun on the side. Dad always insulted me. I didn't care about that, but he'd never insulted Mom. He berated her, sure, always let her know she could have cooked a better meal, kept the house cleaner. Stupid stuff, but he'd never hit her so low before. It made me furious, and he laughed at me. That's when I knew he'd keep poking at Mom over and over again to get at me, so I hit him, knocked him down, and I would have kicked him, but Mom stepped between us."

Thane's eyes went wide with shock, but he still refused to look at his old friend.

"I don't get it," Gaff said, putting down his pen. "You left River Bluffs because you hit your dad?"

Walker's hands curled into fists. "Dad had never pushed Mom before, but he must have decided it was worth it to twist the knife in me. He'd keep doing it, so I left because I knew I'd hit him again. And again. I despised him, and I needed to get away from him. The thing is, later that night, when I told Mom I was moving out, she said she was going, too. She said once Dad got started on someone, he never quit. He'd make her life miserable. Dad wouldn't have crossed the line except to needle me. So how could I just leave her?"

Gaff frowned. "But if she'd filed for divorce, she'd have gotten a decent settlement. It sounds like she'd earned it."

"I asked her about that. She thought Dad would do everything to keep us from getting a penny, and he'd drag the proceedings out as long as he could. She hadn't worked in thirty years and had no job skills, but she said she'd rather live in poverty than battle Dad for months."

Jerod shook his head. "All she needed was a good lawyer. She'd have done all right."

Walker shrugged, looking doubtful. "I don't know. I didn't think she'd ever leave him. All I could think about was if Mom walked out on Dad, we'd have to leave town or Dad would find her and heckle her all the time."

Thane's voice came out as a deep growl. "I get that. I understand. But why couldn't you return my calls? Let me know you were alive?"

"Alive?" Walker stared. "Why wouldn't I be alive?"

"Think about it!" Thane jumped to his feet, his voice raised. "You disappear in the middle of the night, and no one knows where you went or what happened to you. I thought Darby found out you were going to slip away, lost it, and killed you both. I even went to the cops to see if he buried you on his property."

Walker shook his head, stunned. "Is that what happened? Cops tracked us down, but they said someone had reported us missing, and Mom thought it had to be Dad. She begged them not to tell anyone they'd found us."

Thane's face turned so red, Jazzi worried he'd explode from anger. He asked again, "Why wouldn't you return my calls?"

Walker looked down at the floor. "Mom made me promise I wouldn't talk to you. She was afraid I'd tell you where we were and Dad would get it out of you somehow. Or that you'd drive to see us and he'd follow you. I never even dreamed..." He swallowed hard. "I wanted to see you so much. She knew that. I needed somebody to talk to. I needed a friend, but Mom had put all of her trust in me. I couldn't let her down."

Thane rammed his fingers through his hair in frustration, then jammed his hands into his pockets. Mumbling to himself, he stomped outside onto the newly built deck. They could watch him pace back and forth through the windows. Finally, he flung the door open, walked straight to Walker, and crushed him in a hug. "You made me sick with worry, but jeez, I've missed you. I always missed you."

Walker's shoulders sagged with relief. "I didn't want you to worry about me. That's why I called you before we left. I thought you'd put two and two together. You knew my dad."

"I put it together wrong." Thane pushed away and went back to his chair. He locked gazes with Walker. "What now?"

"No idea," Walker admitted. "I thought the old man would live forever, that he was too mean to die."

"Are you a suspect like I am?" Thane asked.

"You're a suspect?" Walker stared at him in surprise.

"Long story, but do you have an alibi?"

"People can vouch I never left Dayton. I played cards at Mom's house until midnight, and then a neighbor pounded on my apartment door at three. He was drunk and couldn't figure out why his key wasn't working. I got him to his place and helped his wife get him settled, then I had to be at work at seven."

"What about your mom?"

"Mom? Why would she be a suspect?"

"She's on our list." Gaff, as usual, didn't mince words. Jazzi supposed most detectives didn't. He gave Walker a long look. "Darby found out she'd remarried, called her."

"Your mom remarried?" Thane inhaled and let out a deep breath.

"After a while, when she felt safer, and after she met Gene, she changed her mind."

"Walker can tell you about that later, but for now, I'm interested in the message Darby left him." Gaff explained about the safe they'd found buried under the slab of cement. "It's meant for you."

Walker tossed a nervous glance Thane's way. "That was the safe Dad kept in the office, remember? I stored contracts in it. Why do you think he buried it with my name on it?"

"I thought he might have booby-trapped it."

Walker seemed to consider that a possibility. "Do you think he wrote some terrible curse for me to read after he was gone?"

Ansel's eyebrows rose, surprised that a son would suspect his dad of being that vindictive.

"The safe's still in my trunk," Gaff said. "Never got someone to help me carry it into the station."

"Do you remember the combination?" Thane asked.

"Yeah, but…"

Jazzi didn't blame Walker for not being enthusiastic about opening it.

"Let's find out what's inside it." Gaff handed Ansel his car keys. "You and Jerod are young and strong. You can carry it in."

Jerod grimaced. "It won't let out some noxious fumes or something, will it?"

"Only one way to find out." Gaff wasn't as concerned as Jazzi thought he should be.

The two guys went to get the safe, and Walker pushed out of his chair. He rubbed his palms on his jeans. "Even my skin feels itchy, I'm so nervous. What have you done in the last two years, bud? Give me some kind of distraction."

"Fumed about you for the first one, then met Jazzi here's sister and fell hard. We bought a house and moved in together a while ago."

Walker actually grinned. He must not have expected that. "I didn't think any woman would put up with you."

"Neither did I." Thane laughed. "What about you? You left everything behind."

"I bopped from job to job for a while, then started driving a truck for a cement company." He stopped to chuckle at himself. "It's in my blood, I guess."

Jazzi saw the men climb the deck steps and hurried to open the kitchen door for them. They carefully lowered the safe to the floor. Walker stared at it and took a step back.

"Well?" Gaff motioned for Walker to get on with it.

With a deep breath, Walker crouched in front of the safe. He turned the tumbler and moved aside before he lowered the handle to open it. Only one envelope lay inside. Walker poked it, and when nothing happened, he took it out and opened it. He scanned the top sheet of paper, and his jaw dropped. "Darby left me everything—the house, the business, everything."

Thane rubbed his forehead as if he couldn't believe it. "You're kidding."

Walker read, "Sorry I was a crappy dad. I know this won't make up for it, but I wanted to do something. Call my lawyer for any answers." Walker showed them the paper with the lawyer's number on it. He looked stunned. "I thought Dad would leave everything to someone else just to punish me."

A smile started on Thane's face. "Does this mean you'll move here and run the business again?"

"I sure hope so."

Gaff shook his head, disappointed. "No clues, nothing to point us toward someone who'd hit him in the head with a shovel and dump his body in gravel he was going to deliver. Any ideas, anyone?"

Walker held out his hands in a gesture of defeat. "My dad had a knack for making people mad, even people who usually wouldn't harm a soul. It could have been anyone."

Not the answer Gaff wanted. He stuffed his notepad back into his shirt pocket and started for the door. "I need to call this lawyer to see if I can learn anything. Then I have to find all the people Darby saw and talked to on the Monday he died."

How he meant to do that, Jazzi had no idea. And for the moment, she didn't care. She was just happy Thane and Walker were together again. Whoever killed Darby could wait.

Gaff turned to Walker. "You coming?"

Thane waved the detective away. "I'll drive him wherever he needs to go."

"Works for me." And Gaff left.

Thane settled back at the card table, and Walker sat across from him. Thane stretched his legs and locked his hands behind his head. "Let's take a minute to catch up."

Chapter 11

Jazzi carried one of the thermoses to the card table, along with Styrofoam cups. She usually hated drinking out of Styrofoam—she was sure she could taste the stuff in her coffee—but she didn't feel right bringing her own mug when Thane and Walker didn't have one. She put the two bags of chips on the table, too.

Once everyone had grabbed what they wanted, Walker said, "The first thing I want to do is call Dad's lawyer and see what's up." He shook his head. "It's just like Dad to leave nothing for Mom."

"She remarried. He'd hate her for that. How's she doing?" Thane asked.

Another smile played across Walker's lips. He really was an attractive man. Jazzi tried to think of anyone she or Olivia knew whom they could set him up with. Ansel watched her expressions and shook his head. He knew her too well.

Walker said, "When we left River Bluffs, I got a job with a roofing crew, and Mom got a job at a diner within walking distance from our apartment. Once a certain customer met her, he came in every day at the same time for supper. After a few months of that, he brought a rose every time and left it for Mom. The way Mom talked about him, I could tell she liked him, so I suggested a divorce."

Thane whistled. "How did that go over?"

"Mom was ready, but she still didn't want to deal with Dad, so she went through a lawyer. In theory, Dad dealt only with him, but somehow, he must have figured out where Mom was living. He said he'd pay five thousand dollars to get rid of her. She took it."

Jerod shook his head. "She got gypped."

"She just wanted out of the marriage," Walker told them. "When the divorce was final, Gene asked her to marry him. Now she works only two days a week, and they're really happy together."

Thane reached for more chips. "So if you leave Dayton to move back here, will she mind?"

"We'll be in easy driving distance. And Gene's friends love her. She has a happy life. She'll be okay as long as I drive to see her once a month."

"That's good." Thane pulled the bag closer. "I always liked your mom."

"Everyone did. It was Dad they tried to avoid."

Thane finished his coffee, took one more handful of chips, and said, "I'd better get back to my job. Where do you want me to drop you off?"

"I'm staying at a hotel in town. I'll call Dad's lawyer from there."

When they got up to leave, Ansel turned to Jazzi, his eyebrows raised in a question. She knew her Viking enough to nod. He said, "Why don't you and Thane come to our house for supper tonight? Olivia, too. You can tell us what the lawyer said."

"You sure?" Walker sounded pleased with the invitation.

"You don't want to miss Jazzi's cooking," Thane told him. "I'll pick you up and drive you there. What time?" He turned to Ansel.

"Six?"

"We'll see you then." Thane led Walker to his van.

Jerod stood. "If we hustle, we still have time to stain the deck. I'd like to cross that off our list."

A good idea. At the rate they were going, every project was going to take longer than they'd expected. With the three of them working together, though, they finished faster than usual. Jazzi tapped the lid back on their can of stain. Before Jerod could think of something else, she said, "Can we leave early? We have to stop at the store to buy stuff for supper, and everyone's coming at six."

Jerod started cleaning up the work site. "Sure, why not? My Franny would be freaking out by now, you're cutting it so close. Just be here bright and early tomorrow morning. We still haven't gotten permission to finish the driveway, so we'll tackle the garage next."

While Jazzi and Ansel helped him, Jazzi thought about their list. After the garage, they were going to tear off the front porch and rebuild it. Then the house needed a new roof. After that, hopefully, they could finish the driveway. Then, and only then, they'd start on the inside of the place.

Lord, they had a lot to do! She pushed those thoughts aside and started toward Ansel's van. Ansel called for George, but the pug didn't move, so he went to pick him up and carry him. Was there ever a more spoiled dog?

They all left together, and on the drive north, Jazzi planned a menu and the ingredients she'd need for tonight.

Chapter 12

Ansel searched to find a parking spot anywhere close to the grocery store but had to settle for pulling into a slot out in the boondocks. Jazzi prepared herself. The store was going to be bumper-to-bumper carts.

Ansel grabbed one of the smaller ones and wheeled it toward the produce aisle. "Where to?"

"Salad things." She grabbed a head of lettuce and a box of baby spinach, radishes, carrots, and mushrooms. She had a can of pickled beets at home and stale bread to make croutons. "Goat cheese," she added.

Ansel parked their cart behind three women who were busy reading labels on every cheese in the case. With his long arms, he stretched between them to get the goat cheese. The younger woman glanced at him and smiled.

"Anything else you need?"

"This is it." He smiled, too, and her eyes lit up, but then he went to stand beside Jazzi.

The woman went back to her shopping.

"Next?" he asked.

"Chicken breasts and a box of brownie mix." She walked alongside him and chose bone-in, skin-on breasts. He bought the Ghirardelli mix for brownies marbled with caramel. Then they stood in line to pay.

"No starch?" he asked.

"Green pea risotto, but I have everything to make that at home."

When they finally left the store and made it into their kitchen, they had to start cooking right away. Jazzi didn't let herself glance at the flowers she'd put in the heavy crock by the sink. They needed to be trimmed and arranged, but she'd do that later. Inky and Marmalade came to stand next to her, meowing while she rehydrated dried mushrooms in the microwave to start the stuffing for the balsamic-glazed chicken breasts. She was making a mushroom-goat cheese filling. Ansel mixed the brownies while she reduced the ingredients for the glaze. But the cats didn't bother Ansel. They stood, one on each side of her, meowing to be fed until she couldn't stand it anymore and stopped to fill their bowls.

Ansel chuckled. "Your cats know we're here to serve them."

She glared at them, purring as they ate. "I didn't know cats were so demanding."

"Farm cats know their place in the world. Ours were happy with squirts of milk when we hooked the cows up to the machines."

"Those were the good old days when you lived with your parents."

He snorted. "Glad they're behind me."

George came to stand close to Ansel, looking hopeful, until Ansel went to fill his bowl, too. "See? He's learning bad habits from your felines." When George glanced longingly at the stove, Ansel shook his head at him. Sounding stern, he said, "Chicken has to cook before you eat it. I don't want you to get sick."

A firm voice had never deterred George, but he understood about cooking. He finished his dry food, then went to his dog bed to put his head on his paws and sulk.

Jazzi's chicken took a while to prep since it was a one-dish wonder. She had to make the rice mixture to spread on the bottom of the casserole before adding the glazed breasts. But once it was in the oven, she could hurry upstairs to shower and change. Ansel's brownies went in before she finished, so he went up ahead of her. When they were both ready, they finished the salad together. Then Jazzi glanced at the countertop near the sink. "Doggone it!"

Inky couldn't knock the heavy crock over, so he'd bitten off the heads of half the flowers. When Jazzi glared at him, he nudged his head against her leg to pet him.

"You're horrible." But she bent to stroke his black fur anyway. Marmalade cried for attention, so she petted her, too. She glanced at the clock. Better get busy. They were pressed for time. As she scooped up dead flowers to throw them in the trash, she glanced out the window over the sink. Gray clouds scuttled overhead, and more leaves had changed color in the woods at the back of their property. It was a perfect evening to hibernate inside and share a meal.

As Ansel walked past her, he patted her fanny. "Your flowers look great. We'd better set the table."

Jazzi placed silverware next to the stoneware plates Ansel had set on the table. They'd just finished when Olivia gave a quick knock at the door, and she, Thane, and Walker came in.

Walker took a deep breath. "Boy, it smells good in here."

"The food's just about ready. Let's get drinks. What do you want?"

The girls chose wine, and the guys grabbed bottles of beer.

She carried the chicken dish to the table and put it on a trivet. Then she went back for the brownies while Ansel got the salad. Silence reigned for a few minutes while everyone filled their plates, then conversation started again.

"What did the lawyer say?" Thane asked. "Is everything legit? I keep waiting for it to be a big joke, that your dad left a note that said 'Ha, ha, the money's gone and the company's bankrupt.'"

Walker laughed. "I kinda worried about that, too, but everything's in order. Gaff told me he called the law office, too, and the only time the lawyer saw Dad was to make out the will. Dad even left money I could use right away to pay the drivers and keep deliveries going."

"I bet the lawyer thought of that," Thane said.

"I don't care whose idea it was. I'm just grateful for it. I went to see the drivers today, and they were relieved they were going to get paid on Friday and they'd keep their jobs. It was great seeing them again."

Olivia pushed a black olive to the side of her salad dish. Ansel loved them, but she didn't like olives of any type. "How did it feel walking into your dad's office again?"

Walker's fork paused in midair. "Surreal. Like coming home when I didn't think it would happen again. The place was a mess. Dad must not have filed anything for a few months. Bea couldn't even dust in there. Every surface was covered."

Jazzi swallowed her bite of risotto. "Bea?"

"Dad's housekeeper. She comes every Monday to clean the office, and Earl said now that Mom's gone, she cleans the house, too. Dad was always nice to Bea. Mom used to suspect they were having an affair."

Thane choked on his sip of beer. When he stopped coughing, he asked, "Do you think they were?"

"I think the only thing Bea wanted from Dad was a paycheck."

Jazzi didn't voice her thoughts, but Darby was killed on a Monday night. Had he tried something inappropriate with Bea? Or had she seen anyone come or go who might have argued with and killed him? She made a mental note to call Gaff later and tell him about Darby's housekeeper.

The conversation drifted from Darby and the will to Thane and Walker's pasts and growing up together. The two trotted out memories, good and bad. By the end of the night, Jazzi felt like she knew Walker a lot better. He was a good man. Too bad she didn't know a wonderful female to introduce him to.

By the time the three of them left, it was inching toward nine, but Jazzi still called Gaff. When she told him her news, he sounded excited. "We needed a new lead. This is good. I'll pick you up when I go to question her."

Jazzi didn't argue. She was involved in this case because of Thane, and Thane was involved because of Walker. If she could help either of them, she would.

After they cleaned the kitchen, she and Ansel relaxed in front of the TV for an hour, pets stretched beside them. Then Ansel headed upstairs. When he looked at George at the bottom of the steps and said, "Later," even the cats knew what that meant. They flopped on the floor to wait. When he held out his hand for her, she grinned.

"I thought you'd be too tired."

Ansel's blue eyes sparkled. "When you look as hot as you did tonight? I'm not dead."

Her tight jeans brought her luck. And she'd worn a lower scooped neckline than usual, but she hadn't thought he'd noticed.

"What man can resist a woman who smells like roast chicken?"

She sighed. "You had to go and ruin it."

"I'll make up for it."

He would, too. To heck with it. Who cared if he didn't smell her Chanel?

George whined, and Ansel pulled her toward the bedroom door. "We don't need an audience."

Nope, all she needed was Ansel. Everything else could wait.

Chapter 13

After work on Thursday, Jazzi took more time than usual showering and getting ready to go out. She was happy with what they'd gotten done on the fixer-upper today. They'd installed a red tin roof on the garage and new gutters, and they'd gotten a good start on new siding. The paint on the clapboards had bubbled so much, they'd decided the wood must have been green and would never hold a coat of paint. The best thing to do was to cover them, so they'd tried to match the siding to the yellow brick of the house.

She glanced at herself in the bedroom mirror. She and Olivia had girls' night out once a week. Ansel and Thane had known that when they moved in with them, and now the guys met and went out together, too. Olivia was a hairstylist and always looked trendy and put-together, so Jazzi made an extra effort when she was with her.

When Jazzi came downstairs, Ansel sat up and took notice. "Should I go with you this time to act as a bodyguard? You look hot."

Her thick, wavy, honey-gold hair fell past her shoulders, and her long, flowered dress hugged her curves. "And who's going to protect me from you? This is my night to yak with my sister."

He laughed. "Picky, picky, picky."

"Where are you and Thane going?"

"Thane invited us to the American Legion off State Street. He says the food there's great. He invited Walker along, too. What about you?"

"We both need a Henry's fix again."

Ansel grinned. "That's your favorite hangout. Beat off any guys who hit on you and come home to me."

"Always." And that was an easy promise to keep. No one could tempt her more than her Norseman. She grabbed her sweater on the way out the door. October nights were downright nippy now.

On the drive downtown, she thought about Walker. She was glad he was going with the guys. He probably needed something fun. It had to be hard to bounce back into Darby's business and pick up where Darby left off.

When she reached Henry's parking lot, every space was filled, so she had to park on the back street. The aromas coming from the kitchen made her mouth water. Barbecued ribs was a standard Thursday night special, but she was in the mood for their filet sandwich with fries. She passed Olivia's car on her way inside. Her sister, who kept close tabs on her weight, usually ordered fish or a salad for supper.

Olivia surprised her tonight and went with the ribs, a baked potato, and coleslaw. "I didn't have time for anything but a snack for lunch. The salon was crazy busy."

They sipped their wine and made small talk until their food arrived. It got even quieter after that. When their hunger wasn't quite as sharp, Jazzi said, "You told me at the time, but how did you meet Thane? It doesn't seem like you two would hang out at the same places."

Olivia smiled. "A friend of mine dragged me to a TinCaps game. Baseball isn't my thing, but she swore the food and drinks at the stadium were worth the trip, and there was going to be fireworks at the end. Thane went with a friend, too, and his seat was next to mine. He spilled popcorn all over me when he was trying to slide past people to get to it, and he apologized over and over again until it struck my funny bone and I started to laugh."

"Did that hurt his feelings?"

"No, it loosened things up. We ended up talking through most of the game, then all four of us went out for drinks after the fireworks. Dave and Shari are still together, too. We play cards with them once a month."

"A happy ending." Jazzi smiled. "How long had it been since Thane lost Walker before he met you?"

"A year. I nabbed him at the right time. He was a mess when he talked about Walker. Then we got together, and four months later, his lease was up, so I invited him to move into my apartment. When my lease was up, we bought our house."

Jazzi rolled her eyes. "You'd have won over Thane even if Walker never left town."

Olivia pursed her lips, looking thoughtful. "I don't know about that. Both of those guys like to fish and camp out. They hunt. In winter, they bowl and shoot pool. They were happy with the buddy system, but I took one look at Thane, and I decided to snag him in a weak moment. Now he's happy I did."

Jazzi stared. "I always thought Thane chased you, not the other way around. I mean, tons of guys were after you."

Olivia wrinkled her nose. "Thane just looked like a solid guy, you know. Someone you could depend on. He's not gorgeous, like your Ansel, but I love his crooked nose and long chin. Did you know Walker's the one who broke Thane's nose? They were playing basketball and Walker's elbow connected with Thane's cartilage."

"Ugh."

"Yeah, Thane said it hurt like heck."

"How's Walker doing? Is it hard for him to get back into the groove of the cement company?"

Olivia gnawed the meat off the last rib. She wasn't kidding when she said she was hungry. "He helped run the business for so long, he said it fell right into place for him, but Darby didn't keep track of things, so he's still trying to sort everything out. I'm glad he's back in River Bluffs. One of the reasons he left is that he was so ashamed of himself for losing his temper and punching someone when he was mad. He said it scared him that he'd lost control like that."

"It would be hard to keep your cool when Darby kept needling you." Jazzi took the last bite of her sandwich and reached for another fry.

"We weren't raised to take any guff from anyone," Olivia said. "If we punched someone, they deserved it."

Jazzi glanced outside the big windows at the front of the restaurant. Almost dark. The days were getting shorter. She drained the last of the wine from her glass.

When the waitress brought them each their check, Olivia grinned. "I've been thinking. You and Ansel bought a house, and Thane wanted a house. You're getting married in less than a month. You remember that, don't you? I still haven't seen a wedding dress. But wouldn't it be nice if Thane got the itch to get married soon?"

Jazzi paid for her meal and left a generous tip. "I didn't think you wanted to get married. I thought you were happy living with Thane."

"That's what I tell him. I'm hoping he'll be like Ansel and the less I push marriage, the more he wants it."

"And if that doesn't work?"

"I'll drug him and use hypnosis to get him to the altar."

Jazzi laughed. Her sister always had a plan.

Chapter 14

When Jazzi padded downstairs on Friday morning, Ansel had coffee and pumpernickel toast waiting for her. She had a thing for pumpernickel with cherry preserves. She glanced at his empty place. "Not hungry?"

"I shouldn't have eaten the whole sausage roll I ordered last night. The thing was huge."

"You could have brought home a corner for me. You didn't have to eat it all." She'd craved one ever since he'd first mentioned it.

He grinned. "But I *did* have to. It was delicious."

"Well, then, no wonder." Inky came to sit beside her foot. Where Inky went, so did Marmalade. She bent down to pet them before finishing her breakfast, then went to make sandwiches to pack in the cooler. When Inky smelled deli ham, he came running, stretching to place his paws on her knee. His meow was a strident demand. Her black cat believed he was entitled. Marmalade stared up at her hopefully. Jazzi tore off small pieces to toss to them. When George saw that, he sauntered over, too. She never favored the cats over George, so she tossed him a few. While Ansel filled the two thermoses, she filled the pet bowls with dry food and tossed two bags of chips into the cooler.

"Ready?" Ansel called for George and headed to the door.

Jazzi followed. On the drive to Southwood Park, she asked, "Did you have fun with Thane and Walker last night? We were both tired enough when we got home, we didn't talk much. Maybe we were talked out."

Ansel grimaced. "We did all right, but Walker was pretty upset. Gaff called his mom and talked to her and her new husband yesterday. He considers them suspects since Darby called Rose."

A cat ran in front of the van, and Ansel braked. Jazzi watched it streak across the street to a front porch, where it scratched at the door. She let out a shaky breath. She hated running over any animal, but a pet was worse. Once her nerves calmed, she returned to their conversation. "Why did Gaff question the new husband? Gene didn't even know Darby."

"Because Walker says he's really protective of Rose. He'd do anything for her."

"Ah, so if Darby upset Rose, he might go have a word with him."

Ansel nodded. "Walker's mom and Gene both vouched for the other one being home that Monday night, but they would, wouldn't they? So they're still on Gaff's list. He even asked the local authorities there to ask around to verify that Rose and Gene were home that night. That bothered Walker."

"Pretty much anybody who knew Darby is a suspect right now unless they have a solid alibi. It's not like this killer planned things out. The crime screams that someone lost his temper and hit him with a shovel. Whoever it was probably didn't even mean to kill him."

Ansel slowed and turned into Southwood Park. Jerod was digging in the back of his pickup when they parked behind him. "Hey, cuz!" he called. "You don't have a pair of spare work gloves, do you?"

She opened the back of Ansel's van and tossed him some. Tugging them on as they walked to the house, he patted his leg for George to follow them. The pug made it to the back deck and huffed as he lay down. After depositing the cooler and thermoses in the kitchen, they got busy on the garage's siding. When it was done, Jazzi stepped back to get a good look at it. "It looks great, a good match to the house."

Jerod glanced from the garage to the three-story, yellow-brick home. "The exterior of the house doesn't need a lot, but I think it would look better with a more impressive entrance."

Ansel raised an eyebrow. "We didn't plan for that, but the front stoop isn't much to brag about. The roof covers the door, and that's about it. The two benches facing each other seat only one person on each side. What have you got in mind?"

"The back deck came out so nice, I thought we could make the porch longer and deeper. Two rocking chairs could go on one side and a porch swing on the other, with a roof over everything."

Ansel narrowed his eyes, envisioning it. "It would take more time, but I think we have enough materials to make it work. It would be a cheap way to add curb appeal."

"Then let's do it." Jerod reached for the circular saw to cut through the pillars that held up the small, peaked roof. Ansel grabbed a crowbar to lift stair treads off the steps. Jazzi went for the wheelbarrow.

It didn't take long to rip off the porch and throw all the debris in the dumpster. Then they got busy, measuring for Jerod's new plan. Once again, they started with a base, laid a new floor, and put up new pillars. Once the roof was on, Jazzi again walked far enough away to see how everything looked. She shook her head.

"The pillars look too small, out of proportion, and they're too rustic. We need to cover them and add molding to make them more elegant." Jazzi glanced at the long windows. "We should add shutters, too."

Jerod and Ansel came to stand beside her. Jerod rubbed his chin. "Yup, you're right. That's an easy fix. The pillars are strong enough; they do the job. We just need to box them out. I can stop to buy molding later to finish them."

They broke for a late lunch before they put tin on the roof's plywood. They used the same red tin they used on the garage. It went a lot faster than shingles. They voted to stay later than usual to get the work done. By the time they finished staining the wood, Jazzi's back ached, and she was getting grumpy.

"Are we still on for Saturday?" Jerod asked as Ansel carried George to the van. The pug was worn out from watching them.

"Ten o'clock," Jazzi answered.

Jerod rubbed the back of his neck. "Let's make it ten-thirty. Franny and the kids are going to want a slow start tomorrow."

"I won't argue with that." Jazzi liked slow starts on Saturdays, too.

Jerod handed her the work gloves she'd loaned him, but she shook her head. "Keep them. I have more."

He made a face. "Good, because I have a feeling Franny borrowed mine to clean out the garden and forgot to put them back."

Franny might not be much of a cook, but she kept a huge garden and froze enough fruits and vegetables to see them through the winter. Come to think of it, Jerod's wife loved almost anything that involved working outside.

Ansel gently put George on the back seat and gave Jerod a wave good-bye. Jazzi rode shotgun, and they started for home. He tapped his fingers on the steering wheel. "We didn't go anywhere last Friday, and I'm in the mood to eat out. What do you say?"

"After your sausage roll last night?"

He gave her a dirty look. "Eating with Thane and Walker isn't the same as a date. I'd like to take you somewhere tonight."

"Do I need to dress up?"

"Nothing fancy as long as it's tight."

She laughed. "Your favorite jeans?"

"And a low-cut blouse."

"I can manage that." She'd bought more sexy items for her wardrobe since Ansel had moved in with her.

They didn't hurry when they got home. They played with the cats and fed all three animals before they took their showers and got ready to leave.

When George saw them in their "go out" clothes, he pouted, but the pug was one spoiled dog. He'd live. So would the cats. It was her and Ansel's night to have fun. No talk about house projects. No chats about Darby and murder. Just eating and flirting and getting in the mood.

Chapter 15

When Jazzi and Ansel walked into TGI Fridays, Jazzi's friend Leesa stood up at a nearby table and waved to them. "Over here!" she called.

So much for date night, but Jazzi had hung out with Leesa since high school, and Ansel liked her and her husband. They were part of their Friday-night crowd.

"Didn't expect to see you two here." Leesa beamed as they seated themselves. "What have you been up to?"

Ansel gave a wicked grin. "Jazzi is working another murder case with Detective Gaff."

"No, not another one!" Leesa turned to Jazzi, who hurriedly explained.

Leesa's husband, Brett, shook his head. "I hope Gaff's paying you to help with his investigation."

"I'm doing it as a favor to Thane."

Brett stared her down. "You're too freakin' nice. You need to start telling people no. You run a business. Your time is money."

Jazzi didn't argue with him. Brett was a financial analyst and tended to be more aggressive than most of the people she knew. It had taken her a while to get used to him. He and Leesa balanced each other out. Leesa tended to be quiet and studious. Probably why she was an English lit prof.

Ansel bumped his knee against Jazzi's, his way of showing support, and changed the subject. "So, is Riley mastering trigonometry yet?"

Leesa laughed. Riley was their two-year-old son, and she was always bragging about how smart he was. "Not yet. Give him another month."

Brett jumped in with, "He *has* learned how to remove the lid from his sippy cup, though, and then he dumps his drink all over the floor."

"He gets time-outs for that," Leesa said. "Let's hope he learns what's acceptable and what's not."

The conversation turned to kids and jobs. Jazzi was listening to Leesa tell about Riley finding the lipstick in her purse when she saw Earl being led to a table. He was with a trim, silver-haired woman. Once seated, they leaned across the table to hold hands. Jazzi sighed. She remembered that Earl was divorced and lived alone. Neither he nor the woman looked young. They must have finally found romance.

The waiter brought the food to their table, and Jazzi didn't think about Earl anymore. They all dug in. When the waiter returned a little later with second glasses of wine, Earl glanced in her direction and noticed her. Jazzi nodded a hello, and he looked shocked. He grabbed the woman's hand and tried to yank her to her feet, motioning to her to leave.

What the heck? Maybe the woman was someone *else's* wife, and Earl felt guilty.

He leaned to talk to her, and the woman looked over at Jazzi. She frowned, then leaned in to have a serious discussion with Earl. Only then did Earl seem to calm down. Odd. Why would Earl care if Jazzi saw him? She didn't know who the woman was, so what did it matter?

Leesa interrupted her thoughts. "Did I tell you that I'm only teaching three classes this year? I wanted to spend more time with Riley."

"That's great!" Jazzi was happy for her.

Leesa took a sip of wine. "Every time I turn around, he's grown more and he's doing new things. I don't want to miss out."

Brett gave his wife an indulgent smile. "If we're going to have a second child, we need to get started, or it will be forever before you work full-time again."

Leesa raised her eyebrows. "My parents are keeping Riley overnight. No time like the present."

Ansel chuckled. "Would you guys like some alone time?"

Leesa blushed all the way to her hairline. "We have to eat first. We'll need energy and stamina."

Brett gawked. "You're serious, aren't you?"

Jazzi could tell her friend had already thought this through and decided they were overdue to make baby two.

At Leesa's steady gaze, Brett blinked, surprised. "Okay, then, let's skip dessert."

Leesa's green eyes sparkled. "Clean your plate."

Jazzi watched them both dig in. Ten minutes later, Leesa's pasta primavera was gone, and Brett's filet mignon was history.

Brett waved the waiter over, paid the bill, then pushed to his feet. "Will you excuse us?"

Ansel grinned. "Good luck."

Jazzi couldn't help but chuckle. When she watched them go, she noticed that Earl and the woman he was with had gone, too. A lone Styrofoam box sat on the table. They must have packed up their dinners and left without one.

Ansel placed his hand over hers. "Are you in a hurry?"

"Not me. We have plenty of time." He could take that however he wanted to. And his question could have had a few different meanings.

He leaned back in his chair and stretched out his long legs. A waitress stopped passing out food to stare at him, then quickly recovered, and finished serving the table. Yeah, Ansel was that hot, especially when he smiled the way he was now. "I think we should go for broke and order another drink and dessert."

"I like the way you think."

He motioned for the waiter. Once they ordered and were alone, he grew serious. "You have everything planned for our wedding reception—the food, the drinks, decorations. But you still haven't bought a dress. That's not a Freudian slip, is it? Did I rush you too much?"

She shook her head. "Things just got busy, that's all. I was going to go shopping with Mom and Olivia after work some night, but then Darby got killed, and Thane's a suspect, and I've been going with Gaff on interviews. I'd go on Saturday, but Mom and Olivia work at the salon, and we're working on Jerod's basement. Most places are closed on Sunday. And anyway, we have our family meal then."

"You're sure that's all?" A trace of worry tinged his voice. "You're looking forward to getting married?"

She pursed her lips. "I've probably put off standing in front of a mirror, trying on dresses. You know I'm horrible at shopping, and I worry I'll buy something that makes me look terrible…"

He laughed. "*Nothing* can make you look bad, but if that's all it is, Jerod and I will work on the fixer-upper on Monday, and you can go to find a dress. Your Mom and Olivia have Mondays off."

Their drinks came, along with a large slice of chocolate cake that they'd share. Jazzi dipped her fork into the rich dessert and took a nibble. "Wow, this is good."

"Will Monday work for you?" Ansel asked.

"It's perfect, and I'll try to look like a beautiful bride."

"You won't have to work at it." He took a bite of the cake, too. "You're delectable, just like this dessert."

He meant it, too. The man was delusional, but she loved that about him. Then she frowned. "Gaff might call me to go with him to see Darby's housekeeper."

"No problem; we'll work around it."

That made her smile. Every girl wanted to interrogate someone before trying on wedding dresses. Just her luck.

Chapter 16

Jazzi and Ansel woke up early enough on Saturday morning that they booted the pets out of the room for some couple time, then showered before they went downstairs. After feeding their furry beasts, they drove to Jerod's house. It was a crappy day—dark gray clouds, a stiff breeze, and occasional rain. Thankfully, they were working inside.

October weather in Indiana was known to bounce from mild to dismal in days. They'd been lucky so far at the fixer-upper. That's why they were trying to get all of the outside work done while the weather was tolerable. If it rained, they could start a project inside and then finish outdoors once the sun shone again. Cement was pickier, though. Jazzi hoped Gaff would give them permission to work on the driveway soon.

George didn't like nippy weather, so Ansel had to carry him into Jerod's house. Gunther and Lizzie came running and squealing when they saw Jazzi's Viking. He put down the pug, picked them up, and held them upside down by their ankles as they giggled and twisted. Jerod laughed at them before shooing them away.

"We have a late start today, and we have to get busy, or you won't have a new playroom."

They must have wanted the basement to be finished, because they turned to leave when Franny called them into the kitchen. "If you finished your snacks, throw your paper plates away."

Ansel turned his head to hide a grimace. The man wasn't a fan of paper plates.

Jerod gave a smug smile. "Just wait till you have kids. Doing dishes several times a day isn't all it's cracked up to be. Paper will start looking like a godsend."

Ansel frowned, clearly unsure whether to believe him. "Kids are that much work?"

Jerod shook his head. "Grasshopper, you have much to learn."

They started down the steps to the basement, staple guns in hand. The first job was to install a moisture barrier. They were working together, so that went more quickly than Jazzi expected. Next, they started building the frame for the drywall. For that, they brought out the big artillery—their nail guns. While Jerod sawed the two-by-sixes to the proper length, she and Ansel nailed them in place. Sawdust flew in the air, adding to the musty basement smell. The whine of the saw biting into wood drowned out most conversation.

They finished one long wall before Jazzi glanced at her watch. She was surprised to see that it was almost one. No wonder she was getting hungry. She held up a hand, and when the sawing and pounding ceased, she said, "Ansel and I are ordering four pizzas for lunch. We want to treat the kids and make life easier for Franny."

"You just don't want Franny to cook something for you," Jerod said.

Ansel shrugged. "There's that, too." The man had no tact when it came to food. He took it seriously.

With a laugh, Jerod nodded. "I won't argue with you, but I bought deli meat to make sandwiches."

That was so sweet of him. Jazzi shook her head, though. "You can have that some other time, but we really do want to treat the kids. What kind of pizzas do you guys like?"

She ended up calling in an order for delivery for one large cheese pizza, the kids' favorite, a thin crust supreme for her and Franny, and two meat lovers' pizzas, one for Jerod and one for Ansel. They went back to work for the twenty minutes before the delivery guy knocked on Jerod's door.

Franny broke into a grin as Ansel paid and tipped him. "You didn't have to buy our lunch, but thank you."

Ansel glanced at Gunther and Lizzie. "Someone told us the kids like pizza."

"We do!" Gunther cried, jumping up and down. "It's our favorite."

"Good. Let's dig in." Ansel watched Franny carry paper plates to the table and pinched his lips together. Good man. He didn't say a peep.

Over lunch, Franny said, "You won't believe the story my mom told me when I saw her this week. She works part-time as a produce person at the grocery store, remember?"

Jazzi nodded. Franny and her mom were close. They called each other a few times a week and got together a few times a month. "What happened?"

"Two weeks ago, Mom was stocking the big center displays when a couple of older men started arguing with each other, and pretty soon, they were pushing and punching and knocking all the oranges and apples onto the floor. Mom had to call for help, and the manager walked the men out of the store and told them never to come back."

"Old men went at it like that?" Jazzi reached for another slice of pizza. "You'd think they'd know better."

"Not these two. Mom said the one had a mustache and sideburns she'd never seen before except on the cartoon version of Yosemite Sam."

Jazzi couldn't believe it. "That sounds like Darby, the dead guy we found in our gravel."

"What did the man look like who was fighting with him?" Ansel asked.

"Long gray whiskers. Mom said his beard was big and bushy."

Jazzi stared. "Earl said Darby's best friend was called Whiskers."

Jerod went to the refrigerator for another beer. He brought one back for Ansel, too. "Sounds like Darby was arguing with everybody lately. Something must have gotten his dander up."

"He argued enough to make somebody so mad he…," Jazzi stumbled to a stop. Two kids were hanging on her every word.

Franny looked at the pizza crusts on Gunther and Lizzie's plates and the three slices left in the box. "If you've had enough to eat, you're excused. I'll save the rest for later."

The kids ran off to watch TV. Franny leaned back in her chair and laid her hands on the round of her stomach. "Has Detective Gaff talked with this Whiskers?"

Jazzi shook her head. "No one knows his real name. None of the drivers know where he lives either."

Franny was beginning to look uncomfortable. She glanced down at her feet. "Thanks for the lunch, but I need to put my feet up. My ankles are swelling."

Jerod stood and came around the table to help her up. When she pushed out of her chair, her hand moved to the small of her back. "You okay?" he asked.

"Just part of being pregnant." Franny started toward the couch, and they returned to their work in the basement. By the time they left at five, three sides of the basement were framed.

"I can finish the last wall," Jerod said. "And I'll buy drywall for next Saturday."

As they started up the stairs to leave, Jazzi called, "See you tomorrow at our place!"

"What's on the menu?" Jerod was pretty serious about food, too, when his wife wasn't cooking it.

"A cassoulet and apple crostatas."

"What are those?"

Jazzi rolled her eyes. Maybe Jerod wasn't that serious, after all. "A cassoulet's a white bean dish with chicken, lamb, and sausages." Actually, she usually cooked duck instead of chicken, but there were going to be fifteen people tomorrow if Walker came. She'd decided to budget a bit. "A crostata's just a rustic pie with the bottom sides rolled up and over the apples instead of a top crust."

Jerod licked his lips. "I like beans. Sounds good. See you then."

Ansel carted George to the back seat of his van. On the drive home, Jazzi said, "Can you believe two old guys brawling in a grocery store?"

"Some people get worse with age," Ansel told her. "But if Whiskers was willing to throw punches in the produce aisle, who's to say he wouldn't lose his temper and hit Darby in the head with a shovel?"

Jazzi had thought about that, too. "There has to be a way to find Whiskers. They were drinking buddies. They must have had a favorite bar."

Ansel chuckled. "Do you know how many bars there are in River Bluffs?"

"Almost as many as the number of churches?"

"Maybe more. Too many to go door to door, that's for sure. But if you're up for it, I'll volunteer to do a bar crawl with you on the south side of the city."

She snorted. "We wouldn't be able to walk after the sixth or seventh one."

"Shows what you know. You just don't hold your liquor well."

"And that's a good thing. Then I'm not tempted to drink a keg by myself."

He laughed. "I wasn't alone when we finished it. I had friends. Jerod was there, too. Maybe we should buy some classy wine for tonight. What's for supper?"

"Sirloin tips over buttered noodles. A can of green beans. That's fast."

"And delicious. Yup, it's a red wine night, for sure."

When he stopped to run into the liquor store, her thoughts returned to Darby and Whiskers. She'd gotten the impression they were longtime, good friends. What had gotten in the way of that? Or did they enjoy fighting and brawling with each other? No, she felt like Darby had been building up pressure for some reason and was as ready to blow as an active volcano. Whoever had been with him when he spewed hadn't taken it well. And a shovel must have been handy.

Chapter 17

Jazzi sipped her morning coffee while sautéing cut-up sausage links on the stove. A cassoulet took a few hours to make, so instead of her usual Sunday morning routine, she started it right after she fed the cats and George. Ansel, bless him, was cutting a boneless lamb roast into cubes. He tossed them in a bowl with olive oil; when he finished, he sprinkled them with salt and pepper. Jazzi had sautéed the chicken breasts by the time he finished.

"Walker told Thane he was coming, didn't he?" Ansel asked as he went for another cup of coffee.

"Yeah, I think he's going to be a regular from now on." She was making it easy for herself and had bought eight cans of northern beans. Ansel opened them and drained them while Jazzi started browning the lamb cubes. Once seared, she added chicken broth and red wine to the pan and put them in the oven. In an hour or more, they'd be tender.

Ansel refilled her coffee cup, too. "If we keep adding people to our family, we're going to have to buy another portable table." They already had one that they put next to their long farm table.

"We're just gearing up. Wait till we add more kids to the mix." She chopped onions and garlic to add to the diced tomatoes and beans. Seasonings came next.

Those finished, she pushed the big roasting pan aside to wait for the lamb while she and Ansel started making the crostata. Usually, she made desserts a day ahead, but she hadn't been in the mood after they got home from Jerod's house.

When she put the desserts in the oven, she ran a critical eye over the house. It hadn't been dusted.

"It looks good to me," Ansel told her. "If anyone runs a white glove over a shelf, he's come to the wrong place."

She smiled and shrugged. He was right. The meal was about getting together, not trying to impress anyone. She and Ansel had an hour to relax, so they flopped on the couches across from each other to read the morning paper and enjoy the last of the coffee.

Jerod, Franny, and the kids were the first to arrive, as usual. Franny pinched her lips, embarrassed, and said, "I forgot to buy anything for the vegetable tray. Do you have enough food without it?"

"No worries." Jazzi hugged her and led her into the kitchen. She always tried to serve snacks while people had their drinks, and Franny's eyes lit up when she saw a cheese ball and crackers.

Jerod's parents, Eli and Eleanore, came next. They joined Jerod and Franny at the kitchen island and teased Gunther and Lizzie for choosing slices of American cheese on saltine crackers instead of going for the fancy stuff.

Next came Jazzi's mom and dad. Ansel went to greet them. "Hi, Cyn. Doogie." He and her parents got along well.

Her dad slapped him on the shoulder. "You still have time to run, boy. She hasn't bought a dress yet."

Her mom patted his arm. "Don't you worry. We're going to remedy that. We won't let her marry you in jeans and a T-shirt."

Ansel laughed. "Doesn't matter, as long as she marries me."

"Not gonna happen. I'm going to see my daughter dressed up for once." Jazzi's dad came to hug her and hand her two bottles of wine before stuffing cash in the jar to donate to the meal. Jazzi knew she'd spent more than she should have this time, but she didn't care if she went over the usual amount and had to put in extra.

Thane and Olivia arrived with Walker. They introduced him and explained that he'd recently lost his father. Everyone went to greet him and make him feel welcome. The last to arrive were Gran and Samantha. When her husband had died, Samantha had moved in with Gran, and it had been a blessing for both of them.

Jazzi poured a glass of red wine for Gran and took it to her. Her Granny liked a drink before and after dinner. Gran took a sip and smiled. "Good stuff."

"Ansel picked it out."

"Your boy has good taste." Gran sipped again, then narrowed her eyes at Walker. She raised her voice. "Your father was really ashamed of himself for driving you and your mother away."

Walker stared at her, stunned. "How do you know?"

Gran's focus turned vague, and she tapped the side of her head. "Sometimes I see things."

Thane nodded. "She does. We can't explain it, but she's always right."

Gran's attention returned to her wine. "Did I see a cheese ball on the buffet?"

With a nod, Jazzi went to fetch her a snack.

People drank and munched until the buzzer on the oven rang. Jazzi went to take the cassoulet out of the oven, and Ansel said, "Ready to eat?"

People got in line to serve themselves while Ansel carried the salad and dressings to the island. Jazzi placed the hot cassoulet on a heavy trivet farther down.

Everyone settled into their usual places, and Walker took a seat next to Thane. No one talked for a few minutes while they started their meals. Walker looked at Jazzi and said, "I've never had anything like this before. My mom made bean soup, but nothing like this. It's delicious."

"Jazzi likes to cook." Franny's voice was filled with pride.

That was one of the reasons Jazzi loved Jerod's wife. She was as happy with other peoples' achievements as she was with her own.

Ansel turned to Walker. "How's it going with your dad's business? Thane said he left it in a mess."

Walker laid down his fork and wiped his lips with a napkin. "It's the darnedest thing. The business is already starting to pick up, but it's going to take a while before it's as successful as it used to be. I found a wad of money rolled up with a rubber band in Dad's desk drawer, though. A lot of money."

"A hundred and fifty thousand?" Jerod asked. "Because Darby came to look through the house we're working on and told us that he'd saved some money and was thinking about flipping houses during the slow months for cement work."

Walker frowned. "He saved it? How? I'm worried I'm going to have enough start-up cash after the slow season. I talked to Dad's lawyer, and he didn't have any idea where it came from."

Thane snorted. "Knowing your dad, he might have stuffed money under his mattress all these years. He didn't trust anyone, not even bankers."

"I'm going to go back through the books to see if I notice anything I missed before. When I told Gaff, he looked into Dad's bank account, but he couldn't find anything either."

Jerod got up to go to the kitchen island for seconds. "Anyone else want more?"

Walker nodded and stood to follow him. Frowning, he said, "Dad must have been worried about money, too, if he was thinking of doing a fixer-upper."

Gran sipped the last of her wine. "Your dad has a lot to be ashamed of. He treated the people who mattered the most to him poorly."

"And the person it hurt the most was himself." Walker shook his head, then smiled. "But I'm having the best meal of my life with friends who mean a lot to me, and I intend to enjoy it."

Conversation flowed again, and Ansel reached over to put his hand on Jazzi's knee and squeeze it gently. "You were right," he said quietly. "Walker needs a family, and who's better than we are?"

Who indeed? The man had been through some rough times, and she suspected he was going to go through a few more. He'd need them.

Chapter 18

On Monday, they started roofing the main house. They could put the tin over the existing shingles since the plywood base was solid. Jerod figured with the three of them working together, they could finish that and install new gutters.

Before climbing a ladder to get to work, Jazzi studied the front of the house.

"I know that look." Jerod sighed. "What are you thinking?"

"We need to paint the front door. Maybe red to match the roof. The mustard yellow doesn't stand out."

"A deep blue or green would work, too," Ansel said.

They voted on forest green. "But first the roof, then the paint," Jerod told them.

They were eating lunch when Gaff called. "Bea can see us this afternoon. Can you still come?"

"Want me to meet you there?"

"No, you're doing me a favor. Besides, you're not that far out of my way. What if I pick you up at two?"

They'd have the roof done by then. "That'll work fine. I'll be ready."

When she hung up, Jerod said, "Let's change up our plans. The gutters will go faster if all three of us work on them. What if Ansel and I paint the front door and put a fresh coat of white paint on the windows' trim?"

"Good, I'd rather you waited for me on the gutters."

Jerod grinned. "You're a glutton for punishment, cuz. You always like to be here for the heavy lifting."

"I just want to make sure you do it right. But I think green trim that matches the shutters would make the yellow bricks stand out more."

Ansel agreed.

Jerod laughed. "Whatever works. Franny always makes those decisions at our place." Lunch finished, they returned to the roof, and by the time Gaff pulled to the curb, Jazzi was climbing down the ladder, that job complete.

"Is this a good time?" Gaff asked as she got in the car.

"The roofs are done. The guys are going to wait for me to do the gutters."

He looked surprised. "Is that a good thing?"

"Yes, this way I won't feel guilty leaving them."

Gaff rubbed his hand across his forehead before pulling away from the curb. "I'm taking up a lot of your time."

"No problem. We all want you to find the person who killed Darby. This is for Thane and Walker."

"Let's hope we learn something new then. We've been hitting a wall lately."

It took them about twenty minutes to reach Darby's place, and Walker came from the office at the back of the property to meet them. "Bea's cleaning the house right now. I'll introduce you to her."

He led them into the split-level. They entered a living room and could see a kitchen through its doorway. Both had wooden floors. A black leather couch with holes in its arms hugged a wall. A wooden coffee table was stained with water rings. Jazzi glanced down a shallow set of stairs to the lower level, which was carpeted, the steps' treads well-worn. A vacuum cleaner ran upstairs, and Walker zipped up there to get Bea. When he led her down to meet them, Jazzi stared. Bea was a trim, attractive woman with short gray hair—the woman who'd come with Earl to TGI Fridays on Friday night.

Bea recognized her, too. "I suppose you're wondering why I told the detective I wouldn't be back in town until Sunday night and then went to dinner with Earl on Friday. I meant to go to Michigan with my sister over the weekend, but she had to cancel."

Jazzi nodded. Plans went awry sometimes. She couldn't help staring at a big bruise on Bea's right arm, though. It was shaped like fingers, as though someone had grabbed her.

Bea put up her hand to rub the spot. "Darby lost his mind on the Monday he died. When I was leaving work, he grabbed me and tried to kiss me. Years ago, when I first started cleaning for him, he grabbed my fanny. *Once.* I made it perfectly clear that he wasn't going to get a better worker than I am, who charged what I charge, but that if he ever touched me again, he'd be looking for someone new."

"And?" Walker asked.

"He never bothered me again."

Gaff poised his pen over his notepad. "What happened on Monday? How did you get away from him?"

She dipped her head, avoiding their eyes. "Earl was waiting to take me home when we got off work. I tried to pull away from Darby, but he wouldn't let go. Earl had to get out of his car and punch him to get him off me."

Walker stared. "Dad knew you weren't interested in him."

"I was starting to worry about your dad. He wasn't the same after you and Rose left him. It was more than being sad or angry. It was almost as if he was mad at himself."

Gaff broke into the conversation. "When Earl punched Darby, was he angry enough to hit him with a shovel?"

"Earl? I was surprised he hit Darby. He's more the gentle type."

"Can anyone corroborate your story?" Gaff asked.

"All the drivers were there. It was quitting time. We were all getting ready to go home. Colin would have hit Darby if Earl hadn't. He was losing patience with the old man."

"Really? Why is that?" Gaff glanced toward the trucks parked at the back of the property.

"Colin's on a job," Walker told him. "So is Earl."

Jazzi wanted to expand the list of suspects. "Is there someone else we could talk to, someone who might know what was eating at Darby?"

"The person who knew him better than anyone is Whiskers, his longtime drinking buddy. They'd known each other since grade school and drank together most nights, but lately, they hadn't been getting along so well. I'm not sure why, and I don't know where Whiskers lives, but their favorite hangout was the bar Shots and Spirits on Wells Street. Whiskers lives within walking distance of it. Darby used to brag that all they had to do was stagger to his place when they had had too much to drink."

"I know that place," Gaff said. "The bartender called us there when I was still driving a squad car. We had to break up a brawl."

Bea nodded. "The bartender will know where Whiskers lives. He took their keys away from them when they weren't safe to drive. He didn't want Whiskers trying to drive Darby home."

Gaff shut his notepad. "Thanks, we'll stop to chat with him." He handed her a card. "If you think of anything, call me."

On the way to the car, he asked Jazzi, "Mind if we drive by there on our way to your fixer-upper?"

"Works for me. We should learn something new."

But the bar was closed when they passed it. "If I pick you up at five, will you go with me to talk to the bartender? People tell you more than me. They might cooperate with a cop, but they don't knock themselves out."

"You'll have to pick me up and drive me home." She wouldn't make Ansel wait at the job site or drive from home to get her.

"That's fair. I'll see you at five."

Chapter 19

The guys had painted the door a deep green when she got back to join them.

"Like it?" Ansel stopped painting trim and climbed down his ladder to stand beside her.

"It's perfect. We need to add a brass knocker now."

Jerod joined them, grinning. "Ansel said you'd say that."

"He knows me too well. The green trim looks good, too." Before, it had been painted mustard yellow, like the door. The color didn't do much to contrast with the yellow bricks.

Ansel studied the results and nodded with satisfaction. "How did it go with Bea?"

Jazzi filled them in as she walked to the side of the house to get a paintbrush and start work.

Ansel looked disgruntled when she finished telling them about Whiskers and the bar. "So, Gaff is picking you up again? I'll wait supper until you get home."

"It might take a while. If you want to eat without me…"

"I'll grab a snack, but I'd rather wait and have supper with you."

She'd feel the same way. She never used to mind eating alone, but since Ansel had moved in with her, it felt weird to eat without him. Supper was when they hashed over each day's events.

"Hey, if Gaff is taking you to the bar, you'll have a designated driver. You could get a little tipsy," Jerod teased.

Jazzi rolled her eyes. "Just what I want to do, especially with a detective."

"It's not *a* detective. It's Gaff. He's almost like family now." Jerod glanced at his watch, then looked at the screen of his cell phone. "She still hasn't called."

Her cousin sounded uptight. "What's going on?"

He checked his cell again. "Franny's mom was visiting today, thank goodness. Franny felt like she was having contractions. Her mom drove her and the kids to the hospital. She promised to call me if Franny was going into labor."

"Isn't she too early?" Worry squirmed through Jazzi. The baby was due in February. This was way too soon.

Jerod's eyes gave away how worried he was. "She carried Gunther and Lizzie to full term. She got so big, so fast this time, she's been really uncomfortable." He stopped and pressed his lips together. "She's going to be fine."

"If you want to leave now, go ahead," Ansel told him. "We can finish the bottom row of windows on this side."

Jerod shook his head. "I always get stuck in a waiting room, going crazy. I'd rather stay here unless Franny's mom calls."

Just then, his cell phone buzzed. He whipped it out of his pocket and listened. When he returned it, he looked relieved. "False labor. Franny's on her way home. She says the false pains feel just like the real ones. When I get home tonight, we're going to have a talk."

Jazzi heard the edge in his voice. "What about?"

"The fool woman was hanging a wallpaper border in the baby's room today. She saw it in a magazine and had to have it. Why she didn't wait for me to hang it, I don't know."

Ansel asked, "Is that what caused the false labor?"

"The doctor told her no more getting on ladders, stretching her arms over her head for a long time, or lifting heavy things. I'm pretty sure he's told her the same thing before."

Jazzi snorted. "You're one to talk. You wanted to hang drywall two days after you sprained your ankle three years ago."

"That's different."

"Of course. I forgot. You're invincible."

He gave her a dirty look. "This is my Franny we're talking about and my baby."

Ansel patted him on the back. "We get it, but take it easy on Franny. She must have really wanted to see what that wallpaper border looked like."

Jerod calmed down a little. "You know, I think I'm going to take you up on leaving early. I want to go hug that fool woman of mine."

They waved him off, then grabbed their paintbrushes. When Gaff came for her, she and Ansel had painted the trim of all the first-floor windows on this side of the house.

Chapter 20

Traffic on Wells Street at a little after five was the pits. A car finally stopped and waved Gaff through so that he could turn left onto a narrow side street and park near the bar. When they walked into the dim interior, it took a minute for Jazzi's eyes to adjust. She was surprised to see that the place was already doing a good business.

"Must be an after-work crowd," Gaff said. He led her to the bar and pulled out a stool for her. When the bartender came to take their order, he showed him his badge. "We came to ask you about Darby Hastings and a friend of his, Whiskers."

The bartender narrowed his eyes. "Is this about Darby's murder? I read about it in the paper. Someone threw him under a pile of gravel."

"We're trying to decide what Darby did last Monday night." He motioned to Jazzi. "She and her work crew found his body."

The bartender blinked, picked up his rag, and began wiping down the bar. Jazzi thought it was probably a way for him to gather his thoughts. Finally, he shook his head. "Whiskers has been one lonely dude without his drinking buddy. They'd been a little off lately, but they still came in together. They were here last Monday."

"We'd like to talk to Whiskers," Gaff said. "Someone mentioned he lives close by."

With a nod, the bartender hooked a thumb toward the side street. "He's the fifth house on this side of the street. He and Darby usually walked here and back, but I still kept an eye on them. They got a little crazy when they started on the rum. Whiskers should be home now. He gets off work at three-thirty."

"Thanks." Gaff handed him his card. "In case you think of anything, here's my number."

The man stuck it in his jeans pocket, then went to fill a waitress's order. Jazzi followed Gaff out the door and down the street. The houses were tall and narrow, with small yards and garages that faced a back alley. The neighborhood had seen better days. One house, on the far corner, had evergreen bushes in front of it, but no other landscaping graced either side of the street. Whiskers's house had faded green siding and a white shingle roof. Everything was taken care of, but nothing new had been done to it for decades.

Gaff walked up the three cement steps to a small stoop and knocked. He and Jazzi waited a few minutes before Whiskers opened the door. His white hair, still damp, was pulled back in a ponytail. Gaff showed him his badge, and Whiskers motioned for them to enter.

"I just got out of the shower. Drive a forklift at a factory." He stopped in the small foyer near the bottom of the stairs. "You must be here about Darby."

"We're trying to track his movements last Monday night."

Whiskers tugged on his beard. He kept it trimmed, but it was thick and wiry. Prominent. "S'pose I was the last person to see him alive—except for the guy who killed him, I guess. We went to Shots and Spirits together, had a few to relax."

Gaff reached for his pen and notepad. "We've heard that you and Darby hadn't been getting along lately."

"Woman problems." Whiskers nodded for them to follow him into the living room. He sank onto the middle of the couch, leaving them to sit on two uncomfortable, old kitchen chairs. Gaff placed his notepad on his knee to write, and Whiskers went on with his story. "Darb and me been friends since grade school. Both had it bad for Miss Timmers, our fourth-grade teacher. No woman that pretty should step foot in a classroom. Gave every little boy fantasies. We lived through that and then met Rose in high school. We fell for her hard. Both tried to win her, but she picked Darby. After that, he always considered himself a ladies' man."

Jazzi stared, and Whiskers threw back his head and laughed.

"Hard to believe, isn't it? He didn't look like much back then either." Whiskers shook his head. "Never knew what Rose saw in him. But it hit old Darb hard when she up and left him. Never thought the boy would leave the cement business either. He took another blow when she filed for divorce, but he almost lost it when she remarried."

"Did he love her?" Jazzi couldn't understand why he'd treated Rose so badly.

"Mad crazy about her," Whiskers said. "But Darby could never show that to anyone. Thought if you let them know you cared, they'd take advantage of you. That, and the man had a mean streak a mile wide. Treated Rose better than anyone, so thought he was doin' good."

"What got between you and him?" Gaff asked.

"Shots and Spirits hired a new bartender a year ago. A woman—Hazel. Everyone calls her Haze. I hadn't thought about females for a long time. Too expensive. But there's something about Haze got my blood racing. Darby was lonely without Rose and thought sure he'd win her, but she chose me. Put a burr up Darb's butt."

"That's what you argued about in the grocery store when you threw punches?" Jazzi would have never guessed they were fighting over a woman.

Whiskers made a face, clearly not proud of himself. "Stupid, huh? But Darby should have been happy for me. Instead, he told me that I should bow out because since he'd had a woman and was used to having one, he needed her more."

Gaff looked up from his notes. "Did you know Darby grabbed Bea last Monday and tried to make her kiss him?"

"Blasted idiot. I ain't surprised. He was losing it. Rose was his rock, and when she left him and remarried someone else, it ate at him. He decided if she'd found someone else, he would, too. And I'd have been happy for him, but he couldn't have my Haze. And he just wouldn't leave it be. He'd never leave anything alone."

Gaff leaned back in his chair. "Do you know anyone who'd be so mad at Darby, he'd hit him with a shovel?"

"A shovel, huh? At the work site?"

Gaff nodded.

Whiskers thought about that for a minute. "From what I can tell, he drove all of them nuts, but they all liked their jobs. Doesn't mean he couldn't have said the one thing that pushed somebody too far, though. He was good at that."

"Did he ever push you too far?" Gaff asked.

"Why do you think we brawled in the grocery store?"

Gaff returned his notepad to his pocket and stood. Jazzi joined him. He handed Whiskers his card before starting for the door. "If you think of anything, call. Does Haze work tonight?"

"Sure does. When you see her, tell her I'll be in shortly. In the mood for a bar burger and fries."

At the door, Jazzi stopped and asked, "Did Darby mention if he was meeting anyone after he left you that night?"

"Naw, no one wanted to spend time with him unless they had to. No one but me, and my patience was getting threadbare."

Once outside, as they walked to the corner, Jazzi said, "You'd think the man would live and learn. He drove away his wife and son. All he had left was Whiskers. Why alienate him?"

Gaff gave her a sympathetic look. "It sounds to me like Darby liked being Darby."

Maybe. But could the man have liked himself? Or did he not care about himself either?

Chapter 21

This time, when they entered the bar, every table was full. A man stood to leave, and Gaff led Jazzi to two empty stools next to each other.

The bartender came. "Back already? Are you off duty? Want a beer?"

"I'm still on the clock." Gaff motioned to Jazzi. "Bring one for her, though, on me."

A beer sounded good, so Jazzi sipped its foam when he put it in front of her.

"Is Haze working?" Gaff asked.

The bartender smiled. "Sure is. She'll make great tips tonight. We have a good crowd. Over there." He pointed to a woman who looked to be five eight, with bulging biceps and short and spiky salt-and-pepper hair. He held up his hand to catch her attention and motioned to Gaff and Jazzi.

She gave a small salute, finished taking the new table's orders, and came to see them, pushing her ticket across the bar's scratched wooden surface. She studied them, narrowing her eyes. "What can I do for you?"

Gaff showed her his badge and introduced Jazzi. "She's helping me on this case."

"Good for you. Woman power, huh?" Haze wore no makeup. Her neck was covered with a tattoo of flames, inked red and orange spikes reaching for her chin. A tattoo of Don't Tread on Me stained her right forearm.

Gaff took out his notepad. "We're here about Darby's murder. Is there anything you can tell us that might help?"

"Whoever did him in deserves a prize. People would take a number and stand in line to watch the old man bite the dust. And he brought it on himself."

"No love lost, huh?"

"He was full of himself. Thought he could pour on the charm and dazzle me. Wouldn't stop coming on to me even after I made it clear I wanted Whiskers."

"How long did you know him?"

"Since I started working here a year ago. He and Whiskers were regulars."

"Did he ever grab you? He latched onto his housekeeper and wouldn't let go."

Haze flexed her muscles. She had to lift weights. Jazzi did heavy work but didn't have defined arms like hers. "The man was stupid, but he didn't have a death wish. I'd have wadded him up in a ball and bounced him off a wall."

Jazzi didn't doubt she could do it. "Would Whiskers have gotten in a fight with Darby to protect you?"

Haze snorted. "I can take care of myself. Whiskers knows that."

Gaff watched Jazzi drain her glass. "Want another one? I'm driving."

"Thanks, but Ansel's waiting to eat supper with me. I don't want to fill up on beer. And I don't drink much on an empty stomach."

"Smart girl." Haze nodded approval. "What kind of a name is Ansel?"

"Norwegian—tall and blond."

"He's yours?" Haze asked.

"We're making it official November eighth."

"*Really* smart girl," Haze amended. She shrugged. "I've never tied the knot, but I'm growing partial to Whiskers and River Bluffs. Always moved from guy to guy and town to town before. I'm not getting any younger. Maybe it's time to let some grass grow under my feet." She grinned. "Who knows? I might even let Whiskers drive my Harley. He's been bugging me to."

Was there a man alive who didn't have a thing for motorcycles? If there was, Jazzi hadn't met him. "I wasn't in any hurry to get married, either, but then I found a keeper. I'd be stupid to lose him."

"I like you, girl. If you come back, I'll bring you a free beer. Drag your boyfriend along, too. I'd like to meet a Norseman."

Would Ansel be safe around Haze? She might have to hang a no touching sign around his neck.

A man two tables over motioned for Haze. "I've got to go, guys. Customers are calling."

Gaff laid a five-dollar bill on the bar and got up to leave.

"Come back anytime!" the bartender called after them.

Gaff shook his head. "I don't get that reaction too often, but when I bring you with me, people like to talk. Thanks for tagging along."

They walked down the street to Gaff's car. "No problem, but we're not making much progress. I want to clear Thane's name."

"He has lots of company on the suspect list," Gaff told her. "It sounds like anyone who met Darby might want to do him in."

It did sound that way. But something had made somebody madder than usual. Jazzi wondered what that was.

Chapter 22

Jazzi called Ansel to let him know she'd be home soon. She didn't want to talk about the case on the way there, so she tried a distraction. "What have you been up to besides work?" she asked Gaff.

"Ann and I babysat the grandkids last weekend. Our two boys and their wives went camping together, so we watched our granddaughter..." He paused when Jazzi interrupted him.

"How old is she? You told me, but I forgot."

"That's easy to do if you don't see kids. She's five. Right between our two grandsons, seven and four."

"Whoa! They're active at those ages, aren't they?"

"You'd better believe it. They still go to bed early, though. A good thing, or Ann and I would have crashed before their parents came to pick them up. We were exhausted."

Jazzi got a kick out of how much Gaff liked being a grandpa. "Let me guess. Now you can't wait to get them back."

He chuckled. "They make you stay young. How about you? Is everything ready for the wedding?"

"Just about. We're having the ceremony and reception at our house. The only thing I don't have yet is my dress."

Gaff frowned. "That was the first thing my daughters-in-law did. Couldn't wait to try on dresses and find the perfect one."

"I don't want anything too fancy. We're trying to keep everything small, inviting only family and really close friends. A full-length dress would be too formal."

"Our older son did the big church wedding and reception. Expensive. My other son did a small church wedding, but his wife still wore a long gown with a train. Both girls have them saved in the backs of their closets."

"No train for me, but my family's so excited, I want it to be a good time for all of us. Gran still talks about the engagement party Cal catered at the house. He and Aunt Lynda never made it to the altar, but I have every intention of filling his house—*my* house—with wonderful memories."

"You already have. I want you to adopt me so I can come to your Sunday meals."

Jazzi laughed. "I think your Ann likes having you home on the weekends."

"She keeps telling me that." He grinned. Jazzi had met Gaff's wife, and she was perfect for him—warm and open. She oozed charm.

Gaff pulled in her driveway to drop her off. As she slid out of the car, he called, "Buy yourself a pretty dress!"

"Will do." She gave him a wave good-bye and headed to the back patio and the kitchen door. When she walked inside, Ansel turned from their six-burner stove, looking proud of himself. "Supper's almost ready."

She sniffed the air. "Something smells good."

"Chili and cornbread. If you get the drinks, I'll carry the food over."

Inky and Marmalade raced to greet her. "You guys were a little slow." Stooping to pet them, she asked Ansel, "Have you already fed them?"

"It's either that or they won't leave me alone. They had to tear themselves away from the big front window, though. They've been watching a chipmunk run back and forth." He put the pan of cornbread on a trivet and went back for the chili.

When the cats ran back to the window, Jazzi grabbed Ansel two beers and poured herself a glass of wine. She carried them to the kitchen island and sat on the stool next to his. "Thanks for making supper."

"I got the recipe off my phone. It has a little heat. Thought we'd try something a little spicy."

She wasn't as big a fan of spice as he was. Okay, in all honesty, she was a wimp. He dished them each a bowl while she cut pieces of cornbread. Then he dug in, lurched back, and grabbed for his beer.

After watching him, Jazzi took a teeny bite, gasped, and gulped down wine. Could you catch your tongue on fire? Burn your tonsils? Melt your teeth?

He spooned a little of the evil mix over his cornbread. "If we eat them together, they'll balance each other out."

Right. His face turned red, and he emptied his bottle of beer. He put a hand to his throat. "That stuff's freakin' dangerous."

Jazzi moved to her cornbread. She was hungry, but not desperate enough to turn her stomach into a furnace. "What did you put in it?"

"A couple of jalapeños, a habañero, hot sauce, and chili powder."

She decided not to state the obvious. Her lips felt numb. "It's too spicy for me."

He looked at the Dutch oven, full of chili. "Do you think the pets would eat it?"

"I thought you liked George."

He pushed his bowl away. "I hope it doesn't melt the garbage disposal."

She laughed and leaned over to hug him. "Hey, you tried something new. I give you credit for that. What if we grill some sausage links to go with the cornbread?"

He tossed a dirty look at his cell phone. "Ten people gave this recipe five stars."

"Maybe their taste buds are made out of asbestos." She dug two packages of smoked sausage out of the fridge and turned on the burner for the stove's grill top. In ten minutes, she and Ansel were back at the island, eating their meal. The chili had gone the way of the disposal, and Ansel cleaned the pan to "remove the evidence."

She told him about Whiskers and the bar while they ate. "Haze wants to meet you, but I think she might like you a little too much."

Finished eating, she carried the dirty dishes to the sink to rinse, and he loaded the dishwasher.

"I'm not afraid of women with tattoos. Not when I have you."

"Haze looks like a woman who could handle spicy," she told him. "She'd probably want more."

"I'm ignoring that."

The couches called to them. When she glanced at the side table near hers, three brides' magazines were fanned out to catch her attention. "Is this a hint?"

He got up to sit next to her, scooting the cats out of the way. "I marked the pages of the gowns I like."

She was afraid to look, but he picked up the first magazine and turned to page forty-seven. "What about this one?"

Could there be more flounces and seed pearls on a dress? And what would she do with a train that long? She shook her head. "Too fancy."

He flipped to page eighty-three. She stared. "Really? The neckline dips almost to the model's belly button."

"You have great cleavage."

"That shows more than cleavage. I might as well go topless. What's next?"

He showed her one gown after another. When he closed the last magazine, she gave him a look. "Are you sure you don't want a royal wedding? You didn't pick one dress that wouldn't work in a cathedral with twenty bridesmaids in attendance."

"Just because we're getting married at home doesn't mean you can't go all out."

"The whole point of getting married at home is that I want to keep everything simple."

"Well, maybe I don't."

She stared. Had seeing all of the fancy gowns and wedding accessories disappointed him with their plans? "You should have thought of that before."

"Why? You won't even go to the bother of buying a dress."

Ouch! She stood, hands on hips. "I'm going with Mom and Olivia. Things have just been busy."

"Too busy to buy a dress. Maybe you can order one from Amazon."

She gaped. "Maybe I won't go to the bother. I have some white slacks in my closet."

"Fine, I think I still have a pair of coveralls from the farm."

She glared at him. "Maybe we rushed this marriage thing. After we lived together a while, Chad didn't like the way I did things either." She tried not to think about her former fiancé. Things had turned ugly before they broke up. She turned and started for the stairs. "I'm done talking to you. I'm going up to read."

"Fine." He stretched out on his sofa. "I'm watching TV."

She stomped up the steps, so angry her hands curled into fists. She grabbed her book off the nightstand and marched to the guest room. Idiot man could sleep with his dog tonight. The cats looked confused but followed her to the smaller bedroom and jumped up to be with her. It took a long time before she could concentrate on the novel's story, but her heartbeat finally settled, and she lost herself in its pages.

An hour later, she heard Ansel climb the stairs. He came to find her, carrying two glasses of wine. He held one out to her. "A peace offering. I'm sorry. I caused our first spat."

She blinked at him. "You call that a spat?"

"It's part of being a couple, isn't it? We can't always agree on everything. But I did rush you into marrying me, and you've done everything to make it a great ceremony. You'll find the perfect dress, too. I'm getting anxious, that's all."

She let out a long breath. "I *will* get a dress, even if I have to drive to Indy to find one, but I'm running out of time. I know that."

"Most dresses need to be fitted. That takes a while."

She patted the bed next to her, and he sank onto it. She took the wine from him and held up her glass to clink with his. "Have you found a suit?"

"It's getting tailored as we speak."

"You didn't tell me."

"It's a secret." He smiled and sipped from his glass. "I don't like having you mad at me. If we're over our fight, I think we should have makeup sex."

She laughed. "You're pretty sure of yourself, aren't you?"

"No, but I know I got your blood pumping enough that you probably need something to help get rid of all of that pent-up energy."

What she needed was something to make things right again. And great sex sounded like the perfect fix. They stood and carried their glasses to the master bedroom. Ansel had left the wine bottle there.

Tomorrow, Gaff hadn't planned any interviews. She could spend the entire day at the job site and take a break from murder to concentrate on gutters...and Ansel.

Chapter 23

Wouldn't you know it? It rained buckets on Tuesday.

On the drive across town, Ansel glared at the dark clouds that blanketed River Bluffs. "No outside work today. The rain's supposed to stay until late tonight."

"The weatherman predicted sun tomorrow."

"Let's hope he's right, and let's hope good weather holds, at least until we get the outside projects done."

When they reached the house, Jazzi held the umbrella so that Ansel, carrying George, could huddle under it with her. Rain pounded on it as they ran to the front porch. The hems of Jazzi's jeans were soaked, her gym shoes squishy. Inside, they found Jerod standing in the kitchen, staring out the window. He looked as gloomy as the stormy skies.

"What now?" Ansel asked.

Her cousin waved toward the job list they'd tacked up. "We start on the first job inside. We can't hang gutters in a downpour."

Jazzi read the top item on the list. "Knock down walls. Put up support beams."

Jerod nodded. "I'm in the mood for demolition. I keep watching one good weather day after another slip away. It's making me antsy. I wish Gaff would let us finish the driveway."

"Let's ask him again." Jazzi pulled on her work gloves and reached for a sledgehammer. She walked to the kitchen wall they wanted to remove and started pounding cracks in it. Ansel grabbed the broken edges and ripped big chunks off the studs. Jerod cleaned up behind them, throwing the pieces in the dumpster. When they finished in the kitchen, they went to the dining room and removed that drywall, too. Right away, the rooms looked bigger.

"Now we gut the kitchen," Jerod told them. "I'd like to keep the built-ins in the dining room. What do you think?"

"The corner cabinets are old-fashioned, but they're in great shape. The window seat looks out onto the backyard. Add a cushion and it'll make a fun reading nook."

Jerod nodded. "They might need paint, but they can stay."

They started pulling off cupboards and toting out appliances. There was no way for anyone to hold an umbrella, but the rain had slowed a little. They got wet, but not soaked. The kitchen had been dinky. They finished it by lunchtime.

"Let's eat before we start on the floors." Ansel was used to bigger suppers than they'd had last night. She'd packed extra roast-beef sandwiches, prepared.

Thane and his crew arrived right when they were returning to work.

"Still want a new furnace and air conditioner?" he asked.

"No choice. The old ones are shot." Jerod rinsed his coffee mug and set it on the card table. Everything else in the kitchen was gone.

Thane gave them a thumbs-up. "Opening up this space makes a big difference." He started to the basement, then hesitated. "Did you know Walker found a note with his dad's papers that said 'Fire Colin'? Nothing else. He has no idea if his dad followed through on it or why he wrote it."

Jazzi pursed her lips, thinking. "Darby was having money problems. Maybe he couldn't afford to keep him."

"Walker said Colin's always been a good worker. He plans on keeping him." His crew started carrying furnace parts down the steps, and Thane went to help them.

"Do you think Darby told Colin he didn't need him anymore, they argued, and Colin lost his temper?" Jazzi grabbed a crowbar to pry off old kitchen floor tiles. She groaned when one layer came off, only to reveal two more layers beneath it.

"I'm guessing no one paid much attention to anything Darby said." Jerod sighed. "We just get luckier and luckier with this house." He bent to touch the bottom layer. "Oil-based. Those things stick. We're going to be at this a while."

Ansel grabbed a flat shovel to scoop up the tiles Jazzi had loosened. "Each layer gets uglier than the one before. I'm guessing none of these people spent time in the kitchen."

Thunder rumbled overhead, and the rain picked up again.

"Most old houses have small kitchens," Jazzi said. "Rich people hired cooks, and average people waited for the wife to put food on the table."

"Where's the fun in that? I like cooking with you." Ansel scooped more tiles into their trash container.

Jerod stopped to wipe sweat off his forehead. The house was cool, but they were working hard. "I'm glad times have changed. If I help Franny make supper, we have a fighting chance we can eat it."

Jazzi shook her head at him. "Her cooking isn't that bad."

He shrugged. "It's according to her mood. If her mind drifts to some refinishing project, something burns."

They filled the trash can, and Ansel dragged it to the door. He hefted it up, muscles rippling, and hurried to empty it in the dumpster. He came back soaked. Usually, Jazzi would drool when his shirt stuck to him, but today he looked cold.

"Put your poncho on before you duck outside next time. The men are working on the furnace. We don't have any heat in here."

He nodded. "Forgot about that." He yanked off his wet shirt and pulled on his hoodie. That was fun to watch, but soon he'd get too warm in that. Jazzi grabbed his flannel shirt and zipped downstairs.

"What are you doing?" Jerod called after her.

"Putting this in the drier. That and the washing machine are new enough to keep."

When she came back up, Ansel reached out to hug her. "You're the best."

"I try." She kind of liked the guy.

They went back to scraping off tiles, and Jazzi's thoughts drifted to Darby and Colin again. "Colin never mentioned that Darby fired him. Maybe Darby changed his mind."

Jerod grunted when he hit a tile that didn't give. "Or maybe Colin decided that since the old coot was dead, he just wouldn't mention it."

Jazzi kicked the last few tiles she'd loosened out of her way. "When Gaff interviewed Earl, he never mentioned that he was seeing Bea or that he'd punched Darby to get him off her, and Andy and Colin didn't squeal on him. There might be more they didn't mention."

Ansel snorted. "Then Earl must have dirt he could dish on them."

Jazzi stopped work for a minute to think about that. "Gaff should talk to the three of them again."

"He'll want you to go with him," Jerod said. "We'll have the tiles up by four. Why not have him pick you up then? You wanted shutters and flower boxes for the front of the house, right? Ansel and I will start building those while you're gone. We'll work in the garage so we don't have to worry about sawdust. They won't take much time. And tell Gaff since he keeps borrowing you, he needs to repay us by letting us finish the driveway."

Ah, her cousin was offering her up as a bribe, but it might work. "I'll give it a try." She went to make the call, and when she came back, she was smiling. "It's a deal. Gaff will pick me up at four, and we can work on the driveway tomorrow."

"I knew I hooked up with you for a reason," Jerod told her.

Ansel laughed. "I'm hooking up with her for *lots* of reasons."

"I still want these floors finished," Jerod said. "Let's hit it."

And by the time Gaff got there, the tiles were gone, and Jazzi was ready to leave with him.

Chapter 24

"How's the house coming?" Gaff asked as they drove to Darby's place. No, Jazzi corrected herself, it's Walker's place now.

"We're going to finish the driveway tomorrow since you gave us permission. Then we have gutters to install, shutters and flower boxes to put up, and trim to paint on the higher windows."

Gaff's shoulders relaxed. "Good, because they're predicting colder temperatures next week."

"I heard that, but it's the middle of October. It might get warmer again after that weather system passes. I'm hoping for a mild Halloween."

Gaff looked surprised. "Why? You don't have kids yet. You won't get any trick-or-treaters where you live. The houses are too far apart."

"But Jerod, Ansel, and I take Jerod's kids to my mom's neighborhood to go house to house. I stay with Mom and help her pass out candy while Ansel goes with Jerod."

"That's nice. Your family does a lot of things together."

"I'd miss them if I ever had to move out of town. It would be awful to be like Walker and have a dad who was so mean, you had to run away from him."

"The sins of the fathers..." Gaff shook his head. "Not a punishment from the heavens, just the way it is. It's the kids who pay when the celestial lottery gives them crappy parents."

Jazzi blinked at him in surprise. Gaff was getting philosophical on her. Who knew? "Your family's close, too. Your kids must like you a little."

He laughed. "Yeah, they didn't turn out too bad, but it's just us and the kids. Ann's and my parents took off after retirement, followed the sun."

They were silent for a moment, and the sound of the windshield wipers, swiping back and forth, caught Jazzi's attention. They were getting close to Walker's house. Gaff's expression changed to detective mode. When he turned into the long drive to the outbuildings, he said, "Let's see what the drivers decide to tell us this time."

Jazzi caught the word "decide." She was quickly learning that omissions could be as misleading as out-and-out lies.

Gaff parked by the office door, and when they hurried inside, they found Walker and all three drivers sitting around a table, in the middle of a meeting. Rain thudded on the metal roof, creating a din. Walker looked up and nodded. "Since you wanted us all together, I decided to throw out Dad's idea of tackling a fixer-upper during our slow time."

"How long did you say the business has been losing money?" Earl asked.

"For months now. Dad meant to fire Colin because he needed to cut back on expenses."

Colin waved that away. "He'd threatened to fire me on and off for years, but then he'd look at the workload and realize there was no way he could do without me."

"So you weren't worried?" Gaff asked.

"Not especially. Darby couldn't turn away business because he didn't have a big enough crew. Even he wasn't that stupid."

"What about during the slow months?" Gaff asked. "What do you do then?"

Earl motioned out the window to his heavy pickup. "I put a blade on Betsy and plow snow. I have lots of driveways and small parking lots lined up."

Gaff turned to Andy.

"I paint house interiors and hang wallpaper with a buddy of mine. I wouldn't mind learning new skills, though, if we decide to flip houses."

Jazzi scanned their faces. "Have any of you worked construction or flipped houses before?"

Not a nod in sight.

Gaff motioned for Colin to go next.

"I head up north to a ski lodge. I clean sidewalks and parking lots, do a little maintenance, that kind of thing. I like working outdoors."

Gaff nodded. "Do you have anything else to tell me? Something I should know? The first time I questioned you three, not one person brought up the incident with Darby and Bea. No one even mentioned that Darby had a housekeeper. Did something more happen that Monday that you don't want me to know?"

Colin and Andy glanced at Earl. "It wasn't Earl's fault," Andy said. "Darby wouldn't let go of Bea. Earl had to punch him."

"If it was no big deal, why not tell me about it?" Gaff demanded.

Colin stared. "You're a cop. You're looking for someone to pin Darby's murder on. Earl didn't kill him. He just punched him."

"How can you be sure Earl didn't kill him?"

Colin gave a long sigh. He obviously thought Gaff was being dense. "Because once Darby hit the dirt, Bea ran to Earl, and we all went to our cars and drove away at the same time."

"But Darby lived here. One of you could have come back."

"In the middle of the night? After Darby got back from the bar? Why would we do that?" Colin rubbed his hand over his face. "You're reaching, man. None of us wanted Darby dead. We'd have to look for new jobs."

Unless Darby had already fired them, for real, or threatened to cut their wages. Why *did* someone kill him? Jazzi would love to know the answer. But it felt like they'd hit another dead end.

As the men stood to go to their trucks, Walker asked, "What about flipping a house during our slow time?"

"I don't know," Earl said. "None of us has any experience."

That seemed to sum it up. Earl and Colin left, but Andy stayed behind.

"Do you need to talk about something else?" Walker asked.

Andy turned to Jazzi. "Are there houses that are easier, that take less work, that we could make money on?"

"It's trickier," she told him, "and you wouldn't make as much."

"I'd like to give it a try."

Walker pinched his lips together, frowning. He looked at Jazzi. "I wouldn't lose money, would I?"

She was ready to leave, to call it a day, but heard how nervous he was. Walker was trying to do the right thing for the men who worked for him. Andy sounded desperate enough to grab at anything hopeful. She settled in her chair. "If the house has any major problems you don't know about, you can pour money down a pit." She might as well let them know the dangers that could lurk behind walls and under floorboards. Flipping houses might not be the answer for their slow season.

Andy slammed his fist on the table, frustrated. "I need to make more money!"

Jazzi felt sorry for him, but she was trying to help. "That's why I'm not sugarcoating house flipping. If a furnace is bad, you have to replace it. Same for AC. Plumbing problems? If you can't fix them yourselves, you have to pay somebody. Wiring…"

Andy interrupted her. "I get it! But painting with my buddy doesn't pay half as much as driving a truck. We're already living paycheck to paycheck. My kid's medical bills keep going up. I need some kind of miracle."

Jazzi was fresh out of those. She didn't know what to tell him.

Walker fiddled with some real estate books he'd brought. "What did you usually do this time of year? How did you make ends meet before?"

"Your dad hired me to clean and organize the outbuildings during the slow season. I can do a little mechanical work and looked over the trucks and equipment, have everything in good repair before orders came in again."

Walker frowned, looking confused. "Why aren't you doing that this year?"

"Darby told me he was doing it himself, that he didn't need me."

"Dad?" He shook his head. "That's a scary thought. He never took care of the equipment. He didn't know how."

Chapter 25

Andy looked away, knotting his hands into fists. "All I know is what Darby told me. Where am I going to find a job that only lasts three months? I'm going to go under and take my family with me. And why didn't your old man warn me in time that I wouldn't have a job, so I could look for something else?"

"He probably didn't want to lose you," Walker told him. "And that's why he came up with this harebrained scheme to flip houses. But you have a job now. I'm hiring you to do what you usually did. Business is picking up, and we'll need everything in good shape when decent weather rolls around again."

Andy gripped the edge of the table until his knuckles went white. "Are you serious?"

"Sure am. That's a part of the business I never did. I have no idea how to do it right."

Andy's entire body relaxed. His shoulders straightened with the weight of worry removed from them. "Thanks, man. This means the world to me."

Gaff chose that moment to open his notepad and click his pen. "When did Darby spring the news on you that your work ended with the last cement job this year?"

Andy shifted from one foot to the other. "A week before he died."

"That had to make you pretty upset. Maybe even furious." Gaff narrowed his eyes, studying him.

Andy spread out his hands in a helpless gesture. "Look. I didn't kill him. You can ask my wife. I was home that entire night."

"I'm guessing your wife is so exhausted, nothing would wake her once she falls asleep. You could have crawled out of bed and driven to Darby's, and she'd never know it."

Andy stared. "Who told you? I didn't think anyone saw me. I went, okay? But I didn't kill him."

Gaff gaped. So did Jazzi. He'd lied to them. He'd actually gone to have it out with Darby on the night he died.

Andy ran both hands through his dark hair. "I'd had it. I couldn't sleep. I was going nuts. No matter what I thought of, it wouldn't work, I wouldn't make enough money. So I drove to Darby's to tell him he either hired me for the slow season, or I was done. I'd look for another job."

"Is that when you fought? When you lost your temper and killed him?" Gaff asked.

"No!" Andy dropped his gaze to the floor, not making eye contact with him. "I couldn't find him. I looked in the outbuildings and knocked at his house. His van was in the drive, but I figured Whiskers must have picked him up to go to the bar and they weren't back yet. Either that, or Darby had passed out and it would be pointless to try to talk to him. I finally gave up and went home."

"What time did you arrive at Darby's?" Gaff was already writing in his notepad.

"One-thirty? Two? Somewhere in there. I can't swear to it."

"He was probably already dead and buried in the gravel." Gaff waited for his reaction.

Andy glanced at the dump truck parked on the gravel. He frowned, trying to remember. "It seems to me it was filled, ready to go, but I can't be sure. That's Darby's truck. He's the only one who drove it. I should have told you, but it looked so bad, my coming here in the middle of the night. I mean, I was mad at Darby. Desperate. You'd think for sure that I killed him."

"I still think it's a possibility."

"I'd never do that to my wife. I'd mess up, for sure—leave some evidence or break down when you interviewed me. I'd spill something that would get me caught, like I did now. You didn't know I'd come, did you? My wife can't raise our boy on her own. It's a two-person job. I wouldn't be any help to her if I was in prison."

The man's devotion to his wife and son made Jazzi like him all the more. How many men would decide not to mess up someone because it would affect their families? But she believed Andy. He *did* care about them that much.

Gaff shook his head, looking irritated. "You have motive and opportunity, so you've moved up on my suspect list. Is there anything else you need to tell me?"

Andy shook his head. He turned to Walker. "Am I still hired to work the off-season?"

"I believe you," Walker said. "My dad made me so mad, I left town. I don't think you killed him, so yeah, it still stands."

That was enough to make Jazzi decide. He could come to their Sunday meals for life if he wanted to. "Does this mean you're not interested in fixer-uppers anymore?" she asked him.

"They sound too risky to me. Besides, I'd rather concentrate on this business. We're going to make it."

With a nod, Gaff turned to leave, and Jazzi followed him. He waited for her to share his umbrella before going to the car. She called Ansel once she was in the passenger seat. "Are you at the job or at home?"

"We have only one more pair of shutters to make. Wanna come and help us paint them?"

"We're on our way. See you soon."

Chapter 26

Gaff pulled to the curb and handed her his umbrella. "You have a ways to walk to reach the garage."

She smiled and pulled a small, fold-up umbrella out of her purse. "I'm prepared."

He shook his head. "That's not much, so don't dawdle."

She didn't. She dashed down the side yard and past the open overhead door into the two-car garage. George was lying just inside, out of the rain but away from the sawdust. The shutters were beautiful. The guys had built them with three vertical slabs of wide wood with horizontal slabs near the tops and bottoms. The flower boxes were deep and wide, too, to stay in balance with the big house.

"How'd it go?" Ansel asked as she shut her umbrella and propped it against the wall. The downpour had softened to a steady drizzle.

Before answering his question, Jazzi glared outside, pushing strands of loose hair that had escaped the elastic band behind her ear. "Sure. Now the deluge stops." She told them about Andy and that Walker wasn't going to pursue finding a fixer-upper.

Jerod pried open the can of deep green paint while Jazzi fetched a stir stick and paintbrush. "Good. That wasn't one of Darby's better ideas."

"He was reaching, needed something to save his business." Jazzi propped a shutter across two sawhorses and began painting.

Ansel finished the last shutter and nodded approval. "Looks good. I like the way these turned out."

He and Jerod each hauled a flower box onto their saw horse.

"What's for supper tonight?" Ansel asked as he painted the inside of the box. Her Norseman always thought about what he'd eat once they got home.

"Homemade hash with leftover potatoes and steak. A salad on the side."

"Can we put an egg on top of mine?"

She smiled. "You and your eggs! I can do that."

Ansel looked happy, but Jerod scowled. "Franny insisted on cooking tonight. Since she's far enough along, she's starving most of the time. I can't fill her up. I hope I don't go home to a whole pig roasting over a pit in our backyard."

Ansel laughed. "Does she have cravings?"

"I should have bought stock in barbecued potato chips," Jerod growled. "The woman eats half a bag at a time."

Ansel stopped painting to study Jazzi. "You're going to be gorgeous when you're pregnant."

"Yeah, right." She tried to think about fixing up houses when she could only waddle. How would that work?

Jerod's cell phone buzzed, and when he answered it, he grinned. "No problem, woman. Don't worry about it."

"Is she all right?" Ansel still fretted about Franny. "No fake labor?"

"She's fine. She asked me to grab food on the way home. She worked on furniture for a while this morning, then sat down for a break and fell asleep. Just woke up."

Ansel finished painting the inside of the flower box and started on the outside. "So you were saved by a nap?"

When Jazzi finished painting the last shutter, Jerod was already taking his paintbrush to a bucket of water to rinse it.

"I think I'll treat her tonight," he said, "and buy mild wings and curly fries. My woman would rather have those than filet mignon."

"Hard choice," Ansel agreed. "Depends on my mood."

As they finished painting and started cleanup, Jazzi asked, "Did anyone call Walker to have the rest of the gravel delivered tomorrow?"

Jerod nodded. "He almost thought about having someone else deliver it, but everyone was busy. He said it was going to be a little hard on him, that he'd picture his dad falling out of the truck into our driveway, but he knew we were getting a little worried about the weather. He promised to deliver it first thing in the morning and then come back with cement after we have time to tamp it down."

It would be a relief to check the driveway off their job list. They could hang gutters if the temperature dipped, but cement was more temperamental.

They headed home a little later than usual. The rain showed no signs of letting up, but at least it didn't feel like a monsoon anymore. When they pulled in the drive, Jazzi grabbed George and carried him into the kitchen so that Ansel wouldn't get as wet running from the garage.

George headed straight to his food dish, and the cats rushed to their bowls. Jazzi was finishing feeding them when Ansel stepped inside.

He stood by the kitchen island. "If I whine and purr, will you feed me, too?"

She rolled her eyes. "Is that all you can tempt me with?"

He laughed, coming to stand behind her to wrap his arms around her waist as she opened the refrigerator. "Those come later as rewards for my proper care and feeding."

She turned in his arms and handed him an onion and carrot. "The rewards are mutual, so the workload is, too. Start chopping."

He bent his head to nuzzle his nose into her wavy hair. "Don't forget my egg."

She pushed him away. "Honestly, you have tunnel vision. Once you think about food, nothing distracts you."

"That's because I don't have to choose." He reached for the leftover sirloin tips and carried everything to the island. "I can have it all."

She pulled out leftover potatoes and a small bag of frozen peas. They worked side by side. The hash didn't take long to make, and she opened a bag of salad—a quick meal. But you would have thought she'd slaved over the stove all day. Ansel finished every morsel. George got only a few scraps.

In minutes, they cleaned the kitchen. "First fun, then a shower?" he asked. "We can watch TV in our PJs."

She wasn't about to argue. When Ansel looked at her like that, her entire body tingled with anticipation. When they headed upstairs, the pets flopped on the floor to wait for them. This time, they waited longer than usual, but then Ansel and Jazzi lavished them with attention when they came down. It was a win/win for all of them.

Chapter 27

On Wednesday, Jerod, Ansel, and Jazzi met early at the fixer-upper to tamp down the gravel Earl had delivered but they hadn't gotten to work on. With the yellow police tape finally down, they could smooth it out and form it into a solid base for the cement. A gray, overcast day shrouded the city, but luckily, no rain was predicted. Jazzi was grateful for her heavy flannel shirt. A damp chill hung in the air. She could feel her thick blond hair flatten and cling to her head. She didn't know which was worse—when heat and humidity made her hair curl and frizzle or when cold and damp air made it go flat.

Jazzi lugged a new coffee urn she'd bought, plus the two usual portable carafes, into the kitchen. All the gloom made her crave more java than usual. Ansel carted in the cooler with their sandwiches and chips. George, knowing they'd return shortly, sprawled on the back porch to watch them work. He didn't like lying in wet grass.

While Jazzi raked and Jerod tamped, Ansel finished building frames for the end of the drive. When they were close to finishing, Jerod called Walker. Half an hour later, he arrived with another load.

The man looked good behind the wheel of a big, red truck. Then again, he was big and solid with crisp chestnut hair, so he looked good no matter what. Again, Jazzi wished she knew someone to introduce him to. He backed into the drive, tilted the bed, and began pouring gravel as he moved forward. Suddenly, the truck lurched and started to roll. The slope of the drive made it pick up a little speed, and they watched Walker lean forward to pump the brake to slow it down. Jerod, Jazzi, and Ansel jumped out of the way as the truck rolled toward them. It wasn't going fast, but Walker couldn't make the turn onto the street without slowing down.

He killed the engine and cranked the steering wheel, aiming at a giant, old tree in the strip of lawn next to the drive. The truck slowed slightly before ramming the tree and coming to a stop. Walker jerked forward, but his seat belt held him secure.

Ansel ran to the driver's door and yanked it open. "Are you all right?" Walker, paler than usual, jumped out of the cab. He leaned against the truck to steady himself. "My brakes went out. Couldn't even get the emergency brake to work."

Jerod got down to peek under the truck. His dad was a mechanic, so he'd tinkered on cars from the time Eli had allowed him in the garage. He scooted far enough beneath the big vehicle that his head and shoulders disappeared. When they reappeared, a scowl pulled at his brows. "Looks like someone cut your brakes partway through so they'd go out eventually."

Ansel reached down and offered him a hand up.

Walker stared. "Why would anyone do that? The men like working for me."

"Who usually drives this truck?" Jazzi asked.

"It's Dad's, the only red one. He wouldn't let anyone else touch it."

Ansel frowned. "That's not the truck that came with our gravel when we found Darby's body. Earl drove a black truck."

"If Darby was loading our gravel when he died, wouldn't it have been in his red truck?" Jazzi asked.

Walker rubbed his chin and then looked surprised. "Now I remember. Earl told me Dad's heater had quit working, and he couldn't keep his windows from fogging up. Andy hadn't gotten around to fixing it yet, so he borrowed Colin's truck for the delivery."

Jazzi reached for her cell phone. Before she called Gaff, she said, "It doesn't sound like you were the target. I think your dad was."

Everyone waited while she explained to Gaff what had happened, then Walker looked from one of them to the other, obviously confused. "Why kill Dad with a shovel when his brakes were cut? Why not just wait and let him go off the road at a curve or fly through a stop sign and get hit?"

"Because someone lost his temper and whacked him before his plan could work," Jerod said.

Walker glanced at the truck, its bumper crumpled against the tree, its hood dented. "Someone really had it out for the old man. What do you think Dad did? I know he made people mad all the time, but nothing like this. I could understand Dad bugging someone so much that they picked up a shovel to shut him up. But planning to murder him ahead of time? That's different, isn't it?"

Jazzi jammed her phone back in her pocket. "The brakes were premeditated. It wasn't just a crime of passion. It was worse."

"Someone must have really hated him." Walker licked his lips. "The thing is, he had the same people around him who'd always been around him. Something had to have changed."

Jazzi had no idea what it would be. "The only things I've heard are that the money got tighter for the business and Whiskers got tired of your dad hitting on his new girlfriend."

Walker looked surprised. "Whiskers finally met someone?"

Jazzi nodded. "A new bartender at Shots and Spirits. She chose Whiskers over your dad, and your dad didn't take that well."

"Would you kill someone over that?" Walker asked.

Jerod snorted. "Not me. I'd start looking for the next gal and make sure she was even better than the one who got away." He would, too. He was quite the player in his day.

Walker glanced at his watch. "I thought Gaff would be here by now."

She'd just called him, but they were all getting restless, standing here, playing what-ifs. Jazzi motioned to the house. "I have lots of coffee. Anyone want a cup?"

The men followed her up the front porch steps and into the kitchen. Once there, Ansel went to let in George, and Jazzi filled the cheap mugs she'd bought and began handing them out. They were sitting at the card table, sipping the stronger brew she'd made, when Gaff gave a quick knock and joined them.

"I brought a mechanic with me. Wanted to know if Jerod knows what he's talking about."

"I worked grease monkey with my dad every summer I was out of school," Jerod said. "Glad you brought an expert to tell me I'm right."

Jazzi enjoyed watching Gaff and Jerod together. Gaff liked giving her cousin a hard time. Knew he could take it and dish it right back. Jazzi wondered if that's how he and his boys got along. Suddenly serious, he said, "You guys got lucky the truck didn't pick up speed. The tree's in good shape, but the truck needs some work."

Ansel drained the last of his coffee. His hand was so big, the mug looked like an espresso cup when he held it. "We did get lucky. It's a good thing the tree was there, or the truck would have kept going. Someone could have been hurt."

Gaff opened his notebook. "Okay, start at the top and tell me what happened and your thoughts on it."

They'd given him the details and their opinions when a man knocked on the door and Gaff motioned him to join them.

"My mechanic," Gaff said in way of introductions.

The man rubbed his hands on his blue work pants. "Whoever called it, called it right. The brakes were slit partway, so that they'd work until the driver was on the road. Then they'd give."

Jerod grinned, and Gaff grinned back.

"Thanks for coming," Gaff told him. "I appreciate it. My crew can take it from here. They're checking for fingerprints, any evidence they can find."

"The next time you bring your car in, you owe me a beer. Maybe two." With a wink, the man left.

Jerod rushed to talk before Gaff could start scribbling in his notepad. "Please tell me we don't have to put the yellow tape back up and stop working on the driveway again."

Gaff shook his head. "No, it's Walker's truck we're interested in. And why do you think someone sabotaged it to hurt Darby."

Jazzi tilted her head, thinking. "You said hurt, and maybe that's all the person wanted. I mean, the dump truck is so big, Darby should have survived if it crashed into almost anything."

Walker pushed out of his chair and began pacing. "Maybe someone was mad at Dad and wanted to get even with him, let him know he'd pushed too hard or gone too far."

"That was still a dangerous stunt." Ansel grimaced, upset. "If the truck didn't kill Darby, it could have killed someone else."

Walker slumped back in his chair. "You're right. Someone took a big risk, and for what? What did he want from what he did?"

Gaff tapped his pen up and down on his notepad, his expression far away; he was deep in thought. "It's time to dig further, to question everyone again. Tell your men Jazzi and I will be at your office at four tomorrow to question them again."

Jazzi turned to Ansel and Jerod, but Jerod nodded.

"We'll finish tamping the gravel as soon as everything settles down, and maybe Walker can send us cement later today. There's not as much hurry on the gutters. Ansel and I can start them, and if it takes two days to finish them, that's okay."

Walker nodded. "I'll get the cement here if I have to stay overtime and drive it here myself."

"Thanks," Jerod said.

"You're helping me. I'm glad I can return the favor, at least a little."

"Then everything's settled for now." Gaff stood and started to the door.

"Just one thing," Jazzi said. "I go out with my sister tomorrow night. I have to meet her at Trubble Brewing at six."

Gaff nodded. "Then let's make it three-thirty, so we're not rushed. I'll see you."

Walker watched him leave, then leaned forward in his chair. "I'm going to call Thane and tell him I'm stranded. Do you mind if I hang out here until he can come and get me?"

"Hang out?" Jerod laughed. "We'll put you to work."

"Even better, I'll go stir-crazy with nothing to do."

Jerod started for the door and stopped. "Come to think of it, I'll drive you back to your place so that if a truck opens up and you have some free time, you can deliver our cement."

They stood, and when Jerod and Walker left, Ansel and Jazzi went back to raking the gravel smooth and tamping it down. Hopefully, by the time Jerod returned, the gravel would be done and Walker could deliver the cement. And this time, fingers crossed, the truck wouldn't be sabotaged.

Chapter 28

Jerod returned an hour later and got busy helping them. "Walker's going to use Andy's truck, and Andy's going to look over the other trucks, just in case another one was tampered with. The drivers couldn't believe someone had messed with one of their vehicles. And it really riled them that Walker could have been hurt."

Jazzi leaned on her rake. Her back needed a rest. "They all like Walker, don't they?"

"He's saving their jobs, and they know it. Plus, he treats everyone with respect—something new for them."

Ansel gave the end of the driveway one more pass with his rake before heading to the machine to tamp the last section down. "Did Walker go ahead and call Thane?"

Jerod nodded. "Yup, and Thane invited him to his place for pizza tonight. Walker said he was ready to get away from the job site for a while. Things have been pretty tense since he came back to River Bluffs."

Jazzi felt a stab of guilt. She'd invited Walker to join her family on Sundays, but it would be easy enough to invite him again during the week. Ansel looked at her face and said, "Thane and I are meeting him on Thursday nights, too, so you don't need to worry about him. We're watching out for him."

She let out a long breath. The poor guy had had nothing but problems since he came home.

Jerod took her rake and carried his and hers to the garage. "You're not our mother. You don't have to hold our hands and give us goodies."

"Does that advice apply to you, too?"

He rubbed the back of his neck. "Come to think of it, mother us all you want."

Mollified, her thoughts went back to Walker. "I'm glad he'll spend the evening at Thane's. He needs a distraction."

Jerod grinned. "That's what kids are for. The minute you step in the house, you don't have time to brood. Besides, the drivers have a theory. They think Darby ticked off the wrong person. They said he kept getting more and more worried about the business and more keyed up about finding a woman to live with. The more he worried, the more he drank. They said he was getting hard to be around."

"Was he interested in some other woman besides Bea or Haze?" Jazzi asked.

"Earl thought he'd go after any woman who looked his way. If she was with somebody—like a jealous boyfriend—he didn't seem to care. Some men don't handle that well."

Ansel finished tamping and turned off the machine. The sudden silence made Jazzi rub her ears. He picked up the tamper and joined them at the garage. "Let's eat lunch before we have to work on the cement."

A good idea. They headed into the house, and George, realizing it was sandwich time, followed them. Walker still hadn't arrived when they finished eating, so Jerod said, "We might as well get started on the gutters. Maybe we can get one side done before he gets here."

No such luck. They leaned their long extension ladders against the roof and were cutting the metal sections to fit when Walker showed up. George had left the back porch to do his business but returned when the big truck backed into the driveway, its drum turning to keep the cement mixed. The noise drowned out their voices as they took their places to start smoothing it as it poured.

They worked with long-handled hoes before Walker gave them a wave and, job finished, drove away. After the surface was fairly smooth, they changed to trowels to smooth it more. It took the rest of the day to finish the entire length of the drive.

Jazzi always felt the strain when they worked with cement. Her back hurt. Her arms ached. And her knees smarted from kneeling so long, even though she wore knee pads. Ansel, with all of his muscles, rubbed his back, too. So did Jerod.

"I'm glad we don't do this for a living," her cousin grumbled. "Maybe your body gets used to it, but it stretches muscles I don't use that often. I'm not picking up any kids tonight. They'll have to wait for me to sit down to crawl on me."

They were cleaning their tools when Thane pulled to the curb with Walker. Thane ran a critical eye over the drive and nodded. "Good work." They'd put cones up to block anyone from driving on it and now put their tools away to come to talk to him. "Are you done with the house on Fairfield?" Jazzi asked.

"Our projects don't take as long as yours," Thane said. "We moved on a while ago. We're working on a house out north, not that far from your house, now."

Ansel glanced at Walker. "Are you going to live in your parents' house since you're in charge of the business? It needs a little updating, doesn't it?"

"That's putting it nicely. Dad didn't believe in wasting money on silly things like new floors or furniture. He waited too long. When things were getting downright shabby, he couldn't afford to remodel. Money was too tight. He kept losing jobs because he overscheduled, and the men couldn't get to places on time. It was Dad's fault, not theirs. Things are getting better already, though."

Thane slapped him on the back. "You could use that wad of cash he kept in his desk drawer to spruce the place up and make it your own. Unless you're sick of living there, that is. I mean, you grew up there."

Walker shrugged. "It's so convenient to live close to the business, I don't want to move, but the house holds some ugly memories. I'd like to completely redo it, make it have a different feel—something warm and relaxing. Thing is, I have no idea how to do that. I can't picture how colors and design go together."

"We can give you some ideas," Jazzi said. "I have lots of home magazines you can look at to see what you like and what you don't."

"Thanks, that's a good idea. Right now, the only thing I like is the back patio with the grill and eating area."

A place Darby never visited. Very telling.

Ansel asked, "Are you and Thane up for Thursday night out? Are we still on?"

"I'm in," Walker said, and Thane nodded a yes.

He turned to Jazzi. "Where are you girls going this week? We'll go someplace else—give you your space."

"We decided on Trubble Brewing. The food's great." Both Ansel and Thane were thoughtful about Jazzi and her sister's night out. She and Olivia both tried to support eateries downtown or on the south side of the city. The south part of River Bluffs got a bum rap in the newspapers, and it irritated them. When she and Ansel wanted a quick bite to eat, they stayed north and went to places closer to home.

Thane grinned. "I vote we go to Buffalo Wings and Ribs. It's not far from my place."

Jazzi shook her head. Ansel never turned down ribs. Walker's eyes lit up, too. She knew where they'd be on Thursday night.

Walker glanced at the tree that his truck had hit. The bark was scraped, and some of it was missing. "You should seal that and wrap it with something. The tree's beautiful. You don't want to lose it."

"In Wisconsin, deer used to damage trees in my parents' yard," Ansel said. "I know what to do."

Walker focused on Thane. "You'd think since someone cut the brakes on Dad's truck, that would eliminate you from Gaff's suspect list. Did it? The brakes had to have been slit before you and Dad argued."

Jazzi hadn't thought about that, but Walker was right. "It might eliminate Earl, too." Not that Jazzi thought Earl was the type to kill someone. "Darby didn't grab Bea until quitting time on Monday, and then all the men left at the same time."

"*Someone* killed Darby. He didn't just step on the shovel and hit himself in the head." Ansel started toward the house. It was after five, and Jazzi would bet that he was starting to think about supper. Her Viking liked to have a routine. She'd already disrupted it more than he felt comfortable with when she came home later than usual after helping Gaff.

Jerod rolled his eyes. "You don't think Darby stood on the edge of his dump truck, knocked himself out, then fell in the gravel? We got that, Mister Tall, Blond, and Obvious."

Ansel chuckled. "Too bad you can't come out with us some Thursday night."

"I wouldn't do that to Franny. She'd tell me to go, but then she'd be dead tired when I got back. Maybe we should have spaced our kids ten years apart—not have a new one until the other one could babysit."

Jazzi snorted. "You'd be close to retirement by the time you had number three."

Ansel glanced at his watch again, and this time, Thane took the unsubtle hint. He motioned to Walker. "We'd better get going. It's getting late. See you at Wings and Ribs tomorrow night."

"I'll be there." Ansel helped Jazzi carry the cooler and carafes to his van before he went to get George. Jerod walked with them to the curb and climbed into his pickup.

He rolled down his window to tell Jazzi, "If you're still in the mood to mother us, you used to bring big pots of soup to have with our sandwiches before you met Viking boy. Just saying."

She laughed. "Are you hungry for soup?"

"Not just any soup. *Your* soup. It's better than any restaurant's."

If he was working at flattering her, he was doing a good job. And she had a soft spot for her cousin. "Any type in particular?"

"I've been craving your black bean soup since it got chilly outside."

An easy recipe. "You picked the right one. I'll bring a pot tomorrow." With a smile, he pulled away from the curb.

Ansel slid behind the steering wheel of his van and grinned at her. "You know what goes good with bean soup?"

"Lots of things, but I bet you have something in mind."

"Cubano sandwiches, and no one makes ones I like more than yours."

"You guys are laying it on thick tonight."

He laughed. "It worked for Jerod. What about me?"

"We'll have to stop to buy a pork roast and deli ham—good bread, too."

"My van knows the way." And once they reached the north side of town, he stopped at their usual grocery store.

Jazzi added two oranges and a lime to their cart. "I'll put the roast in the slow cooker when we get home, so it will be ready for tomorrow. You'll have to help me make the sandwiches before we leave."

He gave a small salute. "Sous chef, ready for duty."

As usual, women congregated in the aisles he was in. Jazzi didn't blame them. Eye candy. It was a bonus when something fun happened at the store. How many times did you see a six-five blond with rippling muscles? She thought about her list. "Pork roast." Check. "Deli ham." Check. "Sexy Norseman." Double check. She threw a bag of fresh baby spinach in the cart. "Instead of lettuce on the sandwich."

They went to checkout, paid, and loaded their goodies in the van. George opened an eye and sniffed. The pug could smell deli ham from three miles away.

"You have to wait," Ansel told him on the drive home. "We bought an extra slice for you, and another for the cats to share."

What would he do when they had kids? If a dog could wrap him around his chubby paw, what could a toddler do? That was a thought for another day. Kids weren't high on her to-do list. Ansel knew that and was prepared to wait.

Chapter 29

Jazzi carried grocery bags into the kitchen, set them on the countertop, and turned to glare at Inky. Another glass jar, holding flowers, was broken. "Really?"

The cat stared back at her, looking innocent. Like he was the most law-abiding feline in the world. Pesky beast! She grabbed paper towels to clean up the mess and throw it away. When she opened the cupboard, there were only two mason jars she'd rinsed out. Pretty soon, she'd have to use plastic to hold the bouquets.

The cats came to wind around her ankles, meowing. "I should send you to bed with no supper," she told Inky. He nudged her leg with his head, all sweet and loving. He knew she couldn't prove anything. The cat was too smart for his own good. He kept staring at the deli bag.

She wouldn't give George or the cats any treats until they ate their dry pet food. The suffering was great, but they endured it. Then when Ansel tossed them bits of ham, the joy was enormous. She shook her head as she poured the orange and lime juice over the roast in the slow cooker. She added minced onion, salt and pepper, oregano, and minced garlic. In a few hours, the kitchen would smell like heaven. Pork heaven.

She and Ansel hurried upstairs to shower and change into their pajamas. Then they returned to the kitchen to start supper. She'd thawed shrimp for scampi—quick and easy. While the spaghetti boiled, she and Ansel worked together to make a tossed salad. The cats wouldn't touch shrimp, but George loved them. Ansel tossed George a couple while they ate.

When they started to the living room to relax after supper, George limped after them. He gingerly put weight on his right, front paw.

"Is he all right?" Jazzi asked.

Ansel bent to see. "I carried him to the van and into the house. He hasn't really walked on it much tonight." When he lifted his paw, George whined. Jazzi started to worry. She brought Ansel a flashlight so that he could see better. "Did he hurt himself?"

Ansel's brows furrowed. "It looks like he has a thin sliver of metal between the pads of his foot."

They hadn't taken the time to rake up nails and scraps as they worked. They'd tried to keep them close to the house, though. "It could have come from the roof or the gutters. Can you pull it out with tweezers?"

"I might miss a piece." Ansel reached for his cell phone and called the vet. When he jammed the phone back in his pocket, he reached for his keys. "The vet's still there, working late tonight. He'll look at George if I take him there right now."

Jazzi cleared her throat and stared pointedly at his pajama bottoms. "How well do you know this guy?" Ansel looked pretty alluring in drawstring pants, but they weren't appropriate for being out in public.

Ansel grunted and ran upstairs to pull on his jeans. A few minutes later, he carted George to the van and raced off. Suddenly alone, Jazzi wandered back to the kitchen. By the time Ansel got back, she had the black bean soup cooked and ready to take tomorrow. They were going to have a heavy lunch. She'd try to order something light when she went out with Olivia.

Ansel carried George into the living room and put him on the couch. "George doesn't like going to the vet, but he was a brave dog."

George pricked up his ears, his lips curved as though he was smiling. "Did you get some medicine to fight infection?"

"He got a shot instead, and he didn't even whine." Ansel stroked his fur, a proud doggie dad. Then he and Jazzi settled in front of the TV, and the cats came to snuggle with her. They were going to have a big day tomorrow. They'd start work on the gutters, and she guessed Gaff would want to make the rounds and ask more questions. Then they'd go out. She scrunched deeper on her pillow. She'd better relax while she could.

Chapter 30

A paw batted her cheek. Jazzi opened one eye and blinked. Inky had his face in hers, staring down at her. She glanced at the clock and pushed him away. She had another half hour to sleep.

When the cat jumped off the bed, she rolled over to get more comfortable. Thud! Something heavy hit the floor. She propped herself on her elbows in time to see Inky walk to the next bottle of perfume on her chest of drawers and whack it over the edge. He padded to the next bottle, raised his paw, and looked at her.

The little brat! She swung her legs over the bed, stalked to him, and tossed him into the hallway, shutting the bedroom door. She'd made it halfway back to her warm sheets and blanket when paws tried to turn the doorknob. Could he open the door? She hoped not. Then a body threw itself against the wood. Paws padded down the hall, ran, and leaped at the door again.

What in the world? She yanked the door open, and Inky flew at her. He hit her midsection and dropped to the floor. He sat on his haunches and stared at her, unrepentant.

She glanced at the clock. In ten minutes, the alarm would go off. She might as well stay up. On the way down the stairs, she warned the cat, "If you do that again, you'll be locked in the basement at night. Then you won't be able to get to our door."

He glanced over his furry shoulder at her and stalked to the kitchen, unconcerned. He went straight to his food bowl and meowed. She stared. "You got me up to feed you?"

He meowed more loudly.

"You know there are outdoor cats who have to worry about owls and coyotes, don't you?"

He didn't look scared. She was filling his bowl when Marmalade came to wind around her ankles. What a nice cat. Affectionate, with good manners. She filled her bowl, too. When Ansel carried George down to join them, she poured two mugs of coffee while Ansel fed the dog.

"Little did I know pets would rule our lives." She plopped four pieces of pumpernickel bread in the toaster. Then she took out all the ingredients to assemble the Cubano sandwiches. "Let's get ready first; then I'll help you." During the week, Ansel usually popped out of bed and was dressed, ready to start his day. She liked slower starts, but the last time she'd cooked in her pajamas, they'd smelled like chicken cacciatore until she threw them down the laundry chute and washed them.

The pets didn't bother going upstairs with them. They knew the routine. She and Ansel would wash up, throw on clothes, and be back soon. Jazzi didn't bother with hair and makeup on the job. Her thick, wavy hair got yanked back in an elastic band, and any makeup she put on—except mascara—melted away.

Once back in the kitchen, she laid out bread slices, pickles, mustard, and the slices of pork and ham to assemble the sandwiches. Ansel pitched in.

"How are you going to heat these at the fixer-upper?" Ansel asked as they gathered things to load in the van.

She opened a bottom drawer of the island and pulled out a panini maker and an electric skillet. The skillet wasn't ideal for heating soup, but it would work. That was the problem with gutting kitchens. Until new appliances arrived, there was no stove, no refrigerator.

Ansel helped her load everything in the van and then went back to get George. When they pulled to the curb at the house, Jerod was getting out of his pickup.

"Good! You can help us with the food." Jazzi held the appliance bag and a carafe for him to take.

Ansel carried George to the back porch and gently set him down while Jazzi carried two coolers into the kitchen. Ansel went to bring in the tote filled with cheap bowls and silverware that Jazzi kept for lunches on job sites.

Jerod scowled at George as he set down his load and opened the door for Ansel. "Why the special treatment for King Pug?"

Ansel explained about his hurt paw. "I don't want him off the porch until I rake around the house really well."

"Poor poochie." Jerod patted George's head as he passed him on his way to the garage. "We'll pitch in. We should have done it sooner. Then we'll rake again when we put the gutters up."

They armed themselves with garden and lawn rakes to do a thorough job. Then they got busy on the gutters. The back of the house went smoothly, but the sides took longer. The house was tall, at three stories, and they lost time going up and down the ladders. It had taken them only a day to install gutters on Thane and Olivia's ranch-style home, but they'd never finish that fast here.

From up so high, Jazzi looked over the neighborhood. Every tree blazed with color. Indiana was following its norm—the leaves changing in the middle of October. One reason she liked old neighborhoods was they had so many trees. Some of the new subdivisions were practically bare. It would take years before they had old giants like these.

When the sun shone directly overhead, Jerod scrambled to the ground. "You brought me a feast. I'm gonna enjoy it."

They stopped work and met in the kitchen. Jazzi plugged in the panini maker and pressed the first sandwich. She poured the soup into the electric skillet.

Jerod sniffed the air. "You went for broke. I didn't expect you to go all out."

She nodded toward Ansel. "You wanted soup. He wanted a sandwich. Why not? I don't have to cook tonight."

"Can I work that angle every Thursday?" Jerod held out his plastic plate, and Jazzi put a Cubano on it.

She snorted. "You know me better than that. Begging only works once in a while."

While the second sandwich cooked, Jerod bit into his. "I can't wait. I thought about this all last night. I have to try it. Jeez, it's good. How many did you make?"

"Enough for you to take some home tonight."

He threw an arm over her shoulders. "You're my favorite cousin."

"Yeah, you say that until Olivia offers to buy you a pizza."

Jerod laughed. "I didn't say I was loyal, just appreciative."

Ansel ladled out soup and carried the bowls to the card table. When everyone had their food and sat down, the guys got quiet. That's when Jazzi knew how much they liked the meal.

They took a longer lunch break than usual. When they finished, Jerod leaned back and rested a hand on his stomach. "This is the kind of lunch that makes you want to sit in your recliner and watch a football game."

Ansel fed the last of his pork to George, then drained his cup of coffee. "It's a good thing you don't do this every day, babe. It's going to be hard to get motivated and climb the ladder again."

She gathered the dirty dishes and bowls and went to the bathroom to rinse them. It was going to be a while before they hooked up the kitchen sink. Every drop of soup was gone, so she rinsed the electric skillet, too. She and Ansel carted the lunch things to the van before heading back to their ladders.

Jazzi was putting an end cap on a gutter when Gaff called. "Are you still on for today?"

"Yup, I'm just finishing my section of gutter. The guys have finished one side, and we're going to tackle the rest tomorrow."

"Are they quitting for the day when you leave?"

Jazzi looked down and watched Ansel and Jerod carrying shutters and flower boxes from the garage. "No, they're going to work on other stuff before they call it quits. They go out tonight, too."

"I'm wrapping up paperwork here," Gaff told her. "I'll see you soon."

She started down her ladder and helped the guys rake until Gaff pulled to the curb. When she slid onto the passenger seat, she wrinkled her nose. "It smells like Coney dogs in here."

"I picked up some for a working lunch," Gaff said. "Ate at my desk."

There was something about their local hot dog joint. When you transported the food, the aroma made you drool the entire time you were driving, and it lingered. She wasn't even hungry, and it made her crave one.

Gaff turned onto Fairfield, and they passed the big church on the corner. It was a short distance to Baer Field Thruway. On the drive to Walker's place, Jazzi admired the trees that had changed. She smiled. Walker might not think of Darby's house as home yet, but in her mind, he'd already put his stamp on the company.

A crimson maple and a row of burning bushes set off the house's yard with vibrant reds. Gaff drove past the tri-level to the outbuildings in the back. Three pickups were parked in a row near the door. It must be a badge of validation for a cement driver to own a pickup. But then Jazzi laughed at herself. She drove one, too.

She was still smiling when she followed Gaff into Walker's office. The smile dropped when she saw Walker struggling to hold Colin. Earl pulled on Andy to get the two men away from each other. When they saw Gaff, they tried to look calm, as if nothing had happened.

"What's the problem?" Gaff reached for his notepad.

Andy slumped, and Earl tugged him toward a chair at the conference table. Colin yanked himself free from Walker and stomped to the far side of the table, as far from Andy as he could get. Earl and Walker settled next to them, leaving Gaff and Jazzi to sit at the head of the table.

Gaff repeated his question. "Explain yourselves, or I'll ask Walker and Earl their versions."

Colin pointed at Andy. "The crybaby tried to get me fired."

Andy pushed to his feet. "All I did was tell Walker I saw a shovel with blood on its blade in your locker. I don't think you put it there. You're not that stupid. You'd have thrown it in a river or gotten rid of it. But I think it's the murder weapon, and I thought the detective would want to take it for evidence."

Colin narrowed his eyes, studying Andy. "You didn't accuse me of murdering Darby?"

"If you'd have let me explain, you'd have known that. All you heard was me telling Walker I saw the shovel there, and you tackled me."

Colin pressed his lips together in a tight line, swallowing hard. "All my life, I got in trouble for things I didn't do. My parents, my teachers… when I told them it wasn't me…they'd never listen. I got in enough trouble that eventually everyone pointed at me whenever anything went wrong. I guess it made me jump to conclusions."

Andy visibly relaxed. "Yeah, I get that. There was a kid in my class who was always standing in the hall or going to the principal's office. One time, he went for something I did, but I didn't have the guts to confess to it. I let him take the rap. I've felt bad about that ever since."

That didn't surprise Jazzi. She'd believed Andy when he told them he couldn't kill someone. It would eat at him so much, he'd mess up and get caught.

Walker looked from one of them to the other. "Are you guys cool now?"

They both nodded.

"Then let's go look at this shovel." Walker stood to lead them to the locker. It was like the ones Jazzi used in high school, long and narrow, with a combination lock.

Gaff frowned. "Who else would know the numbers to open this besides you?"

Instead of answering, Colin banged his fist on the door and pulled it open. "I never use the lock. These were made cheap enough, it would be pointless."

They all looked inside at a shovel propped against the back. The hook for a jacket or coat was empty, giving them a full view of it. Jazzi stared at the blade with dried blood on it.

"When did you first see this?" Gaff asked Colin.

"I didn't use my locker today. I left my jacket in my pickup and just wore my flannel shirt. It kept me warm enough. I didn't open it until it was time to meet with Walker. My throat felt scratchy, and I keep hard candy on the top shelf."

Gaff studied the room they were in—a hallway with lockers on both sides that led from Walker's office to the garage. "I'm guessing you keep all of the buildings' doors locked when you leave for the day."

Walker nodded. "And I keep the keys in the house."

"How many sets do you have?"

"Each driver has a set, in case they come in early to make a run. I have a set, so does Bea. Dad's set is missing."

Gaff made a note. "Did your dad keep his keys in the house, too?"

Walker shook his head. "Dad carried his with him. He had this big key ring with so many keys on it, I didn't know what they all were for."

"So, in theory, if someone took your dad's keys, he'd have access to everything on the property."

"Pretty much." Walker glanced at the shovel again, then looked away. "You're going to take that with you, aren't you? It sort of creeps me out that Dad's blood is dried on it."

"I'll get some gloves, try to wrap it, and load it in my car." Gaff tucked the notepad back in his pocket. "After I do that, I'd still like to talk to each one of you again. I have missing pieces, and one of you might know something you don't consider important, but it is. Earl, I'll start with you."

Earl nodded glumly, and Walker told the others, "While we wait our turn, let's go up to the house and sit on the patio. I bought a bunch of donuts this morning. It's afternoon, but they'll still taste good."

They followed him while Gaff went to get his gloves and load the shovel in his car trunk. Jazzi and Earl walked to the office and poured themselves cups of coffee while they waited. Jazzi took a sip of hers and slapped her hand over her mouth.

Earl grinned. "This time of day, it tastes more like sludge, but at least it's wet."

She pushed her cup away. She didn't think she'd ever be thirsty enough to swallow more of that.

Gaff entered the room and took his usual chair. He nodded at Earl. "Let's get to it."

Chapter 31

Jazzi watched Earl clasp his hands in front of him. He looked more nervous every time Gaff questioned him. Gaff studied him, obviously noticing, too.

"Is there something you want to tell me?" Gaff asked.

Earl opened his mouth to talk. No noise came out. He cleared his throat and tried again. "I didn't tell you about Bea and me because I didn't want Bea involved in this mess."

"But she is involved." Gaff clicked and unclicked his pen and kept doing it. It was annoying. Jazzi wondered if he was doing it on purpose to put Earl on edge. "She worked for Darby, and he assaulted her on the day he died."

Earl leaned forward, resting his elbows on the table. "Bea didn't have anything to do with his death."

"Can you prove that? Did she spend the night with you?"

"No, she wasn't ready for that yet."

Jazzi zeroed in on the words *wasn't* and *yet*. "Did you use the past tense on purpose? Have things changed?"

Earl gave a nervous smile. "I hated seeing her so upset, knew it would kill me if anything happened to her, so I asked her to marry me. She said yes."

"Congratulations!"

Gaff cleared his throat. "That's great news and all, but let's get back to the night Darby died. How long was Bea with you?"

Earl hunched his shoulders, his moment of happiness bumped aside. "I took her out for a fancy dinner, asked her to marry me, and ordered a bottle of wine when she said yes. I didn't want the evening to end, so I drove her to Foster Park, and we walked through the flower gardens. It was dark when I drove her back to her car."

Now Gaff leaned forward. "Where was her car? Here?"

Lowering his head, Earl rubbed his hand over his eyes. "She parked it by the office in back, and I drove her there. Darby's pickup wasn't in the drive. The house was dark."

"What time was this?"

"Close to nine. I knew he and Whiskers would be at the bar. I watched Bea get in her car and followed her out to the road."

"You never mentioned that you drove Bea back here that night."

"There was no reason to. Darby was gone."

"But he knew Bea's car was still by the office. He knew she must have gone out with you. Maybe he called her later that night and made her so mad, she came back to have it out with him, just like Andy did."

Earl's shoulders tensed. He gripped the edge of the table. "She wouldn't do that! She knew he'd grab her again. She'd be alone. Who knows what Darby might do?"

Gaff stared at him with steady regard. "She'd just told you she'd marry you. How far would you go to protect her?"

"What? I wouldn't kill a man. I'd do what I did before and punch him. I'm younger than Darby, stronger. I wouldn't let him hurt Bea."

Gaff made a point of staring at a bruise on Earl's temple. "Unless Darby used a weapon. Is that bruise where he hit you? Did he knock you down and go for Bea? Is that when you picked up the shovel and whacked him?"

Earl gave him an odd look. "Do you lie awake at night making up stuff like that? If you have to know, my dog caused the bruise. He got so excited when I came home, when I bent to pet him, he rammed his head into mine. Brute's big enough, I felt it. Left this." He winced when he touched the spot.

"Could Bea confirm that?"

"How could she? She wasn't there. After she got in her car, she drove home, and so did I." Earl let out a frustrated breath. "Look. You're making too much of Darby grabbing Bea. Yeah, it made me mad, but it was just Darby being stupid. He knew Bea didn't want anything to do with him, but he had been acting more stupid than usual the last few months. Something was eating at him, and I think it was more than worrying about money."

"But you don't know what it was?" Gaff turned a page in his notepad.

"None of us did, but he got into arguments with all of us before he died. Wanted us to drive faster, work an extra job every day. Silly, because I saw his appointment book. He didn't even know who he was sending where most days. He wasn't as good at running the business as Walker, but he'd never been that bad."

"Was he mad at you when you drove off with Bea that night?"

Earl's expression grew thoughtful. "No, he looked sad. That's the funny thing. He knew he'd made a mess of things, and he sat in the dirt and covered his face. I thought he was going to cry, but then he pushed to his feet and stalked to his pickup. We all knew he'd run to the bar. That's where he drowned his problems."

Gaff stopped writing and frowned. "What was important enough to Darby to throw him off balance so much?"

"Heck if I know. If a doctor told him he only had two weeks left to live, I don't think it would have bothered him. He'd just drink and squabble with everyone until he dropped over. The most important person in his life walked out on him, and he didn't go after Rose. He didn't crawl on his knees and promise her he'd change. As long as he could sit at the bar and drink away his woes, he was okay."

Gaff dropped his pen, a look of frustration on his face. "That's it for now. Will you send in Andy on your way out?"

Earl didn't tarry. He didn't run, but he was out the door faster than usual.

Gaff turned to her. "What do you think?"

"I think Earl and Bea stopped worrying about Darby the minute she said yes. From then on, Bea would be driving home with Earl and staying there. Darby was on a downward spiral, but no one knows why."

With a reluctant nod, Gaff agreed.

Chapter 32

They had a minute between interviews, so Jazzi went to make a new pot of coffee. The aroma of a fresh brew filled the room when Andy stepped through the door to join them. He sniffed appreciatively and glanced at the pot. "Care if I get a cup?"

"Bring me one, too, will you?" Gaff looked at Jazzi as she went to fill a mug for herself. Andy showed her where the guest cups were kept. Good, no Styrofoam.

Drinks in hand, they settled at the table, and Gaff took a sip before he reached for his pen. "We already know what you did on the night Darby died. So let's take a different tack. Who do you think killed your boss?"

Andy set down his cup and blinked. "I can't see any of us doing it. Darby drove us nuts, but we were used to him. I think it has to be someone new he met. He went to the bar almost every night, and I know he was looking for someone to replace Rose. He'd grabbed Bea, so maybe he grabbed someone else. Who knows? Maybe he even talked a woman into coming back to his house with him."

"But he wasn't in the house when he died."

Andy shrugged. "Could be he told her he had to fill a truck and then they could spend the rest of the night together."

Jazzi couldn't imagine any woman going home with Darby. With his wild hair and bantam-rooster strut, she'd run if he sat at her table. But the world was full of all types. Was there a woman out there who'd find Darby desirable? Maybe that was going too far. Was there a woman who could tolerate him for a night for free drinks and a roll in the sack? She wrinkled her nose and pushed the thought away.

"Did Darby do anything else on a regular basis? Somewhere else we should check?"

"Besides the bar? Not that I know of. He wasn't a churchgoer. I guess he went to buy groceries once in a while. He didn't go out to eat, usually nuked frozen dinners." He scratched his chin, thinking. "He had a pretty small circle of people he got together with."

"Did he have a run-in with any customers lately? Someone who felt Darby had gypped him."

Andy finished his coffee and pushed the cup away. "You know, Colin was telling me about a guy who drove here, fuming, after Colin delivered a truckload of sand at his house. Guess the guy ordered pea gravel and told Darby he wouldn't be home, so to just dump it beside his garage. Darby got the order wrong and swore that's what the guy told him. When the guy said to send someone to take the sand back, Darby refused."

Gaff gave a low whistle. "So the customer ended up with a mountain of sand he didn't want and none of the pea gravel he ordered? It would take forever to move that much sand."

Andy went for more coffee. "Colin said the man was hopping mad, and when he confronted Darby, Darby just egged him on."

"Why would he do that?" Jazzi didn't see any reason to make a customer madder than he already was.

Another shrug. "Because Darby liked watching people blow a gasket. He'd perfected the art."

Stupid, stupid man. Jazzi shook her head. "What happened with the customer?"

"He left eventually, screaming that he was going to call the Better Business Bureau. Like Darby cared. And the guy knew it. It just got him more riled up. Colin thought he might punch Darby, but he looked over and saw him and stormed off."

Gaff sounded a little happier. They had a new lead. "Can you get me the name and information on the man? Walker probably has it in his books."

Andy nodded. "I'm telling you, you're looking at us as suspects, but there are more people out there who could have lost their tempers and killed Darby."

Gaff didn't argue. He laid down his pen and went to reheat his coffee. "I'll ask around more. Maybe Darby started a fight in the bar, too. It might have been before the night he died."

Andy steepled his fingers, waiting for what came next.

"I'm done for now," Gaff said, returning to take his seat. "Will you send in Colin? And if you'd get the name and info for me, I'd appreciate it."

"Will do." Andy rinsed his mug and left them.

Gaff sat back and took a few sips of his drink. "What would you do if you got a delivery of sand you didn't want and the guy you ordered it from wouldn't move it for you?"

Jazzi pursed her lips. They'd never had that happen, only worked with contractors they knew. But she knew her cousin. "Jerod would probably load it in our pickups and take it to the guy's house and dump it in front of his garage doors."

Gaff laughed. "Then he'd have to move it if he ever wanted to park in his garage again."

"Exactly. It would be tit for tat. Jerod has an evil sense of humor."

"The punishment fits the crime." Gaff looked thoughtful. "I wonder if that's how someone felt about Darby and it got out of hand."

"He'd make sure of that." Darby loved to stir the pot.

Just then, Colin walked through the door and plopped into a chair. He put both elbows on the table and looked at Gaff. "Let's get this over with. What do you want to know?"

"Did you come back later the night Darby died?"

Colin frowned. "Why would I do that? I saw enough of the old man every day."

"There wasn't any unfinished business between you?"

"I didn't say that. He was threatening to dock my pay for a load of sand he sent me to deliver. He swore I got the order wrong and cost him a customer. The old fool. He messed up and was trying to blame it on me."

Gaff finished writing and looked up. "Andy said Darby and the customer went at it."

"If Darby had just sent one of us out to collect the sand and another truck to deliver the pea gravel, everything would have been fine. But Darby did the same thing with the customer that he was doing to me. He kept blaming us for his mistakes. The old man was losing it. His fights didn't even make sense. Sometimes he'd stop in the middle of them, scratch his head, and walk away. He knew was being stupid. Something was on his mind that he couldn't shake."

"Any idea what?"

Colin shook his head. "I'd be surprised if his brain wasn't pickled. He drank too much for too long. I asked him once if he wanted to patch things up with Rose and his kid, suggesting that maybe he felt bad about how things had ended with them. He went ballistic."

"Did he threaten to fire you?"

Colin laughed. "He did that every other day."

"What if he meant it the last time?"

A shrug. "So what? The ski resort keeps wanting me to work year-round. I've never stayed in one place before. Spent a year at the most. It's been nine here. If it's over, I'll move on."

Jazzi frowned. She couldn't figure Colin out. "Do you have family around here? Wouldn't you miss them if they weren't close?"

He barked a laugh. "My old man was fifty when I was born. Mom was forty-eight, didn't think she could get pregnant. I came as a shock. She kept telling me I almost killed her, moved around a lot inside, and then she had a hard time giving birth."

"Did they dote on you since you came so late?" He didn't strike Jazzi as a kid who'd been spoiled.

"No, I just wore them out. I had ADHD and drove them nuts. When Mom hit fifty-five, she had one health scare after another. It was a relief when I moved out."

Jazzi put a hand over her heart. She couldn't imagine what it must have been like for him when he was a kid. "You don't seem bitter."

"Why would I be? It wasn't their fault. They were just too old, and I was too scattered. I was too much for them."

How many kids would look at it that way? Be that generous? She liked Colin more. "Do you ever see them?"

"I go home every holiday, make the drive to Ohio. I take them out to eat. Mom shouldn't have to cook anymore. And that's enough to satisfy all of us."

Gaff frowned at him. "Why don't you and Andy get along?"

"Because the weenie never stands up for himself. He has that stupid victim mentality. I want him to grow some balls. He complains all the time that his mom loves his kid sister more. The girl had two kids with her boyfriend, then the creep dumped her, so she moved back home. Her mom loves it, dotes on the grandkids. But she doesn't want anything to do with Andy's boy. Says she doesn't know what to do with him. *He's* the kid who needs the most love."

"What about Andy's dad?" Gaff asked.

"He's a bigger coward than Andy. Goes along with whatever his wife says and hides in the basement with his toy train sets." His voice rose the longer he talked, and he blinked, surprised. "It really gets to me, okay? I keep waiting for Andy to tell them to take a hike."

"He's not like you," Jazzi said.

"That's a good thing. I'm no prize, but Andy deserves better."

Gaff shut his notepad. "Anyone else you think we should talk to?"

Colin shifted in his chair. It looked like he was trying to make up his mind about something. "You know Bea has a thing about men touching her without permission, don't you? Gets a little squirrely about it. Earl's hinted her first husband was abusive. She poured scalding water on him while he slept the night she left."

Gaff clicked his pen to make another note. "Did he file charges?"

"Nope, because she had a fractured rib and a black eye."

Gaff shook his head. "There's too much domestic abuse in our country."

"In our country? We're only a drop in the bucket. Men with tiny penises have to pick on someone."

Jazzi liked Colin more and more.

Gaff stood. "We might as well go to see her next. I'm questioning everyone again. Then Jazzi and I will go to the bar." He was turning to leave when Andy brought him a piece of paper with the angry customer's name and information on it.

"Good luck," Andy said. "I hope you find whoever killed Darby. I'd like this to be over."

"So would I." Gaff nodded thanks, and Jazzi followed him to his car.

Chapter 33

Gaff flipped through his notepad, found Bea's number and address, and called her before starting his car. He talked on his way out of the driveway, and Jazzi gladly listened in.

"I'm questioning everyone a second time about Darby's death. I need more leads, and you might know something that could help. Will you be home for a while?"

When she agreed to see him, he put his cell in the car's drink holder. "That woman must have a lot of anger built up in her. It had to be horrible for her when Darby tried to force a kiss on her."

"Do you think she got so upset, she came back to put him in his place?" That wouldn't be a smart idea, but people didn't always make rational choices when they were afraid or furious.

Gaff crossed the highway and stayed on Hillegas.

Jazzi glanced at her watch. "You remember I'm going out with my sister tonight, right?"

He nodded. "This probably won't take long, and Bea lives on the way to your house. If I have to, I'll cut the interview short."

Satisfied, Jazzi leaned back in her seat and looked out the window. She drove this route a lot, but she noticed so much more as a passenger. They passed Chevy's, where the guys went to get sausage rolls. Once they crossed the bridge, woods lined both sides of the street until subdivisions started appearing. Bea lived in a small white house a few blocks past the place where Jazzi got her cats. There was a small side street that ended in a cul de sac. When Gaff parked in the drive, Jazzi studied the area. All the houses were well kept, including Bea's.

As they walked up the steps to the front porch, Bea opened the door for them. Her living room was a small square with a doorway on the left leading to a galley kitchen. Bea motioned for them to take the sofa, and she sat in a rocking chair across from it.

Gaff reached for his notepad. "I've already questioned all three drivers, so you were next."

She gave him a steely look. "Someone told you about my ex-husband. He deserved a few scars. He left me with a lot of them."

"Was he always abusive?"

"Not when he was courting me. He was all charm and wonderful. Once I got pregnant and quit my job, he started pinching me when I annoyed him. After the baby, he'd give me a smack. I thought I couldn't make it on my own with a kid to raise. When he caught me looking at job ads, he got me pregnant with baby number two. To make sure I was stuck with him, he threw away my pills and demanded his husbandly rights so we'd have baby number three."

Jazzi stared. "Did you have anybody you could run to? Somebody who'd take you and the children in?"

Bea's stony expression grew colder. "My parents were poor. Struggled to raise me and my brother. I wouldn't burden them like that. When I visited, I never told them about C.L., but they noticed the bruises. When he split my lip, we didn't talk about it. They respected my privacy."

Jazzi tried to imagine what would happen if she went to her parents with bruises and broken lips. It would be ugly. Her sister and Jerod might even be worse than Mom and Dad.

Bea read her expression and tried to explain. "My parents loved me, but they didn't have any resources. My brother was determined to do better and made a lot of money, but he divorced himself from us. We shamed him. We never talk."

How sad. Jazzi thought about Earl. "I bet Earl's family will be happy to make you a part of them."

Bea smiled, but it didn't reach her eyes. She was on guard, waiting for Gaff to grill her. "I never thought I'd meet a man like Earl. He invited me for supper at his parents' once, and they treated me so well. They made me feel welcome and told me to come back any time."

"I'm happy for you."

"You heard?"

Jazzi nodded. "Earl told us."

Bea raised her hand. "No ring, but that's fine with me. No need for one." She rocked gently in her chair. "I'm ten years older than he is. That bothered me at first, but he doesn't care about my age. And finally, I decided it doesn't matter."

"It doesn't. You both know what you want."

Bea's smile returned, then she glanced at Gaff and grew serious again. "I'm sure you have more questions."

"How much did it bother you when Darby grabbed you? Enough to make you go back and argue with him?"

Bea grimaced. "Darby was losing control. I was watching him unravel. So, yes, it bothered me, but I wasn't stuck with him like I was with my husband. I could walk away if I wanted to. When Earl punched him, that was enough for me. And then Earl proposed and it didn't matter. I'd drive to and from work with him. Darby knew better than to push Earl again."

Her explanation made sense to Jazzi. She glanced at Gaff. It seemed to satisfy him, too. He looked up from his notepad. "Anything else that might help me find his killer?"

"You're looking in the wrong place. All three drivers could get jobs somewhere else if they wanted to. So could I. Darby made us mad, but we tolerated it because we liked our jobs. Someone didn't feel that lucky. He or she felt like Darby had them in a stranglehold, like they were trapped. Trapped animals and people show their teeth and fight back."

Gaff nodded. "You're not the first person who's said that."

"I don't think any of us killed him," Bea said. "You need to look somewhere else."

With a nod, Gaff closed his notepad and returned it to his pocket. "I promised to have Jazzi home in time to go out. We'd better leave."

Bea smiled at Jazzi. "Have fun tonight. Earl's coming to help me move in with him in half an hour. My life's going to be better."

As they walked out the door, Gaff said, "That woman deserves a happy ever after. I can't stand men who hit women."

"Earl will put her on a pedestal. She's probably never known the amount of love he's going to give her." Jazzi fastened her seat belt and looked at her watch. "Oh, boy, I'm going to have to throw on something decent and rush to meet Olivia."

"Sorry, Jazzi, but thanks for your help."

She was glad she'd gone with him today. The drivers and Bea had faced problems and grown stronger, better. It was inspiring.

Chapter 34

Ansel made a point of looking at the clock when Jazzi walked into the kitchen. "What was Gaff thinking, keeping you so long? You told him you were meeting Olivia tonight."

She kicked off her work boots and left them by the door. "I'm glad I stayed. It made me like every person who worked for Darby more."

Ansel's frown deepened. "He didn't have any right making you this late. You don't even have time for a shower."

She glanced down at her work clothes. "I gotta move it. Wish me luck. Olivia's going to give me grief when she sees me."

"You're not the one she should lecture."

She wasn't going to win this argument, so she ran upstairs. Ansel was usually easygoing, but if he thought she had been mistreated, he got protective. She'd better make herself look presentable or he'd hold it against Gaff.

She tossed off her flannel shirt and worn jeans, hurried into the bathroom, and washed her face. A little foundation and blush made her look more polished, then she took more care with her eye makeup. She let her hair down to spill over her shoulders. A touch of lipstick, and she was ready to get dressed. She frowned at the clothes in her closet. What would please Ansel? She pulled on a long dress that was fitted to her hips before falling in soft folds to mid-calf. She chose knee-high leather boots to finish the outfit.

When she walked downstairs, Ansel looked at her and shook his head. "You just did that to annoy me."

She frowned. "You don't like the dress?"

"I love it. You look gorgeous, and it only took you twenty minutes. You flew around to look good just so I couldn't fuss about Gaff."

She shimmied her hips, making the skirt swirl around her legs. "Did it work?"

He came to pull her close. "I almost wish we were staying home tonight."

Being surrounded by the Norseman's arms, being pressed against his hard body, had definite perks. "Darn, you feel good."

He chuckled, the sound rumbling in his chest. "It's hard to stay mad at you."

She tipped her face for a kiss. "Good. That way, we can both have fun tonight."

His lips claimed hers, slow and delicious, sending shivers through every part of her body. The kiss deepened, and she could swear her bones melted. Then he stepped away. "You'd better get going. So had I."

Fiddles! She wanted more, but now wasn't the time. Olivia would be on the way to Trubble Brewing to meet her. They walked to their vehicles and went their separate ways. Traffic was heavy as she drove into town and pulled into the brewery's parking lot five minutes late. She rushed inside and saw Olivia sitting at a booth, waiting for her. A man hovered at her table, trying to flirt. Her sister, with a curtain of dark blond hair and a willowy figure, had to beat men off.

"Sorry, I have a boyfriend," she was saying. "I'm here to meet my sister for girls' night out."

The man gave a smarmy smile. "Does your sister look like you?"

"She's taken, too." Olivia looked toward the door and saw Jazzi walking toward her. "There she is. Time for you to go."

The guy didn't budge. "Well, lookie here. One's thin and the other one's curvy. The best of both worlds."

Olivia's brown eyes flashed a warning. "You're not taking the hint. Do I have to call the manager?"

His smile turned nasty. "I'm leaving. I hate teases."

When he turned and walked away, Jazzi sat down. "Did you lead that poor man on?"

"Yes, I sipped my wine in a come-hither way."

Jazzi laughed. "How's life? Did you have a good day at the salon?"

Olivia wrinkled her nose. "Mom had a client come in who'd fried her hair trying to bleach it at home. It looked like straw. Took lots of treatments to make it even a little soft."

The waitress came, and Jazzi ordered a glass of zinfandel. Once they were alone again, she asked, "How's Thane?"

"Good, but he keeps hoping Gaff will arrest someone for Darby's murder. It's not like he's the only suspect, but it doesn't feel good being on Gaff's list."

Her wine arrived, and Jazzi took a drink. "Gaff's trying. There's not a lot to go on. He's going to start expanding his list of suspects."

"Good, because Thane can't picture any of the drivers as a killer. He likes all of them. They were decent to him when he stopped at Darby's to see Walker." Olivia tilted her head, studying her. "You look good tonight. That dress would make a great style for your wedding. Maybe we can find one in white or cream on Monday."

"Monday?"

Olivia blew out a breath of frustration. "We promised Ansel we'd take you shopping and find something decent for you to wear. You keep putting it off, so Mom and I have decided to kidnap you this Monday. We won't stop shopping until you have a dress and shoes."

"It's just that I've been away from the job site a lot in order to go with Gaff as he questions people. We're close to getting everything on the outside of the house finished. Then we won't have to worry about the weather."

Olivia shrugged. "If you can go with Gaff, you can go with us."

Jazzi was about to argue that the Monday after this one would be better when the waitress came to take their order. Jazzi had spotted a specialty burger on the menu and went with that. Olivia ordered the macaroni and cheese with pulled pork on top. When her sister splurged on calories, she didn't mess around.

Alone again, Olivia said, "You're going to buy a veil, too, aren't you?"

"For a wedding at home?" Jazzi had just finished listening to Gaff interrogate suspects, and now she was under the gun.

Olivia rolled her eyes. "It doesn't have to be anything major, but you're going to be a bride. Doggone it, you should look like one."

Her sister cared more about fashion than she did, but Jazzi was trying to up her game. "I'll get a veil."

Olivia smiled. "And Mom scheduled manicures and pedicures for all of us."

"It's too early. They won't last. I kill my nails every time I rip out drywall or refinish floors."

"Wear gloves."

"I do for drywall, but they're clumsy when I use a sander."

Olivia reached for her wine. So did Jazzi. They drained their glasses, and the waitress came to see if they wanted another glass. Instead of asking for a bottle, which seemed appropriate at the moment, Jazzi smiled and nodded.

When the food came, Olivia dug in. "This is heaven on a plate." She didn't stop eating until the waitress brought their second glasses of wine. Then she narrowed her eyes, studying Jazzi. "How are you wearing your hair? If you tell me you're going to pull it into a ponytail, I'm kicking you under the table."

Jazzi swallowed her bite of hamburger. Whatever the seasoning on it was, she'd love to be able to buy a bottle of it. "I haven't thought about it."

An exasperated sigh. "Really, sis! Mom and I are both hairdressers. We can make it look any way you want it."

"Up in a loose knot? Soft and sexy?" Ansel liked it when she let her waves flow freely or, if her hair was up, when stray strands escaped her elastic band.

"We'll have to find the right dress for that. Nothing too severe."

Jazzi hadn't ever worn anything severe. She couldn't carry it off. She decided to change the subject. "Are Mom and Dad doing anything exciting?"

Olivia's eyes lit up. "They're talking about going to New Orleans with Eli and Eleanore. Doesn't that sound like fun?"

Dad had been talking about taking a vacation with his brother and his wife for a while now. The conversation turned to traveling, and she and Olivia finished their meal on a happy note.

When they separated to drive home, Jazzi thought about how much fun it would be if she and Ansel took a trip with Olivia and Thane. She'd have to run that by him sometime. Maybe they could start small and spend a weekend in Michigan, up by Luddington, to see how that worked.

Once she reached their house, she parked her pickup in the garage beside Ansel's van. He'd beaten her home. When she walked through the door, she found him sitting at the kitchen island, feeding a few leftovers to George and the cats.

"We didn't eat supper at home, and they missed out," he told her.

She sat on the stool next to him and leaned into him. He wrapped an arm around her and grinned. "Did you miss me?"

"We haven't had enough us time." She loved hanging out with him.

"Tomorrow's Friday, and then we have Saturday together."

"We haven't finished Jerod's basement."

He grimaced. "And on Sunday, your family comes for our meal."

She rubbed her cheek on his arm. "For the next few days, we'll just have to touch each other every chance we get."

"I'll rent a scary movie for Saturday night."

She frowned. "I was thinking of a chick flick."

"No, you get mushy and laugh when we watch those, but you don't cling."

He had a point. "No guts or gore."

"I'll find something creepy." Ansel had this belief that if she got scared enough, she'd want him to hold her, which would put her in the mood for petting and other things when they went upstairs. Silly man. She'd want that if he whistled and nodded toward the stairs. It didn't take much.

Chapter 35

On Friday, they started early and took a short lunch break, so that by the time Gaff came to pick her up, the gutters were finished. All of the outside work was done except painting the rest of the window trims. Jerod assured her that he and Ansel could cross that off their list on Monday while she was shopping. A good thing, too. Rain was predicted for late Monday night, and it was supposed to linger for most of the week.

She slid in the car and glanced at Gaff. His expression looked as dark and foreboding as the upcoming thunderclouds. "You okay?"

He pulled from the curb with a grimace. "When I called to tell Darby's customer I wanted to stop to talk to him, he got belligerent right away. Turns out I arrested his brother a year and a half ago for robbing a convenience store. I didn't recognize this guy's last name, but that's because his mom had remarried. There's not one person in the family who hasn't been hauled into the station for something—drugs, public intoxication, you name it. His mom spent time in jail for soliciting before her boyfriend bailed her out."

"Have any of them been charged with murder?"

"Not yet." Gaff turned east on Paulding Road. They passed the Catholic high school and kept going. "Eddie has a foul mouth and a worse attitude. If he gets to be too much for you, give the signal and we'll leave. I can go back later on my own."

She appreciated his concern, but she worked a job where she dealt with lots of men. The majority of them kept things professional, but she'd met a few who were on the rough side. Their language tended to be salty or worse. She imagined Eddie must make them look like saints.

"When we leave Eddie's, we'll drive to Shots and Spirits and see what we can learn there. If Eddie gets too cranked up, I'll owe you a beer."

She laughed. "Why does every man think a free drink will even any score?"

His lips twitched. "Because it works once in a while?"

"I doubt it. If a woman accepts it, she was probably already interested or on the fence."

He glanced her way. "Afraid that's about the best compensation a cop can offer a sidekick."

"In that case, I'll take it."

The town's housing subdivisions were behind them before Gaff turned onto a narrow, asphalt road. Farm fields stretched between long, gravel driveways that wound far back from the street. Gaff slowed and turned onto a drive that led to a run-down farmhouse with junk cars scattered in its front and side yards.

Gaff turned off the engine and looked at her. "We're here."

It was a sorry-looking place. If anyone had ever painted the clapboards, it didn't show. She followed Gaff to the front porch. They waited until Eddie finally answered the door. He sneered at Gaff and motioned for them to step inside. So many engine parts littered the living room, it looked more like a garage with a couch and two chairs than the inside of a house.

Eddie flopped onto the couch. His straggly hair was as greasy as his hands. "I was hoping to never see you again."

Gaff checked out the stains on the chair cushions and remained standing. "The feeling was mutual. Let's hope we can get through this in a hurry. Then I'll be on my way."

"After you drove so far?" He stared at Jazzi's chest. "Looks like you brought me a booby prize to loosen my tongue."

He waited for her to be impressed by his wit. She wasn't. She folded her arms over her breasts and stared at him.

He shrugged. "Not the friendly type. But then, she hangs out with cops. That's a strike against her right there."

Gaff pulled out his notepad and pen. "I came to ask you about Darby and the sand he delivered to you."

Eddie sat up and gripped the arm of the couch. "That's what this is about? Did that son of a..." He glanced at Jazzi and then at Gaff. "Did the old crook finally rob the wrong person? Did the Better Business Bureau fine him for being such an...?" He stopped. "He owes me a load of pea gravel."

"I heard about your argument with him. How mad did he make you?"

Eddie narrowed his eyes. "Why?"

"Someone went to his company in the middle of the night, had a row with him, and hit him over the head with a shovel."

Eddie laughed. "Probably broke the handle. That man had a head as hard as a mule's."

"It killed him."

Eddie jumped to his feet. "And you're trying to pin it on me?"

"Where were you on the first Monday of October?"

Eddie paced to a side table and grabbed his cell phone. He scrolled through it and looked up triumphantly. "I spent the night with my baby mama. Her government check came that day, and she owed me some money."

"She'll vouch for that?" Gaff scribbled down the information.

Eddie grinned. "She'll remember. I gave her a good old time."

Gaff wrote down the woman's name, address, and phone number when Eddie gladly shared it with him. Then he returned his notepad to his pocket.

"That's it?" Eddie asked.

"That's all I have for now." Gaff started toward the door and held it for Jazzi.

"This has been so neighborly. Feel free to drop by any time," Eddie called after them as they walked to Gaff's car. "I'll put the kettle on."

Once behind the steering wheel, Gaff grumbled, "That whole family thinks they're too darn clever."

Jazzi glanced in the rearview mirror and saw Eddie standing on the porch waving good-bye to them. "It could have been worse."

"If you hadn't been there, it would have been. They get on my nerves."

If Jazzi had seen the best of Eddie, she didn't want to see his worst.

On the drive to Wells Street and Shots & Spirits, Gaff drummed his fingers on the steering wheel. "That was a dead end. I'll check with Eddie's girlfriend, but if her check came that day, he'd be there for his money. It was a long shot anyway, but you never know. Sometimes those lead to something."

They hit the five o'clock clog of traffic again before they found a parking space two blocks down from the bar. When they walked inside, they got the last two stools available. The bartender finished filling an order, then came to see them. He raised an eyebrow at Gaff. "You're here again. You buying another beer for the lady?"

Gaff nodded. "She's earned it."

He laughed. "Hanging out with you should earn her a gold star. What'll it be?"

"A Michelob." It was on tap, and the mugs were frosty cold.

He went to pour her drink, then grinned at Gaff. "Working on a Friday, huh? No rest for the wicked."

"Every person we talked to said that Darby was losing it, getting more volatile all the time. Did you notice that?"

"Oh, yeah, he fought with Whiskers almost every time they came in here. Never used to happen."

"Because of Haze?"

"I thought so at first, but that was only part of it. When Haze first got here, those two strutted their stuff like roosters trying to impress a hen. But before she even settled on Whiskers, the two of them got into yelling matches until I had to toss them out a few times. I told them if they kept it up, they were done here."

Jazzi put down her mug and licked her lips. "Could you hear what they were fighting about?"

His gaze slid to her engagement ring. "You're a real pretty girl who doesn't put on airs. If you'd hook up with me, I'd buy you a bigger diamond."

She shook her head. "I wouldn't wear it. I asked for something that wouldn't snag while I hammered or sanded."

He looked surprised. "That's a first. Just makes me like you more."

Gaff grunted. "You should see her boyfriend—big and tall like a Viking. Steer clear of her. Back to Darby. Did you hear what he was arguing about with Whiskers?"

He gave Jazzi one more look before answering. "Something about money. Whiskers swore Darby owed him money, but as soon as everyone looked their way, they both got quiet."

"Money can turn friends into enemies." Gaff paid for the beer and added a generous tip. He looked around the crowded bar. "Does Haze work tonight?"

"Nope, she and Whiskers left on her Harley. They rented a lake cabin for the weekend."

Gaff got to his feet. "Figures. Today's been a bust."

The bartender grinned. "It's Friday. Take Saturday and Sunday off, chill out for a while. Haze will be back on Monday."

"Tell her we'll stop in to talk to her." With a nod to Jazzi, he headed for the door, and she followed him. If Gaff didn't want to take the weekend off, she did. She was ready for some quality time with a Norseman.

Chapter 36

Once they were in the car, Gaff turned to her. "Do you have to be home in a hurry? Do you have time for one more stop?"

"Who else do you want to see?"

"Walker's mom and her new husband drove over to see him today. I'd like to question them in person instead of over the phone. Walker gets defensive about his mom. I thought it might help if you were with me."

"Does Walker know you're coming?"

"I warned him."

Curious, she asked, "How did you know they were coming?"

"I called to set up a time to drive to Ohio to see them, and they said they'd be here after his mom got off work at the diner. Her husband took the day off. They're going to stay overnight and spend all day tomorrow with Walker."

Jazzi nodded. "I'll call Ansel and tell him I'll be later than I expected. We're going out for sausage rolls for supper tonight, so there's no hurry for me to get back."

Gaff turned onto Main Street to drive to Walker's place. "I'm taking Ann out tonight. We're going to the Oyster Bar, have reservations for seven o'clock."

"It's a little pricey, but the food's delicious."

"It's tradition," Gaff told her. "Tonight's our anniversary."

"How many years?"

"Thirty-three. The woman's a saint for putting up with me all this time."

Jazzi had met Ann when she invited Gaff and her to swim in their pond one hot summer day. She got the impression that there wasn't much that would throw Gaff's wife. She was a warm, down-to-earth woman. "No kids invited?"

"Not tonight. Just Ann and me. She invited the kids and grandkids for supper on Saturday."

"You're going to have a wonderful weekend."

He nodded. "Once I get this over with, I won't be on duty till Monday morning."

When they turned into Walker's drive, Jazzi noticed an SUV parked near the tri-level's front door. She'd heard all good things about his mom, Rose. She bet Walker had missed her since he'd moved here.

She stood to the side as Gaff knocked on the door. Walker opened it, looked at Gaff, and scowled, but he held it wide to let them in.

"Thanks for coming with him, Jazzi." He led them into the kitchen. "Mom started cooking the evening meal. I offered to take her and Gene out, but Mom brought everything to make one of my favorites."

The aromas from the stove made Jazzi's mouth water. "Spaghetti?"

He nodded. "With a Caesar salad and garlic bread." When his mom looked at him nervously, he gave her a small smile. "Mom, this is Detective Gaff and Jazzi." He motioned to the kitchen table. "And this is Mom's husband, Gene."

Rose was an attractive woman, pretty, not beautiful, and petite. Jazzi wondered where Walker got his height. He got his coloring from his mom.

She turned the burner on the stove to low, put a cover on the sauce, and went to join her new husband at the kitchen table. He reached across the smooth wood surface to give her hand a small squeeze. Walker took a seat next to her, and Gaff and Jazzi sat facing them.

Gaff placed his notepad and pen on the table. "When was the last time you saw Darby, Mrs. Gilbert?"

"Please, call me Rose. I think it was about three months ago."

Walker turned to her, surprised. "You drove to River Bluffs to see Dad?"

"No, he tracked me down somehow and drove to Ohio to confront us. Just knocked on our door one day and insisted I go home with him. When I told him I *was* home, he got agitated."

He stared. "You never told me Dad came."

"I didn't want to worry you."

"Did he know you'd remarried?"

She gently touched his arm. "He assumed that was why I asked for a divorce."

"Did he get loud and angry? Did he threaten you?" Walker's hands tensed into fists.

"Luckily, Gene had only gone to the drugstore because Darby got weird, not nasty. He told me nothing had gone right for him since I left."

Gene curled an arm on the back of her chair. "He wanted Rose to divorce me and remarry him. He wouldn't stop talking about it. I finally had to threaten to call the police to get him to leave."

"Had he been drinking?" Walker asked.

His mom nodded. "He shouldn't have been driving, but we didn't try to make him stay to sober him up. We just wanted him out of our house, but after he saw us, he kept calling me, over and over. He'd always said I was his good luck girl, and he believed his luck abandoned him when I left."

Gene gave a snort of derision. "It wasn't the same as missing her. He wanted his luck back. Pathetic, isn't it?"

Rose tsked. "Darby was never good at expressing his feelings. He'd never be able to tell me he missed me."

Gene shook his head. "We finally had to block his calls."

Gaff looked up from his notes. "Are you a jealous man, Mr. Gilbert?"

"Gene. Call me Gene. No, not really. I'd never marry a woman I couldn't trust. I trust Rose."

Rose smiled. "I stayed with Darby till Walker was grown. I'm loyal to a fault."

Gaff nodded toward Gene. "Is he protective?"

Jazzi could see the light bulb go off over Rose's head. She realized where Gaff was leading. "Yes, but he's smart, too. He wouldn't drive to River Bluffs to kill Darby. He'd hire a lawyer or talk to the police."

Gaff turned back a few pages in his notepad and scanned his information. "According to your previous statement, you and Gene were playing cards the night Darby died."

Rose nodded. "Our company didn't leave until midnight."

Gaff flipped back to where his new notes were. "Plenty of time for you to drive to River Bluffs and back before work."

Walker's gray eyes went wide. "That doesn't mean they did."

"When Andy came to have it out with Darby, he saw a black SUV pull into the driveway. Its headlights lit up his pickup, and then it backed up and left. He thought it was the newspaper delivery guy, but you drive a black SUV, don't you? Andy said it had a dent on the driver's side, like someone had backed into it."

Rose stammered, "That has to be a coincidence."

Gene let out a long breath. "I brought a lawyer's restraining order to hand to Darby myself. I wanted him to get the message—leave Rose alone."

It was Rose's turn to stare. "When did you leave the house?"

Gene grimaced. "I told you to go to bed while I changed into my pajamas. You were so tired after the card game, I knew you'd go right to sleep. I gave you ten minutes, then drove to River Bluffs. I left a note on the kitchen table, but you'd never gotten up during the night, so I just threw it away. That way, you didn't have to worry."

Jazzi studied the three of them. There'd been a lot left unsaid between them to protect the other person.

Gaff's shoulders stiffened, and his gaze drilled Gene. "What happened when you met Darby?"

"That's the thing." Gene shrugged. "I never got to see him. He wasn't here when I knocked on the house door or at the office. I waited a good two hours, but he never came back. I knew if I didn't start home, I wouldn't get back in time, that Rose would catch me. So I left."

"And you expect me to believe that?" Gaff's voice was harsh.

"You asked me a question, and I answered it. I drove home with the restraining order, and I mailed it to him later that day. If you looked through his mail, you probably saw it."

"I have it." Walker got up and walked to a desk in the front room. When he returned, he handed it to Gaff.

Gaff studied the postmark. Tuesday, the day after Darby died. He rubbed his jaw and gave Gene a long, hard look. "You were at the scene close to the time Darby died. That moves you to the top of my suspect list. After you lost your temper and slammed Darby with the shovel, it would be easy for you to drive home and mail the restraining order to throw us off."

"Like I said, I never saw the man. I don't think he was home."

An acrid scent drifted to the table. Jazzi sniffed and wrinkled her nose. "Something's burning."

"The sauce!" Rose jumped to her feet and rushed to the stove. When she took the lid off the heavy pan and gave the contents a stir, she sighed. "The bottom's black. We'll have to throw it away."

"No problem, Mom. I'll take you two out for supper."

Rose returned to the table, looking defeated. She slumped into her chair. "What now?" she asked Gaff.

"Neither of you leave Dayton until we clear you. I might have more questions for you later." Gaff looked from one of them to the other. "Anything else you should tell me?"

"You should keep looking," Walker growled. "Neither of them killed him."

"Let's hope facts bear that out." Gaff closed his notepad.

Walker stood to show them to the door. He looked at Jazzi. "Gene's a great guy. He'd never hurt anyone."

Jazzi nodded agreement. She couldn't swear Gene hadn't killed Darby, but she sure hoped he hadn't. "Will they be here on Sunday? You could bring them to the family meal."

He shook his head. "They're leaving right after breakfast, but I plan on coming. You gave me an idea, though. I'm going to call Thane and Olivia and see if they want to go out with us tonight. Mom always loved seeing Thane. Maybe that way we won't talk all night about Gene driving here."

"Hope you have a nice visit." She hugged him. He was beginning to feel like part of their group. "See you on Sunday."

She followed Gaff to his car and slid inside. On the drive across town to her house, Gaff sighed. "I wish people would just level with me from the beginning, but they rarely do. It always looks worse when we find out later."

Jazzi chewed on her bottom lip. "I think I'd be too afraid to tell you up front, too. If it looked like no one would ever know, it would be tempting not to mention it."

Gaff grinned. "I get that. Good people tell lies. That's why I keep questioning them. Sometimes, eventually, the truth pops out."

It was Friday night, and people were driving more recklessly than usual. Everyone was in a hurry to be somewhere. At the second stop where drivers ran red lights, Gaff grumbled. "They wouldn't do that if I drove a squad car."

"No, but then you wouldn't be a detective either. And you make a good one."

He laughed. "I'll keep that in mind." When he finally turned into her drive and left her off at the back door, he called, "Thanks for going with me."

"No problem! Have a great anniversary, and enjoy tonight."

He smiled. She had a feeling every time he thought about his Ann, it made him happy. That made her think about Ansel. Her Norseman was waiting to take her out to eat, too. And tonight, nothing tempted her more than a sausage roll. She hurried inside to see him, George, and the cats. He'd want to know how Gaff's interview with Walker's parents went. Boy, she hoped Gene wasn't the killer.

Chapter 37

Ansel went to the refrigerator and poured her a glass of wine while she kicked off her work boots and came to join him. "Hey, babe." He wrapped her in a warm embrace.

He smelled like Irish Spring, his blond hair still damp. She inhaled his scent. "They should make a soap called Norse Nuance or Viking Musk. Something that sounds strong and sexy."

"Nuance?" He snickered, stepped back, and dropped onto a stool. He pushed a plate with hummus and veggies to her. She nibbled, then sipped her wine. "How did it go?" he asked.

She sank onto the stool next to his and turned so that they were bumping knees. She rubbed her foot up and down his calf. "No Whiskers and Haze, but Walker's mom and her husband came to see him, so we stopped for Gaff to question them."

"Good. He can check them off his list."

"It moved Gene higher." She told him about their visit.

"Not a brilliant idea. Gene shouldn't have driven to River Bluffs to see Darby, but I wouldn't have told Gaff about that either."

"Neither would I. It would make me look guilty for sure."

Inky jumped on the island's countertop to demand attention.

"You're not allowed up here." Ansel scooped him up and set him on the floor.

Jazzi bent to pet both cats. Marmalade, as usual, acted like a lady and meowed for her strokes. "Walker wasn't too happy that Gaff put so much pressure on his parents, but he understood that that's his job."

"Gaff's a great person, but I wouldn't want him to interrogate me. Cops make most people nervous."

They munched happily together until Jazzi finished her wine. "I'm going to throw a chuck roast in the slow cooker for a quickie version of beef barbacoa at Jerod's tomorrow, then I'll run up and take a shower so we can go out to eat." Hummus was a skimpy appetizer after a long day of work.

"Put on your tight jeans," Ansel called after her.

She did better than that. She wore a low-cut red top, too. Ansel always complimented her when she wore red, said that it went great with her blond hair and blue eyes.

When she came downstairs, he grinned. "I got dessert early. You look good enough to eat."

She wasn't touching that line. Instead, she asked, "Are you hungry now, or would you like to relax a little before we leave?"

They ended up playing with the cats and spoiling George before they finally left the house. When they reached Wrigley Field Bar and Grill, business was starting to pick up. By the time they'd leave, it would be packed. She ordered the sausage roll—a massive thing—and Ansel ended up ordering the pork tenderloin sandwich with breaded mushrooms. Neither of them was eating light tonight.

The waitress brought their beers, and Ansel took a long drink before glowering across the table at her. Uh-oh, had she irritated him? Was he tired of her traipsing after Gaff?

But then he said, "My sister called today. My parents want to come to our wedding. So do Bain and Radley."

She hesitated. She didn't know how to answer him. "I don't have a problem if they come. We have plenty of room, but they're your family, and I know you don't want them here."

He took another swallow from his glass. "I already caved when I went to help them with the house and barn roofs and stayed until Dad could manage his crutches to milk the cows. You know how much I didn't want to see them then, but Adda made me feel guilty. I sure don't want to see them now."

Adda must have tried to wheedle him into inviting his parents. Ansel had a soft spot for his baby sister, but he could be stubborn when he dug in. And he was in no mood to forgive his parents and brothers anytime soon. "Why does Adda think you should invite them?"

He sighed. "Because she has a big heart and a small memory. They treated her like crap, too, but she still rushes to rescue them when they need her. Family doesn't toss you out the minute you graduate from high school and divide the dairy farm between your older brothers. They left her as high and dry as they did me."

"Whatever you decide is fine with me," she said. "Will Adda still come if your family can't?"

"She said she and Henry are excited about coming and staying with us a few days." He shivered. "Mom and Dad would expect us to entertain them, too. Bain would never pay for a hotel room, so he'd expect free room and board. I'd like to see Radley, but he knows how I feel."

"Can you invite Radley, but not the other three? He still lives at home. If he comes, will your parents make it awkward for him? They can't stay mad at him too long. They need his help on the farm." And sadly, that's what decided most issues with Bain and Ansel's parents.

Ansel drained his glass and motioned for a refill. When the waitress came with another cold bottle of Coors, she brought their food, too. Steam rose from Jazzi's sausage roll, but she couldn't wait. She cut a small bite and blew on it. The sausage and marinara sauce were drowned in melted cheese. She made a small, happy noise when she ate it, and Ansel laughed.

"You've been waiting for one of those since Thane, Walker, and I went to Chevy's."

She nodded. "How's your tenderloin?"

"They're always good here." He tasted a mushroom cap and had to chug down his beer. "Too hot. I'd better wait."

Jazzi playfully rubbed her foot against his. "The wedding's not that far away. What are you going to do?"

"Do you think I should invite them?"

She shook her head. "Not if you don't want to. My family doesn't cause me angst. I don't have these kinds of worries."

He grimaced. "That's not much help."

She swallowed another bite of food. "All right, let me ask you this. How much would they ruin your mood if they came?"

He scowled, took another sip of beer, then shrugged. "I'd mostly ignore them. And I'd tell them they could spend one night, then get up and go home."

She blinked. "You'd really tell them that?"

"They let me spend one night at home when I graduated, then told me to get my bags and be gone."

Put like that, he had a point. She went on. "It would make Adda happy if you invited them. Then she wouldn't always be in the middle."

"But they'd use her every time they wanted something from me. Besides, that's her own fault. She could tell them to take a hike."

Jazzi shrugged. "I give up. You have to make up your own mind."

"Will it bother you if they come?"

"Honestly? Yes, but I'd just keep my distance. You'd have to be the one who put clean sheets on the beds for them. We'll have to buy air mattresses and have your brothers stay in the same room as your parents. It's big enough."

"I'll lay sheets out. They can make their own beds. If they don't like their room, they can stay in the garage."

She rolled her eyes. Their house had only three bedrooms, but they were all good-sized.

Time to change the subject. "Is everything outside done at the Southwood Park house except painting the window trim?"

He leaned back in his chair and forked up more mushrooms. "We'll have everything finished on Monday. While you're shopping." He pointed the fork at her. "I'm excited about the dress. We live together. I think you should model it for me."

"Dream on. Bug me about it and I'll buy a white muumuu."

"I'd still know what's under all that volume."

He was impossible. "You don't get to see the dress until I walk down the stairs at our wedding."

"I might take one look at you and faint with joy."

"When you gain consciousness, we'll finish the ceremony."

He laughed. "There's no negotiating, I can see. Love that about you. babe."

His mood better, they dug into their food in earnest. There were no leftovers to take home for George, so Ansel stopped on the way to buy him a junior roast beef sandwich. He bought a second one to split between the cats.

"We've had a good night. Our pets should, too."

Once home, they relaxed and enjoyed the evening before he walked into the other room to call his sister. While they talked, she stayed in the kitchen, adding seasonings to the roast in the slow cooker. Then he called his brother Radley. When he joined her again, his mood was less festive.

"Well?"

He wore a sour expression. "They're coming. Radley said Bain put Adda up to calling for them. I feel like I've been outmaneuvered by my oldest brother again."

"It doesn't matter." Jazzi came to wrap her arms around him. Her head fit under his chin, and she leaned into him. "Bain's a jerk. Radley isn't. And you're more generous than any of them. You did the right thing."

He squeezed her tight. "Let's watch some TV."

There'd be nothing frisky tonight. But they didn't have to be at Jerod's until ten tomorrow. There would be plenty of time to start Ansel's day right.

Chapter 38

Jazzi was the aggressor on Saturday morning, and Ansel loved it. The pets waited outside their bedroom door until they were done. After quick showers, they went down to feed the poor starving beasts before they got ready to drive to Jerod's.

Inky hovered to see where Jazzi was headed next, and when she reached for her work boots, he glared. Most Saturdays, she puttered around the house in the morning, dusting and sweeping. The cats didn't like it when she left for work. In a huff, he leapt onto the countertop next to the sink and stalked to her flowers. He batted the base with his paw, and it didn't move. He tried again. Then he turned to stare at her.

She smiled. "Yup, try to move that crock." It was heavy stoneware. It wasn't going to budge.

Undeterred, Inky grabbed a long stem with his teeth and bit off the flower. The little brat! Jazzi had to admit, she was impressed. He went to grab the next one. "Don't do it," she warned. "That's a rose. It has thorns."

He started to chomp, then jumped back with a yowl. This time, he whirled toward her with a hurt look, and she immediately felt guilty. He'd expected better of her.

"Sorry, I tried to tell you." He jumped off the countertop and stalked away, miffed.

Ansel had watched the whole thing and shook his head. "You ruined his fun."

"He'll think of something else. Maybe I should have let him demolish the flowers. They're easy to replace."

Ansel glanced at the clock and went to gather the food she'd made for lunch. "We'll have to see what Inky comes up with later. We have to go."

Jazzi enjoyed the ride to Jerod's house. Once they left the city and drove down the highway, the houses were set farther apart. On the back seat, George whimpered, and his feet moved as if he were chasing a rabbit in his sleep. Not that he did that when he saw one in their backyard. It must be that, in his dreams, he was an action dog. When they pulled into Jerod's drive and George saw where they were, she watched him steel himself for the onslaught of small children. She grinned and picked him up as they walked to the kitchen door.

Jerod glanced at the slow cooker Ansel carried and her tote bag. "What did you bring this time?"

"The stuff for barbacoa tacos." She plugged in the cooker and set it on low.

Jerod took a deep breath. "I'm going to miss having a private chef when we finish the basement."

Ansel frowned and looked around. "Where are the kids?"

"Franny's mom's taking them to Science Central today. Gunther's been wanting to go for a while now."

Jazzi had gone there with her friend Leesa when Leesa's son, Riley, turned two. An English professor, Leesa was all about providing her child with a maximum number of learning experiences. Thank goodness, the learning was so much fun, he didn't suspect anything. "It's a great place for kids. Adults, too. I enjoyed myself there."

Ansel glanced around again. "Where's Franny?"

"Out in her woodworking shed. She got a great price on some serious tools for furniture making. She's playing with them."

Ansel looked surprised. "She's going to start building furniture now instead of just refinishing it? Has she ever tried that before?"

Jerod nodded. "She took a class once, simple stuff. She's determined to make all of the furniture for the basement, and I wouldn't put it past her."

They headed to the basement, and Ansel toted George down with them. The dog gave a huge sigh and sank onto his side. No kids. Life was good.

"I took a few shop classes in high school," Ansel said. "I built a bookcase with a top drawer. Really enjoyed it."

Uh-oh, Jazzi could hear the enthusiasm in his voice. Building furniture had sparked his interest.

Jerod had stacked the drywall in the back half of the room, and they got to work. They wanted to finish the entire project next weekend, so that Jazzi and Ansel would have a weekend free to get ready for their wedding reception. Hopefully, next Saturday, they could install the hanging ceiling and trim.

There was no small talk while they worked. They'd done this a zillion times together, and they had a set routine. Every piece of drywall was nailed in place by the time they stopped for a late lunch.

"Franny's not eating with us?" Jazzi asked.

"She loses track of time when she touches wood. I'll give her a call." He picked up his cell phone. "Jazzi brought food. You hungry?" he asked. He grinned as he told them, "She's starving, didn't realize it until she stopped working on a table leg. She'll be here in a minute."

"She can make table legs?" Ansel asked.

Oh, boy, Jazzi could see a woodworking shop in her future. She put the shredded meat in the taco shells and passed them to the guys. She opened containers filled with diced jalapeños, scallions, and radishes, along with shredded cabbage.

"No cilantro?" Jerod asked.

"I don't like it. Didn't have any," she told him.

"I like it."

She gave him a stare. He got the message. "There's plenty of other stuff," he decided. He made up two more tacos for Franny, so her plate was ready when she met them at the dining room table.

"Jerod said you got new toys." Ansel opened another container of corn taco shells. Two tacos wouldn't satisfy him and Jerod.

Franny's whole face lit up. "I got a used lathe from a carpenter who's retiring and all the tools that go with it. He had some how-to books for me, too." She went on, explaining some of the projects she'd played with this morning.

Ansel listened carefully. "I've always wanted to try my hand at woodworking."

"Then why don't you?" Jerod asked. "You've got plenty of room for a workshop in your basement."

"Stop encouraging him." Jazzi glanced at her Viking. Too late. His blue eyes gleamed with excitement. She was probably already doomed. He'd talked about dividing the space into two rooms, finishing one as a playroom and keeping the other as a work area.

Ansel glanced at her. "Would you mind if I built chests and china cabinets down there?"

"Not as long as the dust doesn't come upstairs. I'm not that into housekeeping." During good weather, he spent most of Saturday outdoors working in the yard. Once the weather turned crappy, he'd need something to do. A lathe might be a good fix.

He grinned. "I'm taking that as approval. I'll start looking around. Maybe Franny and I can work on projects together."

"We could make a cradle and a crib." Franny looked at Jerod. "We never had a real baby changing table. I could build one."

"You have until February," he told her. "I can help with the simple stuff."

They chattered about woodworking all during lunch, then Jazzi helped Franny store the leftovers before she joined the guys downstairs. Franny hurried back to her shed.

They taped and plastered for the rest of the afternoon. The basement was a big area, and it took longer than they expected. When they finished, Jerod wiped the sweat off his forehead, surveying their work.

"You guys are the best. I can sand it and paint it during the week. If we get the ceiling up next Saturday, I can do the rest."

"You'll need help putting down indoor-outdoor carpet," Ansel said.

"Thane volunteered to help me with that. It's clumsy, but the two of us can get it down."

Ansel nodded, satisfied. "In that case, we're taking off. We're going to have a quiet night tonight before everyone shows up for the Sunday meal."

"What are you making?" Her cousin always wanted to know what to anticipate.

"Chicken potpie, a big salad, and a sheet-pan German chocolate cake." She was taking the easy route and buying rotisserie chickens.

Jerod patted his stomach. "My pot belly's starting to shrink. I have to give it some love."

Jazzi wasn't worried about him shriveling to paper thin. "I think you're making progress."

"And it's all thanks to you." He gave her a quick hug as she and Ansel headed out the door.

On the drive home, Ansel asked, "Want to stop at the store on the way? Do you have a list ready?"

She reached into the glove compartment and pulled out a sheet of paper. "Ta-da! I wrote everything for the whole week. It's going to take us a while."

"Doesn't bother me. I look at everything in the cart and know it's future meals."

Jazzi glanced at the back seat. "Will it be okay to leave George that long?"

"He'll sleep through the whole thing. We'll lock the doors and crack a window, though, so no one steals him."

The pug was so friendly, he'd probably go with anybody who held up a snack for him. When they got into the store, they separated so that Ansel could get all the food on the outside aisles and Jazzi everything she needed in the middle. For better or worse, she knew the store well enough to write out her list that way. They were in the checkout lane in short order, and as Ansel had predicted, George was sleeping when they loaded the bags of groceries into the back of the pickup.

The cats loved grocery day and came running when they walked in the house. Once Jazzi emptied a brown paper bag, she tossed it on the floor for them to play in. It took half an hour to put everything away, and then they decided to make Sunday's dessert and get it out of the way, too. One sheet cake wasn't enough to feed everybody, so they made two.

As Jazzi melted butter with a cup of water, chunks of German chocolate baking pieces, and shortening, Ansel came up behind her and wrapped his arms around her. "We agreed to touch more today." He nestled his face in her wavy hair. She tilted her head to expose her neck, and he nibbled from her collarbone to her jaw.

Her body tensed, ready for more, but he pulled away. "Your mix is starting to boil."

Nuts! She stirred it faster, then turned off the heat.

"I can't concentrate when you're making me all hot and bothered." She motioned for him to start mixing the flour and sugar together in another bowl. When it was ready, she poured the chocolate mix over it. Then she combined the rest of the ingredients and added those, too. She sprayed a pan, and Ansel poured the mix into it. They slid it into the oven, then started the same recipe over again. Jazzi wasn't sure if it would work if she doubled it.

While the cakes baked, they each made a batch of coconut pecan frosting. Ansel shook his head. "The hardest part of making things ahead is not eating them until everyone gets here."

She was tempted, too—by the cakes and Ansel—but she wanted to have a relaxing day tomorrow, so she moved on to making the filling for the chicken potpies. Instead of rolling pie crusts for the top, she decided to make drop cheddar biscuits. She'd whip those up tomorrow, along with a big tossed salad.

Every time she or Ansel passed each other, they reached out to touch or hug. When the cooking was done and the kitchen was clean, they stopped for a serious embrace.

"You fit just right in my arms." Ansel gently rubbed his chin on the top of her head.

She tipped her head for a kiss when his stomach rumbled. Laughing, she looked at the kitchen clock. "We cooked for tomorrow instead of fixing supper. Your tacos must be long gone."

"I'm hungry," he admitted. "Let's throw two pork chops on the grill." She added fresh asparagus stalks to grill, too, and soon they were eating supper. George and the cats had already begged for pieces of rotisserie chicken when she made the potpies, so they tossed them only a couple of small slices.

"That's enough for you, bud," Ansel told the pug, and George wandered back to his dog bed. The cats sprawled across the floor and waited to see where she and Ansel would go next. When they finished up and headed to the living room, the cats sprinted ahead of them. Couch time.

Ansel slid his scary movie into the DVR and scooted closer to the back of the couch to make room for her. She curled into him, and the cats took up spots on the back of the sofa. George, as usual, pressed into his spot by Ansel's feet. They were snug, but happy, and when the movie ended and Ansel told George, "Wait here," the pets expected it.

They'd had a perfect day. Not one mention of Darby or murder, no thumbing through suspects.

Chapter 39

Sunday's meal was easy. She and Ansel lounged on the couches, drinking coffee and reading the newspaper until noon. Ansel looked through the classified ads and found a lathe on sale that he wanted to look at. Then they hustled to shower and dress before Ansel started the tossed salad. All Jazzi had to do was make the cheddar drop biscuits, plop them on top of the chicken potpie filling, and slide them in the oven.

Jerod and Franny arrived with their kids ten minutes early, but Jazzi had put out chips and dips to munch on before the meal started. Franny added her fresh vegetable platter to the table. When Jazzi's mom and dad arrived, she told them about her new endeavor of making furniture. Gran and Samantha came to listen, and Jazzi fetched Gran a glass of red wine. Samantha opted for water. Jerod's parents, Eli and Eleanore, soon joined them, and as usual, Olivia arrived last with Thane and Walker.

The mood was relaxed until Cyn asked Walker, "How's everything going?"

"My mom's a mess." He nodded a thanks to Thane for bringing him a bottle of beer. "Gaff questioned her and Gene when they drove up to see me. Gene never told her that he'd come to River Bluffs to confront my dad and tell him to quit harassing her."

Cynthia, Jazzi's mom, looked shocked. "When was that?"

"The night Dad died. Gene waited to drive here until Mom was asleep, and then he waited as long as he could to have it out with Dad, but he never saw him. Dad was probably dead by then."

"Had things gotten that bad between your mom and dad?"

Walker nodded. "Dad called and harassed her a few times a week until Gene blocked his calls on his and her cells, even their home phone. Then Dad drove to Ohio to harangue her."

Doogie wrapped a protective arm around Cyn's waist. "I'd reach my limit with that, too, if I were Gene."

But Cyn shook her head, an obstinate look on her face. "I know what it feels like to be lied to. It ruins your trust in the other person. Gene didn't level with your mom. I'm sure your mom doesn't think he killed Darby, but that little seed of doubt might be buried somewhere."

Doogie disagreed. "He came secretly so he wouldn't upset her. So why would he confess about coming at all? He'd know she'd worry about that more. Besides, how would he know Darby was buried under gravel in a dump truck? In his mind, it was a wasted trip. Darby never showed up."

"That's what he *says*." Jerod drained his beer and shrugged. "Would you admit it if you lost your temper and accidentally killed someone?"

Walker glared. "Gene wouldn't pick up a shovel and hit someone with it."

"I don't think he did," Jerod said. "But who'd be stupid enough to own up to it if no one could prove it? Let's face it, Gene wouldn't have confessed to coming in the first place if Gaff hadn't asked him about his black SUV and Andy hadn't seen it."

Thane looked rattled. "He did what Andy did. He thought if he just kept quiet, no one would ever know."

Cyn stabbed a finger at the men, determined to make her point. "When Gaff told Walker's mom that Darby was dead, Gene should have told Rose everything then and there."

Gran interrupted. "Darby should have never taken that money."

They all turned to her, surprised.

Walker gave her a sharp look. "What money?"

"He should have given it back to Whiskers." Gran's attention slid to the small plate Jerod was holding. "Those look good." Dropping the conversation, she went to the island for some chips and dip. These days, Gran could change topics in mid-paragraph. Sometimes, Jazzi couldn't keep up with her. And when she reverted to the past and thought Jazzi was her dead sister, Sarah, Jazzi just went with the flow.

But Gran's comments made Jazzi remember what the Shots and Spirits bartender had told them. "Darby and Whiskers were arguing about money lately. That's why they got in a fistfight at the grocery store."

Walker ran a hand through his thick chestnut hair. "How much money was involved? Do you know?"

"No, but I'm going with Gaff to talk to Whiskers on Tuesday."

"Will you tell me what you find out? Dad had a note in the ledger book that he borrowed three thousand dollars and needed to repay it, but he didn't write down who he borrowed it from."

Gunther ran past the kitchen island, and Jerod scooped him up. "No running in the house." Then he said to Walker, "I'd guess it was Whiskers."

Walker handed Thane his empty bottle when he started to reach for it. "At least, that's something I can fix. I can pay back the money. And I can gut Dad's house and completely redo it so that it feels fresh and new. Staying in the same, old surroundings didn't help Mom. It brought back too many unhappy memories. Between that and learning about Gene sneaking here while she slept, this wasn't the best trip for her."

Thane nodded. "I can help you with renovations. I learned a lot when I worked with these guys."

Walker turned to him, grateful. "I was thinking that when business crawls to a stop, that would be a good time for me to tackle the house."

"Let us know, and we'll pitch in," Thane told him.

"We?" Jazzi frowned, but Ansel and Jerod nodded.

Jerod grinned at her. "Come on, cuz. We can help with the big stuff, then Thane and Walker can do the rest."

She sighed. She supposed she was all right with that, but she was tired of working Saturdays, and Walker would be starting up in early December. The holidays always got busy. She'd be scrambling to put up Christmas decorations and baking cookies.

Cyn tried to change to a happier topic. "Are you excited about seeing your sister at the wedding, Ansel?"

He scowled. "Did Jazzi tell you that my whole family's coming?"

With a sympathetic groan, Cyn reached for the bottle of red wine and refilled her glass. "Even the big brother who cheated you out of your inheritance?"

"My sister and her husband, my brother Radley, my oldest brother, and my parents who were perfectly happy to go along with his plans."

"Good lord. You're still going to have a wonderful day, aren't you?" Cyn looked worried.

Jazzi went to put an arm around her. Doogie held one side of her, and she held the other. "We're not going to let anyone spoil our celebration. Since Adda pressured Ansel into inviting them, he warned her that she's the one who's going to have to keep them happy. He doesn't want anything to do with them."

"Then why invite them?" Jerod asked. Jazzi rolled her eyes at him, but her cousin rarely deviated from the direct approach. Tact wasn't one of his strengths.

Ansel was used to him, though. "I want Adda and my brother Radley to feel welcome. Dad and Bain would give Radley so much grief that he couldn't come without them."

"Oh my." Cyn wasn't sure what to make of that, but she'd had her share of family turmoil when she was first married. Her sister Lynda had provided plenty of angst for all of them.

Doogie rubbed his hands together and gave a meaningful glance at the long farm table. "Maybe we should eat."

Thank heavens! It was time to concentrate on food. "Grab a plate while I put the food on the island. Then we can dish up."

Once everyone was settled at the table, the mood cheered up again. George went person to person to beg for scraps, and the cats ditched the party to claim their spots on the living room sofas.

Gran took a bite of the potpie pie and grinned. "You were always the best cook in the family, Sarah."

She reverted to the past when the atmosphere became tense. No matter. Jazzi smiled at her. "Thanks, Gran. I learned from the best. You let me tag along in your kitchen."

"You're going to make Cal a wonderful wife." Cal had been engaged to Jazzi's Aunt Lynda. Poor Gran had them all mixed up today.

The conversation turned back to the upcoming wedding, and Walker raised his beer bottle in a toast to them. "To happy ever after! Thanks for inviting me. Earl and Bea announced to the whole crew that they're getting married soon. They'll be good for each other."

Jazzi raised her wineglass. "Here's to Earl and Bea!"

They drank another round, and Walker looked thoughtful. "It's made me realize I'm not getting any younger. Thane's got someone now, and I'm a few months older than he is. Mom's happily married. She doesn't need me anymore. I'd like to find someone special."

"Use a dating website," Eli said. "That's the modern way, isn't it?" Jerod's dad loved to spend time on his tablet.

Walker grinned. "I've tried, and I met some really unique girls that way. For now, I want to go the old-fashioned route."

"Bars?" Jerod asked.

Franny kicked him under the table, and he flinched. "That hurt." She ignored him.

"You could join a club," Olivia suggested.

Walker took all of their comments in stride. "First, I have to get everything settled about Dad's death." None of them used the word *murder.* "Once that's behind me, I need to get out and about more."

"When you're ready, you'll find the right girl," Ansel told him. "You have looks and personality. Most girls won't turn you away."

If he'd taken his own advice, he wouldn't have ended up with Emily—she of the controlling personality, but Jazzi let that pass. Instead she said, "I hope you guys saved room for dessert."

Chairs scraped, and people lined up for German chocolate sheet cake. Jazzi considered the meal, paired with red wine, a success. And tomorrow she was going shopping with her mom and Olivia. At first, she'd dreaded that excursion, but now she looked forward to it. She'd buy something so pretty, it would take Ansel's breath away, and he wouldn't even think about his family invading their ceremony.

Chapter 40

On Monday, Jazzi helped Ansel load the cooler full of sandwiches and chips, along with the coffee thermoses, into his van. George whined, upset, when she didn't climb in with them. She waved as Ansel backed out of the drive, then once they were on their way, she went upstairs to finish getting ready—applying her makeup with care and slipping on a dress that buttoned from its scooped neckline to its mid-calf hem. She wore heels, even though she'd be on her feet all day, because Olivia had warned her to wear the kind of shoes she'd wear to her wedding. That way, she'd know if the dress she chose was the right length.

Ready, she gave Inky and Marmalade one last session of petting before walking out the door. Glancing at the trees at the back of their property, behind the pond, she noticed that half of them were leafless. By their wedding, all of them would be bare. As she watched, two deer came out of the woods to eat grass. She knew many farmers considered them pests, but she stood for a moment, enjoying their beauty. A gust of wind whipped her loose hair into her face, and she shook herself. Time to shop.

She drove to Olivia's house, where Cyn was probably already waiting for her. Both women walked out of her sister's ranch-style house when she pulled in the drive and idled the truck. Olivia wore skintight, lipstick-red pants with a black sweater, tugged in at the waistline with a red belt. Red stilettos completed the look. Her mom wore a long cobalt-blue skirt with a white, long-sleeved top. Her heels were more modest.

Olivia motioned for Jazzi to park. "There's no way I'm crawling in and out of your pickup," she called. "I'll drive."

If Jazzi were Catholic, she'd have made the sign of the cross. Her sister drove fast or faster. But they'd all survived this long, so she slid onto Olivia's back seat and braced herself.

Mom's face was wreathed with smiles. "We finally have you for a whole day of shopping. That hasn't happened since I took you shopping for school clothes at the end of every August."

Jazzi laughed, remembering. She and Olivia had always looked forward to their annual outing. They were told to find an appropriate outfit for each day of the week, plus two pairs of jeans for after school and weekends. They tried on khakis and leggings, skirts that touched the floor when they knelt—too short wasn't allowed—and a variety of tops. They also chose two Sunday dresses for church. When they were young, their mother was a stickler about their Sabbath wear, but once they reached their teens, their dress code loosened up a bit.

"I don't know which I looked forward to more—the clothes or picking a new book bag and school supplies." Jazzi said.

Olivia snorted. "You always got so excited about new markers. You were good at drawing back then. Do you still ever do it?"

"No. Now I draw up house plans. Not the same thing."

"But that artistic side of you is what makes your houses turn out so pretty," Cyn said.

Olivia drove them to a wedding shop on the north side of town. "Do you still have your wedding dress, Mom?" They'd looked in Mom's photo albums, and she looked lovely in a long taffeta dress with a train.

"No, I kept it for years until I realized that after having children, I'd never fit in it again."

Jazzi stared at her, surprised. "But you're thin."

"Things shift," Cyn said. "I'm close to the same weight, but that weight's not in the same places."

With a shrug, Jazzi kicked that worry to the curb. "You still look good."

"Well, thank you, but I donated the dress to the Salvation Army. I hope some girl felt like a princess, like I did, when she got married in it."

Olivia parked, and on the walk inside, she told Jazzi, "That's how we want you to feel. Like a princess. So don't just buy a dress to get this over with. Take your time and find the right one."

"I want to make Ansel's jaw drop." There, she'd said it.

Olivia giggled. "That won't be hard. That man thinks you're everything and more."

"That's how a man should feel about his wife," Cyn told them. "Your dad still thinks I'm the prettiest woman in every room. He's delusional, but I love him for it."

They were laughing when they stepped through the shop's door. The clerk let them look around a bit before she offered to help them.

Jazzi ruled out anything full-length. The dresses were so beautiful, they took her breath away, but they weren't what she wanted. "We're getting married in our home. I want a dress that's mid-calf, like the one I have on."

The clerk led them to one row of dresses after another. Jazzi liked one that flared at the waist, but the beadwork felt a little fussy to her. Another fluffed with a chiffon skirt, but it felt too girly. Finally, she saw an ivory-colored dress with a boat collar and a fitted top that flowed into soft folds that stopped just below her knees. She reached out to touch the soft fabric.

Her mom looked at her face and smiled. "That's the one. Try it on."

It must be destiny, because it was a perfect fit. When she stepped out of the dressing room, she could hear Olivia and Cyn inhale quick breaths. That was the effect she wanted from Ansel. With a quick nod, she said, "I'll take it."

Next came choosing a veil. She went with something simple—a single layer with a beaded hem. She bought a garter, too. Then Olivia drove to a shoe store, and to everyone's surprise, including hers, Jazzi chose a pair of daring red high heels.

Olivia rushed to hug her. "Who knew my sister had a funky side?"

The next stop caught Jazzi by surprise. "I know you two live together, but this is your wedding. You have to buy something extra sexy." And Victoria's Secret had an abundance of that. She bought scanty lace underwear and a nightgown to remember. She bought the robe, too, not that either of them hid much.

While Olivia waited for her to make her pick, she shopped, too. Armed with a push-up bra and matching thong, she gave an evil smile. "Thane's going to have a good night tonight."

Jazzi secretly believed that was never in question, but she kept her opinion to herself.

They stashed all of their purchases in the car's trunk and headed south to have lunch on the Deck at the Old Gas House. It was a brisk day, but not chilly, and since they were in long sleeves, it felt good to sit outdoors. Two kayaks glided past them on the river while the waiter took their order. All three of them chose the beef tenderloin main-dish salad and a glass of wine.

Mom took a sip of her Chablis before asking, "Do you have everything under control for the big day?"

BODY IN THE GRAVEL

Jazzi nodded. "We ordered a cake. We decided on the menu, and none of it's too time-consuming." When Cyn looked disappointed, she hurried to add, "Ansel's excited about helping me get everything ready. We're making beef tenderloins and pork tenderloins with a cherry glaze. Both easy. Lots of kinds of bruschetta."

"Like the ones you make with the pureed beans?" Olivia asked.

"We were thinking of fancier this time—a blueberry lemon ricotta topping, a Greek topping, and smoked salmon."

"Mmm, what else?" Cyn asked.

"Shrimp and pineapple flatbreads, crab and bacon endive boats, small crab cakes..." Jazzi paused. "More, but I'd have to look at my list."

Mom rubbed her hands together. "I'm not eating a thing all day until your party."

"What about decorations?" Olivia glanced at the candles on the table. "Are you okay with those?"

"I ordered lots of flowers and votive candles. I think we're in good shape."

The waiter came with their food, and they paused until he left. Then Olivia asked, "How bummed out is Ansel going to be about having his parents and Bain there?"

"It rankles. They knew he didn't want them. I wouldn't have the nerve to go someplace I knew I wasn't welcome, but Bain seems to think he should get what he wants."

"Was he always the chosen one?" Cyn asked.

"It sounds like it. He and his dad rule the house. Mostly, he inherited his dad's aggressive personality. Ansel told me he's an in-your-face kind of guy. That, and no one ever stands up to him." Jazzi stabbed some beef and lettuce with her fork. "If you ask me, I think he's jealous of Ansel. Bain might have inherited the farm, but Ansel inherited the looks and brains. Some rich girl threw herself at him when he went home to help on the farm when Bain broke his leg and his dad had knee surgery."

Mom drizzled more French dressing on her salad. "Sounds to me like Ansel got lucky when they gave him the boot. If not for that, he might have been stuck with them for life."

Olivia laughed. "I wish I knew some girl I disliked enough to introduce to Bain."

"What about Radley?" Cyn asked.

"He sounds pretty nice. The rich girl was after him for a while, but he didn't want anything to do with her. That irritated Bain. He thought if Radley hooked up with her, they could plug into some of her money."

Mom set down her wineglass harder than usual. "You're making Bain sound like a completely miserable human being."

Jazzi shrugged. "Guess we'll find out soon enough." She had no intention of letting Bain throw his weight around in her house. She'd pay to put him up in a cheap motel if she had to, and if he irritated Jerod enough, her cousin would keep needling him until he'd be happy to go.

The discussion turned to the flowers she'd ordered.

"Why pink roses instead of red?" Olivia fussed.

"Because they're my favorites. You can have red at your wedding."

By the time they finished their meal, they were giggling and silly, ready to drive to get their manicures and pedicures. Jazzi usually got restless when she had to sit still so long, but Cyn and Olivia kept her talking through the whole ordeal, so she had a good time.

She ended her day before Ansel did and beat him home. He and Jerod were painting window trim on all of the higher windows today. The cats attacked her at the door, and she faithfully petted them before carrying all the boxes upstairs and hiding them in the guest closet. She didn't think Ansel would try to peek at her dress, but she wasn't taking any chances.

When he finally dragged himself in the back door close to six, she had two big steaks ready to throw on the grill. He set George on the floor and grinned. "Your nails look pretty."

It was just like him to notice her manicure before spying the steak. "Thanks, I think this shade of pink will match my wedding bouquet."

"Did you find a dress?"

She smiled. "It makes me feel like a princess. How was your day?"

"We missed you. It took longer to paint everything ourselves."

She laughed. "I thought you might come home starving. I made potato salad and green beans, too."

"Beautiful and kind. That's why George and I love you."

They each shared the events of their day while they cooked supper and ate. When they finished and George padded to his dog bed to lie down, Jazzi shooed Ansel away. "There's not much to clean up. Go take a shower and hit the couch. I'll be there soon."

He'd usually argue, but not tonight. The poor man was drooping. On his way up the steps, he called, "When does Gaff come for you tomorrow night?"

"Four-thirty. We're going to Shots and Spirits to talk to Whiskers and Haze. We won't spend long with Whiskers. He's not the chatty type."

"We'll have a good start on the inside projects by then. We got lucky getting everything done outdoors. It's supposed to rain tonight and keep raining for the rest of the week."

It felt good to have some of the pressure off. They wouldn't be in such a rush from now on. While Ansel showered and changed into his pajamas, Jazzi looked out the kitchen window while she rinsed their dirty dishes and loaded them into the dishwasher. She saw the first raindrops splatter on the cement patio, watched the sky grow darker, and dried her hands just when the downpour started.

She and Ansel met at their couches and settled in to relax. The cats jumped up to snuggle with her, and George curled at Ansel's feet. The perfect way to spend a rainy night. She thought about her day and smiled. Who knew shopping could be so much fun? She might have to try it again with her mom and Olivia. It was too bad Ansel's sister didn't live in town. They could take her with them. Jazzi would have to keep that in mind. Maybe later in the year, they could invite Adda and her husband to stay with them again, as long as they came alone. No parents or Bain. She dreaded seeing them at her wedding. If they so much as said one nasty thing to Ansel, she'd sprinkle cayenne on everything she served them.

Chapter 41

On Tuesday, Jazzi was back in her worn jeans and work boots. When she and Ansel pulled into the fixer-upper's driveway, they left George in the van for a minute, took the big umbrella, and huddled under it to appreciate how the outside of the house had turned out. They'd boosted its curb appeal so high, people slowed down when they drove by to get a better look at it.

"I didn't think we could make it look this good," Ansel told her. He wrapped an arm around her waist and gave her a squeeze. "You've got a good eye—among other things."

She grinned up at him. "It came out better than I expected. It's always nice when that happens."

Feeling satisfied with themselves, they returned to the van to lug things into the house and start work. Rain pummeled the ground outside and bounced off the metal porch roofs. Ansel and Jerod had sawed through the drywall to create a larger opening between the dining room and living room. Jazzi gave it a kick to knock the unwanted pieces out of the way.

"Buyers are going to like this open feel," Jerod said, bending to pick up the fallen chunks and toss them in a trash bag.

"If the owner buys a table with enough leaves, he could seat as many people in here as we do at our house." Ansel grabbed a broom to sweep the dust and dirt into a pile.

"It would be more crowded." Jazzi bent with a dustpan to scoop up debris.

"Who wants to cook for that many people besides you two masochists?" Jerod asked.

"I *like* cooking," Jazzi said, defending herself.

Jerod threw the last of the broken drywall into the bag. "Besides, how many people design their houses to have the entertaining space you two have? You should have gone into catering instead of house flipping."

"Ugh." Jazzi wrinkled her nose, disgusted. "Then it wouldn't be fun. It would be work."

While the guys put the finishing touches on the new, bigger arch, Jazzi stepped inside the first floor's half bath. She grabbed the medicine cabinet over the sink and ripped it from the wall. It joined the drywall in the heavy trash bag. They'd already turned off the water, so she unhooked the sink and carried it outside. She left it on the back porch. There was no way she was dashing to the dumpster. The half bath wasn't a big space, but it served the purpose. There were two more bathrooms on the second floor and another on the third. They'd be a good selling point when they listed the place.

Ansel and Jerod carried out the old toilet, and Jazzi started prying up the chipped ceramic floor tiles. When the downstairs was gutted and cleaned, she started sanding the floors while the guys moved to the second floor. The wood in the living and dining rooms could be refinished, but the kitchen and bathroom floors were too rough. They decided not to try to match the new wood to the old and to go with tiles instead.

By the time Gaff came for her, she'd finished sanding and joined Jerod and Ansel to install blue kitchen tiles with a white pattern. They were going with white kitchen cupboards, butcher-block counter-tops, and blue tiles for a backsplash.

Gaff came to peek at their work. "Ann's never allowed in one of your fixer-uppers. She'll want to redo most of our house. I already have a long enough honey-do list."

"Getting any closer to finding a killer?" Jerod asked.

"Yeah, just not for this case." When Jerod snarled, Gaff chuckled. "Ready?" he asked Jazzi.

She grabbed her raincoat and hurried to his car with him. Once inside, she asked, "How seriously are you taking Walker's dad as a suspect?"

"I hate to say it, but he's at the top of my list. He was there. He was tired of dealing with Darby. And he was serious about keeping him away from Rose."

After the Sunday meal, listening to Jerod make those same points, Jazzi had reluctantly put Gene at the top of her list, too.

Gaff pulled from the curb and smiled. "But that could change today. Maybe Whiskers and Haze will point us in a new direction."

They hadn't before, but stranger things had happened.

Driving to the bar, they had to take a different route than usual. One of the city's underpasses was flooded. Gaff blasted cool air on the windshield to keep it from fogging over as the car's wipers flashed back and forth. The rain pounded the car so loudly, Jazzi felt like she was trapped inside a drum with the slap, slap, slap of the wipers as a steady rhythm.

When they pulled to the curb at the side of the building, not that many cars lined the street. People were hibernating tonight to stay dry. Before heading to the bar, they hurried down the sidewalk to Whiskers's house. A tiny roof covered the front stoop, so their pant legs were sticking to them by the time Whiskers opened the door. He glanced at them and grimaced but motioned them inside.

Two lamps glowed in the living room, unable to compete with the gray of the day. The foyer loomed with gloom and shadows. Gaff closed his umbrella and left it near the front door, and Jazzi took off her raincoat. There was no place to hang it. She hated to drip water on Whiskers's floor, so she said, "What do you want me to do with this?"

Whiskers draped it on the bottom post of the stair railing, letting a puddle form beneath it. Then they followed him farther into the house. Newspapers were scattered on the floor in front of the couch, weighted down by an empty coffee cup. He stepped over them to flop down, and they took the two uncomfortable wooden chairs across from him. Jazzi's chair wiggled enough, she worried that it might come apart.

Whiskers tugged on his beard, studying them. "What do you wanna know now?"

Gaff opened his notepad and rested it on his knee. "We've heard that Darby owed you money, and the two of you were arguing about it. Is that true?"

"Who told you that? Someone at the bar? Well, I guess it was no secret, and it didn't shame Darby none."

"How much did you loan him?"

"Three thousand, the pesky crook. I been putting money aside to buy a motorcycle so I can ride with Haze."

"And he knew that?"

"We told each other most everything."

"Did he tell you about driving to Ohio to harass his ex-wife?"

"Darn idiot. Yeah, he told me. I said all he'd do is cause trouble, but once Darby got something in his head, it was near impossible to change his mind. Why would Rose take him back after she got herself a good man?"

Gaff returned to the question of money. "Why did you give Darby a loan?"

"My old friend needed to get one of his trucks fixed but couldn't come up with the cash. If the truck didn't run, he couldn't make money. Swore he'd pay me back at the end of the week. It hadn't happened by the day he died. Got the feeling it wasn't going to, that he never intended to make it happen. He said he was cutting it thin with his business, but that's not my problem, is it? Wasn't too happy about it."

"How mad did you get?"

"Mad enough to stick a knife in all four tires of that truck."

"What if Darby had caught you at that?"

Darby blew out a puff of air. "What if he did? There'd be fisticuffs. I could still take that old coot."

"Is that what it came to in the end?" Gaff asked.

"Naw, when I told him I wasn't drinking with him no more till I got my money back, he promised he'd get it to me by the end of the month. Darby didn't like drinkin' alone."

"Do you know if Darby owed anyone else any money?" Gaff asked.

"Who'd be stupid enough to hand him cash but me? We been friends so long, I thought he'd come through for sure."

Jazzi frowned, and Whiskers focused on her. "What's botherin' ya, little lady?"

She wasn't little, but she let that pass. She wondered if she should tell Whiskers about the stash Darby hid in a drawer. Gaff hadn't brought it up. Was there a reason? She glanced his way, and he nodded. "We learned that Darby had some secret savings. I can't understand why he wouldn't pay you back."

Whiskers sat up straighter on the couch. "Secret savings? How much?"

"Enough to pay you back and more."

"Blast that man to tarnation and back! Did he make a note that he owed me money? Will Walker pay his debts?"

Jazzi nodded. "I saw Walker yesterday. He saw the note in his dad's ledger, just didn't know who to pay."

Whiskers's shoulders relaxed. "That Walker's a good boy. His mama raised him right. Good thing he didn't get none of Darby's spit and grit."

"I'll tell Walker I talked to you. He'll probably give you a call."

"Is that boy and Thane still tight? They used to be joined at the hip whenever Darby let Walker have a little free time."

Jazzi smiled. "They're friends again. You can tell they go way back with each other."

"Like me and his old man." Whiskers shook his head. "If I'd been smart, I'd have cut Darby loose after Rose left him, but I thought he was just goin' through a rough patch, that eventually he'd settle down and get his act together."

"Maybe he would have if he'd lived a little longer," Gaff said.

Whiskers raised his eyebrows, looking doubtful. "Don't think he'd have held onto his business much longer. Don't know if that would have made him worse or better. With Darby, I'd bet on worse."

Gaff pushed to his feet. "Is Haze working tonight?"

"She ain't here, is she? She won't make diddle for tips tonight. This rain'll keep people away."

Gaff tipped his head. "Thanks for your time. We'll head to the bar to talk to her next."

"Knock yourself out." Whiskers fluffed the couch pillow and stretched out. "Tell her I'll be in later for supper. Might take a nap first."

With a nod, Gaff fetched his umbrella, and Jazzi slipped on her raincoat. It felt clammy, but it would keep her dry. When they opened the door to let themselves out, the rain hadn't let up. They sloshed on wet sidewalks to the bar.

Chapter 42

When they walked into the bar, the air-conditioning hit them. Jazzi shivered. The cold air on top of the cold rain was too much. She took off her dripping raincoat and hung it on a hook near the door. Newspapers lined the floor to soak up the water.

Jazzi rubbed her arms as she took a seat next to Gaff. When the bartender asked for her order, she said, "Coffee. With sugar." She usually didn't take sugar, but it sounded good tonight.

"I made a fresh pot," he told her. "You're in luck."

"I'll take a cup, too," Gaff called after him. He nabbed a second mug as well. When he came back and pushed their drinks across the bar, he grinned.

"The sky opened up tonight. The bar's going to be pretty dead."

"Doesn't seem to bother you," Gaff said. "You don't mind a slow night?"

The man shrugged. "Just as soon be here as sitting alone in my apartment. It's nice to have a low-key night once in a while. No rush."

"Is Haze working?" Gaff had scanned the room. So had Jazzi. She was nowhere in sight.

"She's hanging out in the kitchen, pestering Leroy, my cook. I'll get her for you." He disappeared behind a door marked PRIVATE, and soon Haze wandered out and leaned across the bar to talk to them.

She nodded toward the bartender. "Clay said you two had come in last Friday, looking for me."

So that was the owner's name. "Did you have a nice weekend?" Jazzi asked her. "Clay said you and Whiskers rented a place at a lake."

She gave a brief smile. "Took the boat out every morning and caught a few fish. Hiked a couple of times, but mostly, just relaxed. I needed a vacation. It's been a while. Moving's expensive. Had to work extra hours to get back on my feet."

Gaff took out his notepad, a sign the small talk was over. "Did you know that Darby owed Whiskers money?"

"I heard them arguing about it. All Whiskers would ever say was that Darby was a rotten crook, and a man should be able to trust his friend after all the years they'd known each other."

Gaff took a sip of his coffee as he wrote. "He never told you how much?"

"I got the feeling it was an expensive repair, an engine or transmission blew, something serious."

Gaff rubbed his chin. It was covered with stubble this time of day. "Did Whiskers tell you that he slashed the tires on Darby's truck?"

She frowned. "He failed to mention that. I don't like it when men play tit for tat. That was a cheap trick. He knows I wouldn't approve."

"And Darby never brought it up?"

"Darby wouldn't, would he? He'd have to admit he borrowed money and wasn't paying it back." She thought for a minute. "After Whiskers's little trick, though, I'd call it even. He'd never see a cent of what I owed him."

Jazzi drained her coffee cup, and Clay took it to get a refill, adding sugar again. She agreed with Haze. Buying four new truck tires couldn't be cheap. If Whiskers wanted payback so bad, he'd canceled any debt.

Gaff picked up the thread again. "Did the two men get along better after the tire incident?"

"No." Haze drifted to the coffeepot, too, to pour herself a mug. Only a few tables held customers, and they were nursing their beers, enjoying their burgers. They wouldn't need her for a minute. She went on. "I could have told Whiskers that payback wouldn't make him as happy as pressuring Darby for the cash. Whiskers takes money seriously. He lets himself spend a certain amount on beer and meals each week, and the rest goes into savings and never comes out."

Jazzi grinned. "He told us he was saving for a bike like yours. He must really have a hankering for one."

"We've talked about taking a couple weeks off and riding our Harleys out west, camping wherever we could."

"That's your idea of fun?" Jazzi had no desire to sleep in a tent. The ground wasn't even close to soft enough, even with an air mattress.

"It's not for everyone," Haze admitted, "but we'd like it. I can make a mean meal in a cast-iron Dutch oven over a campfire."

Jazzi would take her word for that. The closest to cooking outdoors she ever wanted to experience was a gas grill in the backyard.

Haze looked at her expression and shook her head. "I thought that you, gutting houses and being a pro with hammers, would be a natural at guy things like camping."

"Not gonna happen. To me, roughing it is when you rent a place with no dishwasher."

Haze threw back her head and laughed. "To each his own, but Whiskers was socking a fair share of money away to buy a Harley as big as mine."

Gaff tried to steer the conversation back to the loan. "Would Whiskers and Darby have made up eventually?"

"Probably, but it would have taken a while. Whiskers felt betrayed. That's a hard pill to swallow."

"Anything else that might have come between them?" Gaff asked.

"Me? That had happened for a minute, but they were working past that."

Gaff absently rapped his pen on the bar a few times, thinking. "Someone said that Darby was flirting with a woman who came in here with a guy. How did the guy take that?"

"Didn't seem to mind. I got the feeling he was more than ready to get rid of her and thought Darby might be his ticket to move on."

That put an end to that lead.

A man at the table by the door raised his beer bottle and motioned for Haze. She turned to Gaff. "Anything else?"

"No, I can't think of anything for now. Thanks for your time."

She grew serious. "A man got killed. He deserves some justice. Come again if you have more questions."

Nice. People didn't always think of Gaff that way, but that was exactly what he was doing—trying to bring justice to a murder victim.

As they ran to the car and Gaff drove her home, he said, "What do you think?"

"Something doesn't add up. If Darby had a hundred and fifty thousand dollars wadded up in his desk drawer, why didn't he pay Whiskers back? Why not fix the truck himself?"

"Maybe he'd vowed never to touch that money," Gaff said. "Or maybe since he knew how Whiskers felt about money, he wanted to hurt him where it counted. Maybe he was getting even for Whiskers winning Haze."

"Darby was that warped." She could see him using twisted logic like that.

Gaff rubbed his eyes in a tired gesture. "Whatever the reason, Whiskers is as high on my suspect list as Walker's dad."

Jazzi played with that idea for a while. "But would Walker's dad have taken Darby's keys and put the shovel he used to kill Darby in Colin's locker? Whiskers knew the cement company as well as the workers. He'd been there plenty of times."

"I don't see that the shovel rules Gene out." The traffic light turned red, and Gaff stopped for it. There were hardly any cars on the road tonight. The rain and gloom ate headlight beams, making it hard to see lanes and street signs. "Whoever put it there might have just wanted to blame someone, anyone, for the crime. He might not have been trying to pin it on Colin."

Jazzi sighed. "The more we learn, the more confused I'm getting."

"That's part of it," Gaff told her. "You just gather information until something clicks into place. We haven't found that missing piece yet."

She was beginning to wonder if they were going to. There were plenty of unsolved crimes, she knew. She hoped this wouldn't be one of them.

When Gaff pulled into her drive, she zipped to the door and quickly stepped inside. Lights blazed, and warmth enveloped her. Home. Maybe here, surrounded by good vibes, she could sort things out. Or not.

Chapter 43

The next morning, Gaff called Jazzi at home before she and Ansel left for Southwood Park. "We have another body."

"Whose?" Jazzi stopped petting Inky in mid-stroke, and the cat turned to stare at her.

"Colin. A guy at his apartment complex was walking to his car and saw him slumped over his pickup's steering wheel."

A chill swept through her body. Colin hadn't hit forty yet, too young to die, "What happened to him?" A heart attack? Aneurysm? No, Gaff was a homicide detective. He didn't get involved unless foul play was suspected.

"Looks like he rolled down his window to talk to someone, and whoever it was shot him in the head."

Jazzi couldn't catch her breath. She gripped the edge of the island's counter, and Ansel reached out to steady her. "Wouldn't someone have heard the gunshot?"

"The apartments are close to the entrance ramp of the interstate. The guy who found him said they hear cars and trucks backfire all the time. They don't pay attention anymore."

"And no one saw anything?"

"It was pouring down rain last night. People stayed in."

"Where was Colin going? Does anyone know?"

"No one we've talked to. The lady who lives across the hall from him was coming in when he was going out, and she teased him that only ducks loved this weather. He told her he'd stay home if he could, but he had some business he had to take care of."

"Was that after work hours?"

"A little after five. She was just getting home from her job. Colin told her he'd gotten off work early since they couldn't pour cement in the middle of a storm."

Jazzi felt a little sick. "We were sitting in the bar, talking to Haze, when he got shot."

"Looks like it."

"What are you going to do now?"

"Make another round of visits. Can the guys spare you today?"

"Where do you want to pick me up?"

"At the house in Southwood Park, if that's okay. It's closer to the station and Darby's cement company."

"Call me when you're on your way, and I'll be ready."

"Will do."

Jazzi clicked off her phone and stared at Ansel. "Someone killed Colin."

He scooted his stool closer to hers and wrapped his arm around her. "Are you going to be okay?"

"I got to know him a little. I liked him."

The cats realized she was upset and jumped on the island to rub against her. This time, Ansel didn't shoo them off. "Want some more coffee?" he asked.

She nodded. "I want some chocolate, too."

He came back with hot coffee and a bag of semi-sweet chocolate chips. "It's the best I can do." They didn't keep candy in the house and rarely had snacks in their cupboards.

She popped some chips in her mouth and let them melt on her tongue, then washed them down with coffee. She glanced at the clock. "We're going to be late."

"I'll call Jerod and let him know. Take your time. He'll understand."

But she got restless sitting there, noodling over one bad scenario after another. She drained her cup and said, "Let's go."

He pulled the van as close to the back door as he could get so that they didn't drown loading the cooler and thermoses into it. He bent his body over George to keep him as dry as possible when he carried him to the back seat. On the drive across town, he said, "If you want to come home after you're done with Gaff, just have him drop you off here. You can watch a movie or something to take your mind off things."

She was one lucky girl. Ansel always tried to take care of her. "I'll probably come back and work some more. I'm better when I'm busy."

He nodded. "I'm down with whatever helps."

He turned on the CD player, and they listened to music as he drove. When they turned into the new driveway at the fixer-upper, he parked behind Jerod's pickup. Pulling up the hood of her raincoat, Jazzi glowered at the sheets of rain. Maybe they should build porticoes on old houses whose garages sat back from the street. That way, people wouldn't have to brave the elements when they carried groceries or supplies inside.

"It was a hot, miserable summer, and now the skies are dumping gallons of water on us. I hope Mother Nature's in a better mood by winter." Ansel didn't grumble about weather very often, but everyone was getting tired of this year's extremes.

She took off her raincoat and left it on a plastic lawn chair on the porch before lugging the cooler into the kitchen. When they walked into the house, they told Jerod what had happened to Colin. Jerod stopped mixing the mortar for the floor and studied her. "You okay?"

The same thing Ansel had asked. She nodded. "I liked him, though."

She knelt to help him lay tile. Ansel would only get in their way, so he grabbed sandpaper and started work on the open staircase in the center of the house, close enough to join in on their conversation.

Jerod scraped mortar across the floorboards. "Does Gaff have any idea why someone shot Colin?"

Jazzi pressed a tile in place and reached for the next one. "It's too soon, but it's going to make it easy to rule out Walker's dad if he was in Ohio yesterday for supper."

Jerod brightened. "I hadn't thought of that."

When Gaff came to fetch her, Jerod asked him about it. "Does Gene have an alibi for last night? If he was in Dayton, he's off the hook now, right?"

"*If* he was in Dayton, which he wasn't. Supposedly, he was on his way home from a business trip."

Darn. That made Jazzi think. She had no idea what Gene did for a living. "What kind of business meeting?"

"He sells machines and parts for a big company. Has to travel out of state sometimes to meet clients."

Ansel came to join them. "Where did his meeting take place?"

"In Illinois. He had to drive right through Indiana on his way home." Gaff shook his head. "He got back to Dayton by nine last night, plenty of time for him to meet Colin in the parking lot on his way."

Oh, crap. His trip moved him higher up the list rather than lower.

"Who knows?" Gaff shrugged his shoulders. "The way this case has been going, it's possible everyone could have been in the parking lot at that time. Walker's gathering the drivers in his office for us to talk to them. It would be nice if one or two of them would have solid alibis."

Jazzi wasn't sure how she felt about that. She'd rather Gene had plenty of company so that he didn't look any worse or better than anyone else. She went to get her raincoat and set off with Gaff.

The rain let up a little before they reached Walker's office. The weatherman had predicted that it would stick around but slow to a steady drizzle for the next few days. It was steady enough that she covered her head with her hood before leaving the car.

Walker, Andy, and Earl sat at the rectangular table, all looking glum. When they took their seats, Walker asked, "Someone shot him?"

Gaff nodded. "The questions are who and why."

Andy spread his hands out. "Colin could irritate people, but nothing like Darby. And they didn't have the same friends. It doesn't make sense."

"Let's start with the simplest thing." Gaff looked at each of them. "Where were you between five and six last night?"

Andy spoke first. "My wife and I were with our son's counselor. She has some new activities she'd like us to try with him."

"And she'll verify that?" Gaff asked.

Andy nodded. Just then, the door opened, and Bea stepped into the room.

"Walker called me and thought I should be here for the meeting, too. He told me about Colin."

"We're checking alibis for between five and six last night," Gaff repeated.

She nodded and looked at Earl.

"We were getting supper ready about that time." Earl winced. "We didn't start until close to six. I had run to the store for some last-minute items. Bea can't vouch for me. I don't have an alibi. She was home, though, talking on the phone with my mom. Mom can verify that."

Jazzi frowned. "Most grocery stores put your time of purchase on your checkout tape. Do you have that?"

"I threw it away, didn't think I needed it."

Gaff poised his pen over his paper. "Give me the name of the store and I'll stop there, see what I can find out."

Earl moved in his seat, looking uncomfortable. "I left the store at five-thirty, and I didn't come straight home. Colin called and told me he could pay me back the fifty bucks I'd loaned him. I drove to his apartment and knocked on his door, but he wasn't home. I decided it wasn't that big of a deal, that he could give me the money later, and left."

Gaff shook his head. "And you weren't going to tell me that?"

"It doesn't look good, does it?"

He flipped a page in his notepad. "What time did you get to his apartment?"

"About five forty-five."

"Do you own a gun?"

Earl swallowed and sent Bea a nervous glance. "A nine-millimeter. I bought it when there was a string of robberies on our side of town. I don't have anything worth stealing, but these guys beat up a man when they broke into his house."

"What about you?" Gaff asked Bea.

"A shotgun."

He leaned back in his chair. "Colin was shot with a thirty-eight."

Both Earl and Bea looked relieved. Gaff looked at Walker.

"I was on the phone with Thane," he said. "He found a great deal on wood flooring he thought would look good in my house. When I hung up with him, Mom called. She was at loose ends without Gene. But I own a thirty-eight. Dad bought it and kept it in his desk." He got up and walked to the metal desk by the front window. He unlocked the top, right drawer and handed Gaff the gun.

"Mind if I take this in for testing?"

He pushed it to him. "I can't remember the last time I shot it."

Jazzi turned to Earl. "When do you guys get paid? Today's Wednesday. How would Colin end up with extra money on a Tuesday night?"

Earl blinked, surprised. "I don't know. Maybe he sold something? Won at cards? He liked poker. He got himself in trouble once when he drove to a casino, but every time he borrowed from me, he paid me back."

That's more than she could say for Darby. Then the words *every time* stuck in Jazzi's head. "How many times did Colin ask you for money?"

"A time or two." He didn't want to tell her.

She wondered if Colin owed other people money, people who weren't as nice or patient as Earl. "Did Colin borrow from many people?"

Earl squirmed more. "He had trouble paying back somebody once, and the guy threatened to break his fingers. That's the time I loaned him two thousand dollars. He got it back to me, though, a little at a time."

Bea shook her head. "You were awfully nice to that boy."

"He was a good kid, just didn't always think things through, that's all."

A kid. He was probably only four or five years younger than Earl, but she thought of him as a kid, too. Maybe because he didn't take anything seriously.

Gaff looked at Andy and Walker. "Did either of you loan him money?"

"I never had money to spare," Andy said.

Walker shook his head. "He never asked. Dad would have never helped him."

Funny, Darby would have turned him away, but he expected Whiskers to bail him out when he was strapped for cash.

Gaff closed his notepad. "If any of you thinks of anything else, tell me. It might help. And Earl..."

"I know. Don't leave town." Earl didn't look happy. "I was better off not having an alibi than being in the wrong place at the wrong time."

"I'm glad you leveled with me. It gives us something new to work with. Money's probably what got Colin killed." Gaff motioned to Jazzi, and they left. Back in the car, he asked, "Are you up for seeing Whiskers and Haze again tonight? After I drop you off at the house, I'll see if I can find out more about Colin's gambling problems."

"Count me in." She hadn't pegged Colin as a gambler, but it fit with his let-the-chips-fall-where-they-may attitude. They didn't talk much on the way back to the house. Colin might have been a little immature, but he didn't deserve to die. And the question lingered: Why had he died?

Gaff pulled close to the back porch and said, "Four-thirty?"

"I'll be ready."

When she walked into the house, the guys were sitting down to lunch. More work still needed to be done on the kitchen floor, but it would go faster with her there. Jerod handed her a sandwich. "How did it go?"

She shared everything she'd learned. When she finished, Ansel shook his head. "I can't see Earl murdering anyone. He comes across as too nice."

"So does Gene," Jerod countered. "All of them do. I guess you can look a murderer right in the eye and never guess what he's capable of."

Jazzi grimaced and went for a cup of coffee. "Enough talk about murder. I have four hours before Gaff comes back for me. I want to think about happier thoughts until then."

Ansel grinned. "Did we tell you that George missed you?"

She rolled her eyes. "You'll have to do better than that."

So they tried. They talked about paint colors and what kinds of knobs and handles to use for each room while she and Jerod finished laying and grouting the kitchen tiles. Once done, Jazzi stood back to admire their work. The mosaic pattern gave the floor a timeless feel. That done, she and Jerod helped Ansel sand the staircase. The wooden steps, spindles, and handrail were all worn. They'd sand all of them—a time-consuming job even in the places where they could use a hand sander. But they were making good progress. She was in a better mood when Gaff returned for her.

Chapter 44

When they reached Whiskers's house, Haze opened the door for them. Dressed in tight, black exercise pants that emphasized her muscular thighs and a form-fitting shirt that hugged her biceps, she looked formidable, even when she hid her tattoos.

"Business has been so slow, Clay let me stay home tonight," she told them. "Tonya needs the extra tips, and if things pick up a little, Clay said he'd help her on the floor."

"Clay's easy to work for, isn't he?" Jazzi asked.

"He's a solid guy. Getting a little lonely since he broke up with his girlfriend, but some girl will snatch him up soon." She took Jazzi's raincoat. "I'll hang this in the mudroom and get Whiskers. Make yourselves comfortable in the living room."

They took the two wooden chairs, as usual. A pair of heavy handheld weights lay on the floor by Jazzi's. No wonder Haze's biceps bulged. She came back with Whiskers in tow and sat next to him on the sofa.

"What can we help you with now?" she asked.

Gaff reached for his notepad. "Colin, one of the drivers for Darby, was shot dead in his apartment building's parking lot last night between five and six. Did you know him?"

Whiskers snorted. "'Course I did. He worked for Darby, didn't he? I was at that cement company a thousand times or more when I had days off and me and Darby were going fishing or barhopping."

"Did he ever talk to you about money?"

Whiskers stared. "Why would he? Do I look like an investment expert?"

Gaff shook his head. "No, I mean did he ever ask to borrow money from you?"

"He knew me better than that." Whiskers tugged at his beard, a nervous habit. "Why would the kid need money? He made good wages, wasn't in debt as far as I knew. Stayed in a cheap apartment."

"Word is he had a gambling problem," Gaff said.

"Didn't seem the type."

Haze patted his thigh. "Neither do you, but you like to put money on those lottery tickets."

"Those don't get me in trouble. Sounds like Colin dipped into more than bingo and scratch-off tickets."

"Earl loaned him money once in a while." Gaff scanned through his notes. "Helped him pay back two thousand dollars once."

"You should never bet what you can't afford to lose." Whiskers grimaced. "The boy should have known that."

"For some people, it's an addiction. We're leaning toward the idea that Darby and Colin both died because of money."

Whiskers frowned and pushed to his feet. "I need a beer. Why would Darby die because of money? The only person he cheated out of cash was me."

Jazzi stared, and Whiskers looked uneasy. She regarded him intently for a moment, then asked, "Did you know that Darby had been saving money for a long time and kept a hundred and fifty thousand dollars wrapped in a rubber band in his desk?"

"Never mentioned it."

She went on. "I keep tripping over him having that money but having to borrow from you to fix his truck."

"Looks like he wasn't gonna part with any of it."

"Either that, or he didn't have it when the truck broke down. We keep thinking he saved the money, but what if he didn't? What if he won the whole thing a short while ago? You knew that, didn't you? And that's why you were so mad that he didn't pay you back."

Haze turned on the couch to lock gazes with him. "Darby never gambled. Laughed at you for wasting your money every week on scratch-offs."

"He was getting desperate. Quick money started to look good to him."

Haze stood to face him. "No. Two months ago, when he was stopping at the gas station to fill up his truck and you asked him to pick up some tickets for you while he was there, he didn't want to take your money. Said the state of Indiana was robbing you. But when you grumbled enough, he promised he'd buy your favorites for you."

"So?" Whiskers squirmed. "He must have decided to buy a couple for himself since he was there."

Haze put her hands on her hips, her expression hard. "That's when you two started arguing about money and you stopped playing the lottery."

Whiskers's face reddened to a deep scarlet. "Shut up, woman! You don't know what you're talkin' about."

Jazzi stood, too. "One of your tickets paid off, didn't it? You won, and Darby kept your money."

"Wouldn't I tell the whole world if that happened?"

Gaff tucked his notepad back into his pocket. "You couldn't prove anything. Darby paid for the tickets. You couldn't prove he used your money."

Whiskers yelled, "He was supposed to be my friend! I should have been able to trust him. I even offered to split the ticket with him since he bought it, but he just laughed at me."

Gaff started to stand, but Whiskers raced into the kitchen. When he came back, he held a gun.

Haze crossed her arms. "What are you going to do? Shoot all three of us? I'm not going to stand here to be a target. Neither are they. One of us will get to you."

"He's got handcuffs." Whiskers motioned to Gaff. "Two of you can lock yourselves to the bottom stair post. It's heavy enough to hold you. That'll buy me some time to get away. Haze, I'll have to lock you in the basement."

"No." She didn't move. "Why did you kill Colin?"

"He played the lottery, too. Figured it out when he heard Darby had that money in his drawer. Promised to stay quiet if I paid him enough. Probably was getting squeezed for a gambling debt."

Jazzi tried to remember the timing that night. "So you told him you'd meet him and give him the money, and instead, you shot him. But we came here at five. You were going to take a nap."

"Thought I'd have a decent alibi." Whiskers sounded disappointed. "You only stayed ten minutes. I'd already set up the meeting with Colin. When you left, I drove there, then hightailed it on back and was on the couch when Haze dashed over to fetch me for supper. Thought I'd zonked out and didn't wake up."

"Why not just pay him off?" Haze asked. "You didn't have to kill him."

"He'd never stop. Every time he lost at cards, he'd hit me up." He waved the gun. "Enough talking. I'll lock you in the basement first, Haze. Then I'll cuff these two to the staircase."

Haze shook her head. "You know I hate that basement. I'm not going down there. Mom used to lock me in the closet for hours, sometimes days. I told you my story."

He pressed his lips together, frustrated. "Sit down, then, and I'll tie you up. And don't try nothing."

She sat in the chair Jazzi had vacated.

"Put your hands behind you." He unhooked his belt. When he bent to wrap it around one of her wrists, she grabbed his gun hand, reached for a weight, and smacked him in the head with it. He fell, and she ripped the gun out of his hand.

Gaff drew the gun from his shoulder holster, too—the reason he always wore a suit jacket. They both aimed at him.

He stared up at Haze. "What did you go and do that for? I wouldn't have hurt you."

"You say that now. How long would it have taken you to decide we were liabilities, too? That maybe you should start a house fire before you walked to the bar and pretended the cops thought I'd killed Darby for some reason. Who else would figure out Darby stole your money?"

"I'd never hurt you."

As Gaff cuffed him, she turned away from him. "I never thought you'd hurt Darby either. But you did, didn't you?"

Jazzi and Haze went to the bar while Gaff called for backup. It was a while before a squad car drove Whiskers to lockup. Then he came to join them. They were each drinking a beer.

"You look like you need one, too." Clay went to pour Gaff a cold one, but Gaff waved the idea away.

"I have to go back to the station. Still on duty. When Jazzi finishes her drink, I'll drive her home first."

Jazzi put her hand over Haze's. "Are you going to be all right?"

Haze shrugged. "He's not the first man to let me down. My friend's boyfriend dumped her, so she's alone now, too. We can share an apartment again. I'll survive."

Jazzi felt sorry for her, but she knew Haze would plug into work and move on. There wasn't much else to say, so when she finished her beer, she followed Gaff to his car and brooded on the drive home. He was brooding, too, she could tell. At least, they could share their down moods.

Chapter 45

Later that night, Gaff called to ask if he could invite everyone to meet at Jazzi and Ansel's house in the morning. "You have plenty of room. It won't be quite as grim as going through everything with them at the station."

"Can Jerod and Ansel be part of the meeting?" she asked. "They've followed everything that's happened so far."

"You three found Darby's body, and they were there when Walker's brakes went out. They're part of the case, too."

They settled on nine o'clock. When she told Ansel, he said, "Make lots of coffee. I'll make a donut run before they get here. I'll call Jerod to let him know."

"Maybe once Gaff closes the case, that will help put it behind us." They'd had a crappy night. She'd never say it to Walker, but the more she learned about Darby and Whiskers, the more the case bothered her. She could see the good in almost everyone she met, but she'd yet to discover it in them. How could two men care so little about the people they loved? They'd tainted her view of humanity, and she wanted to wash the memory away. It would take a while, like trying to scrub a stain off your skin.

When she and Ansel went upstairs to bed, he pulled her against him and held her close. "Jerod and I threw around the idea of forgetting the fixer-upper and going to his place to finish the basement when everyone leaves tomorrow. That way, we could stay home Saturday and start getting things ready for our wedding."

"I'd like that." It was a small thing, but it lifted her spirits. They knew it would, and she appreciated their effort.

He bent to kiss the top of her head. "I love ya, babe. I can't wait until we make it official."

That lifted her spirits even more. Growing old with Ansel rated really high on her happiness list. When she drifted off to sleep, she was ready to wrap things up in the morning and move on with her life.

* * * *

By the time Gaff and Walker and his crew sat around their kitchen table, Jazzi had coffee cups at each place and filled carafes within easy reach. Ansel had loaded rolls and donuts on serving trays to pass around. Might as well have something sweet to wash down the bad taste left by the solving of Darby's murder. Thane took a seat next to Walker, and when Bea arrived, she sat next to Earl.

Jerod walked in next and looked surprised. He glanced at the kitchen clock. "I'm five minutes early. I thought I'd be the first one here."

"Your parents aren't coming?" Jazzi asked Walker.

"Mom asked me to call her when we're done. This whole thing has upset her. She didn't want to hear what Dad did in front of everyone."

Haze was the last person who knocked on the door, and Jazzi led her to join the others in the kitchen.

"This is some place," she said, looking around.

Jazzi motioned to Ansel and Jerod. "We renovate houses. It's what we do."

Gaff cleared his throat and laid his notes in front of him, calling the meeting to order. "You've all heard by now, but Whiskers is the person who killed both Darby and Colin. I thought I'd run through what happened so we're all on the same page."

He started with Whiskers giving Darby the money to buy him scratch-off tickets and went from there. When he reached the part about Colin trying to shake down Whiskers, Earl looked distressed.

"If he needed money, why didn't he just come to me?"

"If his plan worked, he'd never have to pay back his debt," Gaff said. "He didn't know Whiskers that well, though. He misjudged him."

Bea reached to put her hand on Earl's thigh. "You helped him all you could. He knew you were always there for him."

Walker leaned forward, looking as upset as Earl. "My dad stole that hundred and fifty thousand dollars. It should have gone to Whiskers. That means it should go to you now, Haze."

She shook her head. "I don't want a penny of his blood money. Find something good to do with it."

"I was going to renovate Dad's house, get rid of his memory, and make the house mine."

"If it removes every trace of Darby, I'm all for it. Besides, Whiskers left a message on my cell phone, said he signed his house and bank account over to me. By the time he gets out of prison—if he gets out of prison—he'll have a good pension waiting for him. If he dies first, he signed that over to me, too."

Gaff and Jazzi gaped at each other, surprised.

Haze caught it. "I know, I'm the one who ratted him out, told you Darby never played the lottery. And I'm the one who hit him in the head with an exercise weight. I went to visit him in jail this morning and reminded him of that, but he said that's why he fell for me, because I'm a straight arrow. I promised to visit him once a week in prison, and he said that would be worth every penny of his money."

Jazzi stared. "But I think you were right when you said he'd tie us all up and then set the house on fire. He'd have killed all of us."

"I know, but he's giving me something I've never had—some security. I can give him something in return—my company."

Jazzi didn't think she could be that forgiving, but she'd never had to pinch and hustle to keep her head above water either. "Are you going to stay in his house?"

"No, I can't live there, but the money I make selling it can buy me another one. My friend said she'd move in with me, and I won't make her pay rent. That way, she can build up some savings, too."

Walker nodded. "Either way, if you ever need anything, give me a call. I'll be there."

"I might take you up on that. I'll need help moving."

"Done." The expression on his face said he'd help more than that.

Gaff put away his papers. "Any more questions?"

Everyone looked at the door, ready to put Darby and Whiskers behind them.

He stood. "Let's call it a day then."

People filed out of the house until only Jerod remained.

"You sure you want to head to my place? You could start your weekend early, cuz."

She shook her head. "I need to keep busy, get my mind off this. I want to see how your basement turns out."

He grinned. "Good, because it would be hard hanging the ceiling myself."

"I haven't made anything for lunch. Didn't think about it," she admitted.

"With Darby trying to kill you last night? And the meeting this morning? Why would you? I'll throw some hot dogs on the grill." Jerod snatched the last donut. "I'm ordering pizza for supper, eating healthy today."

Ansel started to clear the table, wearing a heavy frown. "He would have tried to kill you, you know. If I'd lost you before I even got to marry you…" He couldn't finish his sentence.

She hugged him. "But I'm here, and I love you. Don't think about it."

He turned to Jerod, visibly trying to shift moods. "We'll be at your house in half an hour."

"See you then. If you're a little late, I won't send a Saint Bernard looking for you." He left them.

The cats zipped into the kitchen once everyone was gone. A good diversion. She'd already fed them breakfast, but what the heck? She split another can of wet food between them. The worst was behind them. Life should get back to normal soon. And then, his parents would come. Ugh!

Chapter 46

The week before the wedding flew by. Jazzi and Ansel cleaned and cooked everything possible ahead of time. Jazzi was putting the last-minute touches on the floral decorations before his family arrived. They'd decided to come in time for supper on Saturday, spend the night, and celebrate with them on Sunday, then drive back to Wisconsin after the reception.

"That's a lot of driving for such a short visit." Jazzi added a half dozen delphiniums to the bouquet of pink and white roses and baby's breath.

"They want to be back in time to milk the cows on Monday morning. They're paying two boys from their church to milk while they're gone, but they have to go to school on Monday."

"You didn't tell them to come at the last minute and get out fast, did you?"

He finished setting the table. "If they didn't like that, they didn't have to come."

A quick trip might be for the best. She worried about how everyone would get along. She'd decided on a slow-cooker stew and a big salad for supper, something simple. They had enough last-minute cooking to do tomorrow. Adda had volunteered to help, but Ansel had warned that might or might not be a good thing.

She was mixing the salad when a gray van pulled up close to the garage. Six people piled out of it, and Ansel went to open the door and meet his family. Jazzi carried the salad bowl to the table and went to join him.

His mother and father led the way. When they reached Ansel, he said, "Mom and Dad, this is Jazzi. Jazzi, these are my parents, Britt and Dalmar."

Jazzi smiled, and his mother gave a timid smile back. The woman was tall and so thin she could double as a wraith. Ansel had said she was frail.

A big, beefy man, his dad didn't offer a hand, scowling at her. "What kind of name is Jazzi?"

She decided not to take offense, but his tone irritated her. "It's short for Jasmine. My mom loves to read. She named me after the heroine in some book she loved."

The man sniffed and moved on. A real charmer.

The two brothers came next. Ansel motioned to the one who was six feet tall and stocky. He walked with a limp. "This is my oldest brother, Bain." The second man was an inch taller with a sinewy build. "My older brother, Radley," Ansel told her.

The whole family was blond with blue eyes. Bain looked grumpy and hadn't even stepped into the house yet. "Adda told us you had a beautiful house, but she thinks everything you do is wonderful, so I wanted to see it for myself. She didn't say you must be rolling in it."

Ansel's voice turned chilly. "We got it for a good price when it was in bad shape and fixed it up."

"How much money did that take?"

"None of your business." The two brothers glared at each other.

Radley stepped forward, bumping Bain out of the way. "Hey, bro, congratulations!" He wrapped Ansel in a bear hug.

"Glad you could make it." Ansel slapped him on the back. His dad and Bain had chosen Radley over him to help run the farm, but Radley hadn't been part of that decision. He'd told Ansel he felt bad when they drove him away.

Radley turned to Jazzi. "So you're the poor girl he tricked into marrying him."

She laughed. Thank heavens someone in this family was happy for them. "It's nice to finally meet you."

"My baby brother hit the jackpot. Got a real looker, and he says you're a good cook, too."

"I lured him with food."

Radley's grin was a match for Ansel's. He wasn't quite as gorgeous as his younger brother, but he was handsome enough. Radley sniffed the air. "Something smells good in here."

"Stew. Supper's ready whenever you get settled."

"Where do you want us?"

"Ansel will help carry your luggage. There are two spare bedrooms upstairs. We put you and Bain on air mattresses in your parents' room unless you'd rather find a spot down here."

He shrugged. "Doesn't matter. It's only for one night."

He moved on, and Adda and her husband came to greet them. Adda turned to Jazzi. "You remember Henry, don't you?"

"Sure do. Come in. I'll show you to your rooms."

Jazzi led the way upstairs while the guys carried suitcases behind her. She'd put Adda and Henry in the same room they'd slept in the last time they came—the caramel-colored bedroom. Ansel's parents and brothers shared the bigger amethyst-colored room next to it. She and Ansel had moved the queen-size bed to one side and had placed two tall air mattresses on the other side.

"What do you need a room this big for?" Bain asked.

"The man who owned the house before us entertained a lot," Ansel told him.

Bain shook his head. "Is your room this big?"

"Bigger, with its own master bath. All of you will have to share the guest bathroom." Ansel waited for Bain to digest that information. Then he glanced at his mother. "What do you think, Mom?"

She put a hand to her throat. "It's beautiful. Everything about it is beautiful. The house, the yard...everything."

Ansel smiled. "We dug a pond at the back of the property with a gazebo. We love it here."

"Why wouldn't you?" His dad looked ticked. "You left the farm, and you've never had it so good."

"Yup." Ansel's blue eyes glinted. "Getting kicked out of the dairy business was the best thing that ever happened to me."

Radley grinned, but his dad's complexion darkened to a deep red. "With money like this, you could have hired us some help when Bain broke his leg."

"I thought with such great management skills, you'd be in good shape." Ansel's temper colored his voice. Good for him! Jazzi did nothing to soothe him. His dad was pushing his luck, and if he kept prodding, he'd regret it.

"I'm just glad you showed up to help us." Radley carried his bag close to one of the air mattresses.

Ansel nodded, his gaze fixed on his dad. "You're lucky I came at all."

Adda rushed into the room and tugged on Ansel's arm. "I want to see your property and pond before the sun sets."

"A walk would be nice," Henry said, joining her. "We were cramped in the van for a long time."

Jazzi couldn't imagine spending hours stuck with Ansel's dad and Bain. She'd need to walk it off, too. She started for the door. "Grab your jackets on the way out. It's chilly once the sun gets low."

George lifted his head as they passed him to go outside.

"Want to come, boy?" Ansel slapped his thigh, but the pug got comfortable again and closed his eyes.

"Not worth much, is he?" Bain said.

Jazzi bit down on her bottom lip. Ansel was a big boy. He could take care of himself.

Ansel knotted his hands into fists and jammed them in his pockets. "We don't make things earn their keep around here. We enjoy George's company, and that's enough."

Bain's expression turned sour, but he didn't comment.

They walked past the two-car garage and over the rise that Ansel had bulldozed into place. Then they followed the edge of the pond until they came to the gazebo.

"I bet you have some good times here!" Radley stood on the built-in bench to get a better view. "You even have a charcoal grill and a picnic table. You can give some good parties."

Dalmar grimaced. "Parties are expensive. You have to feed everyone."

"I have a big family," Jazzi told them. "We like to invite them over on Sundays."

"Every Sunday?" Britt asked.

She nodded. "Just about, but everyone pitches in on the cost. They stuff money in a jar to help cover expenses."

Radley's voice turned wistful. "You must like each other."

"We always have a good time when we get together."

Radley and Adda exchanged meaningful glances, and Jazzi felt sorry for them. Fun wasn't part of Dalmar or Bain's vocabulary.

When Dalmar glared at Radley, Adda twined her arm through Jazzi's. "This has been fun, and I don't know about anyone else, but I'm starving. Did you say supper was ready?"

A great save. Jazzi motioned for them to follow her back to the house. Once in the kitchen, she said, "Ansel, why don't you get everyone something to drink while I carry the food to the table?"

As it turned out, everyone but her wanted beer. Ansel handed out bottles to each person, then placed a bottle of wine and a wineglass by her plate. She put the stew on the table with a huge bowl of parsley potatoes next to it. Radley stood to dish up the stew from the heavy Dutch oven. Adda passed the potatoes, and Ansel passed the salad. Once everyone was served, Radley made an effort at cheerful conversation. "Did you hear that Jezebel got married? Up and hooked up with a forty-one-year-old guy who has even more money than her first husband."

Bain stabbed at a potato. "That girl chased after you for weeks before Ansel came back to town. If you'd hooked up with her, we'd be set."

"Couldn't stand her," Radley said. "She'd be worse than being stuck with you."

Bain's head snapped up, his lips twisted in a snarl. "She might look better if our money gets much tighter."

"I'd rather eat kale every day than jump through hoops for a spoiled, picky wife."

Their father put his elbows on the table and leaned forward. "The price of milk will go up again. We've weathered worse."

"Now, Dalmar, boys, let's enjoy our meal." Their mother looked at Jazzi and smiled. "I've always added potatoes to my stew. I've never made them separately. This tastes wonderful."

"Thank you." Jazzi nodded at Britt's empty beer bottle. "Do you want another drink?"

Britt shook her head. "I only allow myself one. I'd like water, though."

Jazzi got up to get it, and Adda asked, "Have you two decided on where to go for a honeymoon?"

Ansel reached for a second helping of stew. "We're waiting until we finish the house we're working on. By then, it will be past Christmas and New Year's. We were thinking of flying someplace sunny."

"Florida?" Henry asked.

"Maybe Cancun or the Bahamas."

"Must be nice," Bain grumbled.

"I think it sounds wonderful." Adda winked at Henry. "We haven't taken a honeymoon yet. We should think about somewhere warm."

"Like you two have that kind of money." Dalmar smirked, and Jazzi fought back a strong urge to jump to Adda's defense.

Instead, Henry answered. "Selling insurance has been good to me. If Adda wants to travel, we can afford to."

Dalmar blinked. "Are we the only ones who are struggling?"

The others looked around the table. "We're doing all right," Adda said.

Ansel nodded. "So are we."

The conversation wasn't making their father happy. He shot an angry glance their way.

Jazzi had listened to him long enough. She stood and started to collect plates. "I made a trifle for dessert. And there's coffee to go with it. Adda, do you want to help me with dessert plates?"

Adda grinned. "On my way, and we'll talk about happier things while we eat our sweets."

Radley took one look at the layers of sponge cake and pudding buried in strawberries and whipped cream. He smiled with a mouthful. "Heaven!"

Ansel poured coffee for everyone, and when Bain opened his mouth to speak, Ansel shook his head. "Unless it's happy, keep it to yourself. This is our pre-wedding supper. It's supposed to be a celebration."

Bain and his father sulked, eating silently. Everyone else had a good time. When the meal was finished, and they started work on cleanup, Bain and Dalmar stood, arms crossed over their chests, watching them. Obviously, rinsing dishes and loading the dishwasher were beneath them.

When the kitchen shone, Bain pointed to the stainless-steel countertops. "I've never seen anything like this before."

"Restaurant kitchens have a lot of stainless steel," Ansel said. "We like to cook, so we thought we'd try it, too."

"Not on the kitchen island?" Henry asked.

Ansel looked proud when he studied its butcher-block top. "We use it as a buffet when Jazzi's family comes on Sundays."

"How many people?" Bain asked.

"Usually fifteen." Jazzi nodded to the farm table. "It has lots of leaves. And we have a second table we add on the side. So far, we can seat everyone in one place."

"Even if they pitch in, that has to get expensive." Bain shook his head.

Jazzi wasn't about to argue with him about the price of food. "We manage. My mom and sister don't like to cook, so they're happy I do."

Britt wrinkled her nose. "I don't like to cook either, but we can't afford to eat out all the time."

"We *never* eat out," Radley added.

"I like good, simple food that sticks to your ribs. I don't need anything fancy," Dalmar said.

Ansel glanced at the clock. "We had a late supper. Why don't we get comfortable in the living room? Would you like to rent a movie tonight or just sit around and visit?"

Bain's frown returned. "Dad and I had to get up early to milk this morning, and it was a long drive here. I could use an early night."

Radley rolled his eyes. "I got up early, too. Milked, too, but I'd like to stay up a while and visit."

"Suit yourself. Don't wake us when you come to bed," Dalmar warned.

They walked through the living room, and Bain shook his head. "Who needs four couches in one room? How many parties do you throw here?"

"The room's too big for one setting," Ansel said. "So we made two groupings. And we use them, too."

Radley eyed the second group and said, "They look comfortable."

"If you'd rather sleep down here, I'll get you some blankets and a pillow," Jazzi offered. "Then you don't have to worry about making noise when you go upstairs."

"Thanks, I'll take you up on that."

Dalmar snapped his fingers at Britt. "You coming?"

Jazzi stared at him, shocked. What did he think his wife was—a trained dog?

Britt looked torn but went to follow him to bed.

Radley shook his head. "For Mom, what Dad says goes. Too bad. She'd have liked talking with us."

"Her choice." Ansel's voice held little sympathy. He went for another round of beer. "Now that they're gone, let's enjoy ourselves."

Radley grinned and held out his beer bottle for them all to clink together. "Who'd have thought? Our little brother beat us to the altar. Way to go, bro!"

Jazzi sipped her second glass of wine and felt herself relax. They'd survived the night. Tomorrow, they'd be too busy, making the last of the food, to argue. Then her family would come. Lord help Bain and Dalmar if they tried to get a word in edgewise then. And after that, they'd leave. Good riddance.

Chapter 47

Sunday morning turned out crisp and sunny. Jazzi had taken three loaves of tea breads out to thaw the night before—zucchini, banana-nut, and blueberry lemon. Along with boiled eggs, juice, and coffee, she figured that would do for breakfast. She and Ansel had gotten up especially early to start cooking for the reception, but Bain and Dalmar were already in the living room, reading the morning paper, when they came down. Radley must have decided to sleep upstairs because the second set of couches was empty.

The cats had started down the stairs with them, saw the two men, and turned around to go back to the bedroom.

His dad looked at Ansel, carrying the dog. "Mutt can't walk?"

"Stairs make him nervous." Ansel gently set George on the floor.

Bain glanced at his watch. "You used to be an early riser."

"I don't have to milk cows anymore." Ansel started to the kitchen. "Want some coffee?" They'd set the timer for it to start last night.

"Wouldn't mind." His dad didn't get up. Neither did Bain.

Jazzi mumbled insults inside her mind but went to fetch coffee for them. They'd leave after the wedding today. She might never see them again—if she was lucky. "I put some things out for breakfast if you're hungry."

"Yeah, we saw them. We made ourselves some eggs," Bain called.

Yes, yes, they did. The dirty pans and dishes were in the sink to prove it. Bacon grease slicked the inside of the nonstick skillet. She looked in the refrigerator. Luckily, there was enough bacon left to make the crab and bacon endive boats. Jazzi bit her bottom lip to keep quiet. She wanted this day to be pleasant. Ansel poured two mugs of coffee, and she took them to their guests.

When she returned to the kitchen, the cats had slunk downstairs to twine around her ankles. They'd disappear again after she fed them. Last night, Inky had tried to beg at the table, and Dalmar had swatted him away. Inky glared at him as he disappeared into the laundry room. There was no love lost between the cats and Dalmar or Bain.

Ansel cleaned the dirty dishes while she took out ingredients to start cooking. First, she'd make the toppings for the bruschetta and put the three bowls in the refrigerator. She'd assemble everything later. After that, Ansel cooked and crumbled bacon while she started the crab filling for the endive. When that was finished, it went in the fridge, too. Ansel came to help her with the shrimp-pineapple topping for the mini-flatbreads. They were making great progress when Adda, Henry, and Radley joined them in the kitchen. They were happy enough with the tea breads and boiled eggs and settled at the farm table to enjoy them.

Jazzi and Ansel stopped working long enough to eat with them.

"Did you sleep well?" Jazzi asked.

"Like a baby." Adda buttered another slice of zucchini bread. "The bed in that room is so comfortable."

Jazzi looked at Radley. "How did you do on the air mattress?"

"It's bigger than my twin bed at home. Bain and I moved into the house Grandma and Grandpa used to live in, and Mom and Dad let me take the bed I used as a kid. This makes me think it's time to buy something new."

Ansel laughed. "That bed has to be about as old as you are. I'm surprised the mattress is still alive."

"I don't have a problem with mine," Bain called from the living room.

Radley made a face at him. Bain couldn't see it from the other room, but it amused Jazzi.

"My feet hang over the end of the bed," Radley complained. "I wake up feeling like a pretzel. I peeked in your room when I was upstairs. What size is your bed? It looked like it was long enough for Ansel."

"It's king size," he said. "If I slant myself a little, I have plenty of space."

"I peeked in, too," Dalmar called. "You sleeping in a pink room now, boy?"

Did Ansel's dad ever know when to shut up? But his question amused Ansel.

"I sure am. I'm getting in touch with my feminine side."

Radley stifled a laugh, but his dad gave a huff of disapproval. The calling back and forth must have woken Britt. She came downstairs to join them. She wore a pair of faded black slacks and a tan turtleneck with stains. Ansel rose to take her a mug of coffee while she settled at the table with them. Dark circles smudged her eyes.

Jazzi frowned, concerned. "How did you sleep? All right?"

"Your bed was wonderful, but I have trouble sleeping when I'm in new places. Too much stimulation. My mind turns on, and I dither over too many thoughts."

She was probably counting all the reasons she should never have married Dalmar.

Dalmar grunted. "You've never had too many thoughts in your life. You *are* good at dithering, though."

Jazzi turned to stare at the back of the man's head. Would it kill him to say something nice to his wife? If she threw a boiled egg at his head from here, would she hit him?

Britt looked embarrassed but shrugged. "I'm sorry I slept so late."

"Glad you did," Jazzi said. "We want you to enjoy yourself here."

Radley motioned to the array of ingredients spread out on the kitchen island. "Looks like you're making enough for an army today."

Ansel pushed his plate away. He'd tried one slice of each bread and gone for seconds of the blueberry lemon. The man had a thing for berries. "You haven't met Jazzi's family. Not one person gains weight, but they all eat like horses. They'll descend like locusts, and there won't be a leftover in sight."

Jazzi laughed. That was a fair description of their Sunday meals. "I have two really good friends coming, too—Reuben and Isabelle. Reuben used to live in the apartment above mine when I rented a house in West Central."

Ansel gave a worried glance at the other room and said, "Reuben's a black man, married to a white woman. They invited us to their wedding. We're lucky to call them friends."

His dad came to stand in the archway to stare at him. "Is that common here?"

"Sure is, and it works out just fine." Ansel waited.

His dad's lips pressed into a flat line. "You don't expect us to talk to them, do you?"

"I'd rather you didn't. I like them. If you insult them, I won't be happy about it."

His dad's eyes flashed ice cold, and he turned on his heel to return to the living room.

Radley shook his head and stood. "Well, it's about time for me to rinse my plate and pitch in if you need me."

"We're in good shape." Jazzi stood, too. "We bought lots of magazines you can read if you want to, or you can watch TV, or…"

"What if I take you and anyone else who's interested for a ride around town, so you can see River Bluffs?" Henry asked. "Jazzi offered me the keys to her pickup."

"Good idea." Radley glanced into the living room. "You two coming?"

"No need to," Bain called. "No desire to spend time here. After we finish the paper, we'll take a walk to stretch our legs."

The sooner, the better. But Jazzi politely kept her opinion to herself.

"Mom?" Henry looked at Britt.

She went to get her jacket. "River Bluffs is a bigger city than I thought. I'd like to see it."

Adda stayed in the kitchen to help out. "What can I do?"

"What if you and I work on the mini crab cakes together?" Jazzi went to get the lump crab meat out of the refrigerator. When she opened the door, Adda spotted the chocolate-covered strawberries inside.

"I love those!" she cried.

"I didn't make them," Jazzi admitted. "I bought them at DeBrand's."

"What's that?"

"A premier chocolate shop. You wouldn't believe how good their s'mores are. Homemade chocolate and marshmallow. I could eat a tray of them."

"Sometime, if Henry and I come to visit again, can we go there?"

"You can talk me into DeBrand's anytime," Jazzi told her.

They got busy on the crab while Ansel massaged a rub into the tenderloins and left them out to reach room temperature.

"What next?" Adda asked. "This is fun. I've never made any of this before."

"Stuffed mushrooms. My family loves them."

By twelve-thirty, all of the food was ready to go. It would take only minutes to assemble it and put it on the kitchen island. Dalmar and Bain had stared as they walked past the trays of dips and chips as they left the house for their walk. She and Ansel had made those ahead of time.

"Do you people eat anything normal?" Bain growled.

Jazzi glanced at platter after platter, waiting for food to be placed on them. "Lots of times, but not today. We're going all out for our wedding."

Dalmar grumbled, "You people have more money than good sense. You could have bought a new lawn mower for what you spent on this."

Ansel answered, "Luckily, we didn't have to choose."

Bain slammed the door as they left, and Ansel shook his head. He asked Adda, "Do you think they'll enjoy the wedding at all, or did they just come to grump about everything?"

"They wanted to see where you live and what you were doing with yourself. It annoys them that you're doing better than they are."

"What happened on the farm? We were doing all right when I was at home."

"Milk prices dropped, and the need for a lot of repairs hit them all at the same time. They'll get past it, but it's tight right now."

"I don't wish anything bad on them," he said, "but I wish they could be happy for me."

"You know better than that. But Mom, Radley, and I are thrilled you're doing so well. Henry and I plan to hit you up once in a while for a weekend in the big city."

He laughed. "Anytime. Jazzi was already talking about that."

Adda came to hug her. "You make a great sister, but now you'd better go upstairs and get pretty. Ansel can hardly wait to put that ring on your finger."

With a smile, Jazzi ran up the steps. Cyn and Olivia would be here soon to do her hair and makeup. Ansel had bought a suit for the occasion. He hadn't let her see it. "If you can hide your wedding gown, I can keep my secrets, too."

She'd changed into the dress by the time her sister knocked and stepped into the room. Cyn came in behind her. Olivia gave a long sigh. "You look beautiful."

"You haven't fixed me up yet."

"That will make you even more beautiful." Olivia was wearing a rose-colored, form-fitting dress. Her heels matched. She looked as stylish as always, but she grimaced. "Maybe watching you two tie the knot will put Thane in the mood."

Jazzi turned to her in surprise. "Are you ready to get married?"

"I have to pretend that I'm in no hurry so that I don't scare Thane away, but I'm ready to make that man mine. I always have to do the nudging, though. Thane's not like Ansel, begging me to say yes."

"Ansel didn't beg."

"No, he nagged. Same thing." Olivia pouted.

"Maybe he thinks you don't want to rush things," Cyn said.

"Maybe, but I'm going to hint that I'd like to walk down the aisle someday soon."

Jazzi suspected that's all it would take. Thane was crazy about her sister. Olivia frowned at Jazzi's hair. "Okay, time to get down to business. You have so much hair, it's going to take a while to do an updo."

Jazzi heard footsteps walk down the hallway to the two bedrooms on the end. Ansel's family must be getting ready now, too. She wondered where Ansel had gone to get dressed. Probably the laundry room.

At ten till two, her mom kissed her cheek and said, "Knock 'em dead." Then she and Olivia went down to take their seats. Jazzi stared at herself in the full-length bathroom mirror. For once in her life, she *felt* beautiful. At two, the violinist they'd hired began playing the wedding march. Jazzi took a deep breath, opened the door, and started down the stairs. The photographer snapped pictures. People smiled up at her, but she couldn't stop looking at Ansel. With his white-blond hair, blue eyes, and golden tan, his black suit and white shirt made him look stunning. The suit was tailored to stretch across his broad shoulders and narrow at his solid torso. There could never be a better-looking groom. Her pulse picked up, and she beamed at him.

So much happiness flooded her that she felt giddy. The ceremony went by in a blur, and by the time the justice of the peace pronounced them man and wife, she was ready for her kiss. She tilted her face, and Ansel did a thorough job of it. Jerod cheered. So did Thane and Walker. Laughing, she and Ansel walked to the back of the living room and announced, "Let's party!"

People hugged them as they made their way to the kitchen. Ansel's family was the last to congratulate them.

Radley frowned. "I didn't see any table for presents."

"We didn't want any," Jazzi said. "We have everything we need."

"Good, because it cost a lot of gas money for us to drive here," Bain told them.

"We're just glad you came." She knew they were a pain in the neck, but years from now, when they looked back, Ansel would be happy they had been here.

Corks popped as Jerod and Thane opened bottles of champagne. They'd hired a DJ, and music played while people ate and drank. Ansel introduced his family to Jazzi's, and even Dalmar and Bain looked like they were enjoying themselves a little. Walker got them talking about his cement business, and Thane yakked with them about furnaces and air-conditioning. As the afternoon wore on, Radley asked how easy it was to find a job in River Bluffs. Thane told him that someone at his company was retiring. They were looking for a new man to train.

"I'll put in a good word for you if you're interested."

Radley hesitated, but Britt put a hand on his arm. "If you'd like it here, go for it. Your dad and Bain will survive. They can work longer hours."

"Are you just saying that so they don't have to split their profits with me?"

She smiled. "They'll like that, too, but mostly, I want you to be happy."

That was all he needed to hear. "Would I make enough to rent a place while I trained?"

"You can stay with us until you're on your feet," Ansel said. He glanced at Jazzi. "Is that all right?"

"Not tonight." She gave a wicked smile.

Radley laughed. "I'd have to go home and pack, but I think I'm going to go for it. I'll try not to stay underfoot too long."

"The house is big enough, we'll make it work." It would cramp their privacy a little, but it would only be for a while. And Ansel would like having his brother in town.

When the food had a serious dent in it, the men moved the furniture out of the way in the living room, rolled up the oriental carpets, and the DJ put on dancing music. Ansel and Jazzi cut the cake, and Jerod popped more champagne corks. Gran drank enough to hit the dance floor. Even Reuben and Isabelle pulled out their best moves.

Jazzi and Ansel moved from one person to another, grateful they could share the day with so many people they loved.

Two hours later, satiated with food, drinks, and fun, guests began to leave. By seven, Jazzi and Ansel had the house to themselves.

"No work tomorrow," Ansel said. "We can put the house together then. For right now, I've stared at you in that dress long enough. You've never looked more beautiful, but it's time for that thing to hit the floor. I've thought about having you to myself for the last two hours."

When he started for the staircase and told George, "Later," the pets curled up to wait. They might not understand that their owners were now married, but they understood what *later* meant. And this time, they sensed that *later* would take longer than usual.

Please turn the page for some delectable recipes from Jazzi's kitchen!

Potato Salad

I combined Ina Garten's French potato salad with my mom's recipe for potato salad (because I love mayo), and came up with this. Cut 10 small Yukon gold potatoes into chunks (I don't peel them). Boil the chunks in salted water until tender. While they boil, make the sauce.

For the sauce:

In a large mixing bowl, combine:

> 1 cup of Miracle Whip or mayonnaise
> 3 sliced celery stalks
> 1 diced sweet onion
> 2 tablespoons of dry vermouth
> 2 tablespoons of chicken stock
> 3 tablespoons of white wine vinegar
> ½ teaspoon of Dijon mustard
> 2 teaspoons of kosher salt
> 1 teaspoon of coarse black pepper
> 10 tablespoons of olive oil
> 2 teaspoon of dry dill

When the potatoes are tender, drain them, and add the sauce while the potatoes are still hot. Stir together. If the potatoes mush a little, even better. At the end, add 4 hard-boiled eggs, chopped.

Sloppy Joes

My sisters don't like any foods that are too fussy or elaborate. They prefer the kinds of meals I used to make for my boys. (I made them "fancy" mac 'n' cheese once with Gruyère, and they hated it. Now I stick to cheddar.) When I make them sloppy joes, I know I'm safe. They don't like them too tomatoey, though; here's their favorite type:

3 pounds of 80/20 ground beef, browned and drained
1 chopped sweet onion
1 chopped red pepper
1½ teaspoons of garlic powder
1 tablespoon of yellow mustard
¾ cup of ketchup
3 tablespoons of brown sugar
Salt and pepper to taste

Flat Iron Steak Tips and Mushrooms over Buttered Noodles

My husband will eat and enjoy almost anything I cook, but when I make beef, he's a happy man. Steak and potatoes is his favorite. We both love flat iron steaks in almost anything. (They work perfectly in beef 'n' broccoli.)

Boil a bag of wide egg noodles according to the package directions. Be sure to add salt to the water to flavor the noodles while they cook. Brown the steak while the noodles boil. When the noodles are cooked, drain them, return them to the pan, and add ½ to 1 stick of butter. Add salt if needed and parsley flakes to taste.

Cut 1 flat iron steak lengthwise into 3 long strips, then slice horizontally into bite-sized pieces. Brown them in a large skillet in olive oil. Salt and pepper to season. If you want a little more kick, sparingly sprinkle with Canadian seasoning. When the beef is cooked as you like it, add:

> 1 small box of sliced mushrooms, sautéed
> 1 tablespoon of minced garlic
> 6-ounce can of tomato sauce
> 1 tablespoon of soy sauce
> ¾ cup of beef broth
> A light splash of balsamic vinegar

Heat, letting the flavors mingle and allowing the sauce to coat the pieces of steak.

Sausage Rolls

Milk and cheese are not my friends, so I make sausage rolls that I can eat, and my husband loves them without the cheese, too. However, if you like cheese, just add some shredded mozzarella before you roll them up.

I use a roll of pre-made pizza dough. Spray a baking sheet with olive oil or other cooking oil, and place the dough on the sheet.

For the filling:

Brown 2 pounds of Bob Evans (or your favorite) sausage, and add:

1 pint of sliced mushrooms, cooked until they are soft
14 ounces of marinara sauce (or 15 ounces of tomato sauce, a pinch of sugar, 1 teaspoon of Italian seasoning, and 1 teaspoon of minced garlic)

Let the filling cool while you sauté:

1 cup of frozen diced green peppers
1 thinly sliced sweet onion

Top the dough with the sausage mix filling and the vegetables. Add mozzarella if desired. Pull up the sides and the ends of the dough to seal. Bake at 425 degrees for 15–20 minutes until golden.

Printed in the United States
by Baker & Taylor Publisher Services